Praise for the work of
**Barbara Michaels**

"Simply the *best* living writer of ghost stories and thrillers in this century."
MARION ZIMMER BRADLEY

"Michaels has a fine sense of atmosphere and storytelling."
*NEW YORK TIMES*

"Barbara Michaels's thrillers are always a highly satisfying blend of unearthly terrors and supernatural suppositions."
*PUBLISHERS WEEKLY*

"A master of the modern Gothic novel."
*LIBRARY JOURNAL*

"Michaels has a fine downright way with the supernatural. Good firm style and many picturesque twists."
*SAN FRANCISCO CHRONICLE*

"This writer is ingenious."
*KIRKUS REVIEWS*

## Books by Barbara Michaels

Other Worlds
The Dancing Floor
Stitches in Time
Houses of Stone
Vanish with the Rose
Into the Darkness
Search the Shadows
Shattered Silk
Smoke and Mirrors
Be Buried in the Rain
The Grey Beginning
Here I Stay
Black Rainbow
Someone in the House
The Wizard's Daughter

The Walker in Shadows
Wait for What Will Come
Wings of the Falcon
Patriot's Dream
The Sea King's Daughter
House of Many Shadows
Witch
Greygallows
The Crying Child
The Dark on the
   Other Side
Prince of Darkness
Ammie, Come Home
Sons of the Wolf
The Master of Blacktower

# Prince of Darkness

## ELIZABETH PETERS
### WRITING AS
## BARBARA MICHAELS

HarperTorch

*An Imprint of* HarperCollins*Publishers*

❧

HARPERTORCH
*An Imprint of* HarperCollins*Publishers*
10 East 53rd Street
New York, New York 10022-5299

Copyright © 1969 by Barbara Michaels
ISBN 0-06-074509-6

First HarperTorch paperback printing: May 2005

HarperCollins®, HarperTorch™, and ❧™ are trademarks of Harper-Collins Publishers Inc.

Printed in the United States of America

Visit HarperTorch on the World Wide Web at www.harpercollins.com

10   9   8   7   6   5   4   3   2   1

# Contents

**Meet:** Place where hounds and field gather before a hunt

**Huntsman:** Generically: one who hunts. Specifically: one who directs, controls and assists hounds in their pursuit of game. ("Hunter" is used only in connection with the horse and never the rider.)

**Quarry:** Hunted animal

From *The Horseman's Dictionary*, by Lida Fleitmann Bloodgood and Piero Santini. (E. P. Dutton and Co., New York, 1964.)

# Prince of Darkness

# PROLOGUE
## *Meet*

THE TEASHOP WAS LOCATED ON ONE OF THE DINGY discouraged streets on the wrong side of the Thames, not far from Waterloo. Its interior appearance matched the neighborhood. Torn plastic mats failed to conceal the streaked grease on the tabletops, and the floor was strewn with the crumbs of a thousand vanished biscuits. The afternoon sun of September fought its way in through windows begrimed with dust.

It was early in the day for the peculiar meal which only the British could have invented; the hour, and the unprepossessing atmosphere of the shop, perhaps explained why there were only three people in the place: two customers, at a back table, and a drowsy-looking waitress, whose teased blond hairdo was pressed up against the transistor radio which filled the room with the jerky rhythms of modern dance.

The two men who sat hunched over untouched cups of a suspicious-looking dark-brown liquid were in complete harmony with their surroundings. The elder of the two was a tiny man, wizened and bent like a gnome. His sharp nose would one day meet his pointed chin, if the teeth in between abandoned their posts. His eyes were small and close set, and heavily shuttered, not only by drooping lids, but by a kind of opacity; the thoughts that burgeoned inside the domed head, sparsely covered by graying hair, would never be read through those windows. He wore a chartreuse-and-burgundy tweed jacket and a cap of the sort that is associated with gentlemen who frequent the race tracks. His hands were small and delicately shaped.

The younger man's most conspicuous feature was a head of thick flaxen hair which hung in ragged locks over his ears and brushed the back of his collar. The collar was frayed; the suit jacket was shiny with age and seemed not to have been constructed for its present owner. Though slightly built, the man was too thin even for his normal bone structure. His skin had the distinctive grayish pallor which innocent observers might have interpreted as the result of long illness, or—more accurately—long confinement away from the sun. There were good bones under the tight-drawn skin of his face, but his features were marred by their expression. The blue eyes were set too deeply in their sockets, the mouth was too tight, the jaw heavy and arrogant. Like his face, his hands bore the signs of his recent activities; long-fingered and slender, they were heavily calloused, with broken nails and ragged cuticles.

He picked up his teacup clumsily, as if he were not accustomed to handling anything so comparatively fragile as the thick white china, took a sip, and grimaced.

"No wonder so many people are emigrating."

"Sure, and it wasn't for the beverage that a good Irishman like meself would suggest meeting here."

"Irishman, hell. You haven't seen Dublin for fifty years. And do drop the phony accent, can't you?"

"Limerick," said the older man equably. "And be damned to you. Seems to me you've picked up a bit of an American twang yourself."

"My late—er—roommate was an American."

"And what would he be doin' so far from home, I wonder?" cooed the older man. He met his companion's cold stare and bared his teeth in a grin. "Allow me me little eccentricities, lad. So long as I do the job you've no ground for complaint."

"I'll give you that much," the younger man said grudgingly. "You're the best in the business. That's why I got in touch with you."

"That and old friendship, eh?" The older man grinned more broadly, and his companion responded with a slightly upward curve of the corners of his mouth. It could hardly have been called a smile, but it was evidently the closest approximation he could manage to that expression, and the slight relaxation of his taut shoulders indicated that his mood was improving.

"Hardly friendship," he said. "You seem to have flourished since those days, Sam. You're looking older and more wicked than ever."

"I can't say the same for you. How long is it you've been . . ."

"Back?" The younger man supplied gently. "Six days."

"Six, is it? You wired me four days ago."

"Yes."

"In a hurry, weren't you?"

"Yes."

Sam sucked his lower lip. He gave his companion a sidelong glance.

"And what have you been doin' with yerself since then?"

"This and that."

"You've not spent your time in Savile Row, that's for certain," Sam said, with a glance at his companion's shabby suit. He gave his own lapel a complacent tug. "Nor at your barber."

"What's that supposed to mean?"

"Why should it mean anything, then?"

His companion gave him another grudging smile.

"Everything you say means something, you old

devil. Are you suggesting I get my hair cut, or the reverse?"

"Ah, it's a sad world when a man can't make a casual remark without starting nasty suspicions." Absently Sam took a sip of tea, choked theatrically, and settled back. "The reverse. You're right up with the current fashions. Why don't you grow a beard?"

"No beard. All right, Sam, let's have it."

Sam sighed profoundly.

"You didn't give me much time, you know."

"You never need much time."

"In this case I didn't. Most of it's public knowledge." Sam sat up straighter. When he spoke, his accents were unaffected, average American.

"Name of Katharine More. Dr. More. It used to be Moretszki, in case you didn't know."

"She changed it?"

"Not she. She's got a towering pride, but not of that variety. The grandfather changed the name when he came from Russia in the eighteen eighties. He proceeded to do two impressive deeds: make a fortune in real estate and engender twelve children. The lady you've inquired about is the daughter of the second son, Carl. By one of those odd quirks of fate which occur in the best of families, she is the only surviving descendant of that prolific old gent."

"Which makes her the surviving heir to the prolific old gent's money."

"Precisely." Sam shot a keen glance through

scanty lashes at the other man's face; it was impassive as stone. He continued.

"The money went, in actual fact, to the eldest son, Stephan. He had a stepdaughter, child of his wife's first marriage, but no offspring of his own. So the money went to Kate."

"Kate? Not Shakespearean, I hope."

"I think of her that way," Sam said, with hideous sentimentality. His companion winced perceptibly. Sam smirked. "Indeed, but there are suggestions of the shrew. The lady is fairly young—late twenties—very rich, very intelligent—"

"Please." The younger man raised a peremptory hand. "Don't say very beautiful."

"Well." Sam masticated his lower lip thoughtfully. "That she isn't. Not that her face would stop a clock, mind, but she's the image of the lady professor, which is what she was. Everything but the horn-rimmed glasses. She has twenty-twenty vision."

"You would know that." The younger man sounded resigned. "Well, I've never believed in those films anyhow."

"Which films? Oh, I get you; the ones where the frigid old bag takes off the horn-rimmed specs in the last reel and turns out to be Sophia Loren. No such luck, my boy. But three or four million bucks should gild even a withered lily."

"You're a dirty-minded old man entirely," said his companion, in a vile imitation of a brogue. "Professor of what?"

"Assistant prof, to be precise. Of Sociology. Her field is folk-lore and superstition, ethnic survivals in isolated communities, et cetera. She's written one book, on superstition and witchcraft in America. It's been compared with Margaret Murray's work on the witchcraft problem, but is more highly regarded by the scholarly reviewers; traces the cult of—"

"Is there anything you don't know?" The younger man ran a hand through his shaggy hair.

"That's my business, me boy. Information."

"Well, you needn't give me a synopsis. I've read Murray's books, as it happens. She claims, I believe, that the witchcraft of the Middle Ages was the remnant of a prehistoric European religion which survived into late times. The horned god, fertility rites, and so on."

"That's right. Your girl friend has carried the idea one step further. She thinks the Old Religion still survives."

"Oh, it does, it does," the younger man murmured. "The powers of darkness are considerably stronger than the powers of good. What student of world affairs could doubt that? All right, Sam, let us not philosophize. Is the lady still professing? Or professoring?"

"No, she quit after she inherited her petty millions. Retired to the old family homestead."

"Which is where?"

"It's all in my report." Sam indicated the sheaf of papers which lay on the table between them.

"Middleburg, Maryland, U.S.A. No, I'm not kidding. It's a misnomer, though; the town is an unusual place."

"Go on."

Sam settled back in his chair, comtemplated his tea balefully, and settled for a cigar. When it was lit he blew out a cloud of dark smoke that made his companion wrinkle a fastidious nose, and began his lecture.

"Middleburg is one of the oldest settlements in the States, goes back to the early seventeenth century and Lord Baltimore—you've heard of him? Religious freedom, Catholic English fleeing persecution, all that stuff. Well, so the town sat there, peacefully rotting, for three hundred years. About thirty years ago it was discovered by the overflow gentry from Baltimore and Washington. They thought it was quaint, and I guess it was; if you like quaintness. Now the place is transformed, but selectively. The idle rich bought up the old houses and restored them, and built big estates outside town. They've got a committee which supervises new construction; I hear you can't build a house in the area for under a hundred thousand, but that may be exaggerated. Slightly exaggerated.

"The citizens are an ungodly mixture. Along with the inbred descendants of the original boys and girls you'll find some of the bluest blood money can buy. The country club is so exclusive that the President—of the U.S., that is—was recently blackballed. It's huntin' country and drinkin' country. I don't know about merrie olde England, but in the States those two often coincide. How are you at riding? Horses, I mean."

"Fair."

"Oh, that English modesty," Sam said, beaming. "What about hunting? Riding to hounds, I believe it's called."

"I'm not awfully keen these days on hunting things," the younger man said. His tone was calm, even pleasant; but a shiver went up Sam's well-insulated backbone.

"Well, then," he said, studiously contemplating his stone-cold cup of tea, "we'll have to find some other way for you to ingratiate yourself. The lady doesn't hunt, in any case."

"Doesn't she?"

Sam looked up quickly, but his companion's face was as affable as it ever permitted itself to be.

"Want more tea?" he asked, more disturbed than he cared to admit.

"God forbid."

"All right, five more minutes and you can be on your way to wherever you're going, and I'll be on my way to—wherever I'm going. Where was I? Oh, yes, the town. If you want to know more about it, there've been articles in some of the glossier magazines. They like their privacy, in Middleburg—for a variety of reasons, probably—but they can't keep all the curious out, and it is a strange place, with the mixture of old and new. The old boy, Kate's Uncle Stephan, was one of the people who bridged the gap. He had the dough, and his mother was a daughter of one of the old families. A Device, no less. All right, shrug, but in Middleburg that means something. Uncle Stephan was a weirdo himself. Didn't marry till late in life, a widow with a child. He brought the kid up after his wife died, but never officially adopted her; that's why the dough went to Kate when he kicked the bucket. She's got the girl living with her now. They tell me she's quite a dish."

"Your slang is at least twenty years out of date. All right, you've given me a picture of the lady, and a damned unattractive one it is. What about her weaknesses?"

"Rumor says she hasn't any."

"Rumor. What about you?"

"A compliment, is it?" Sam grinned. "Praise from Caesar . . . I'll admit I've found a few weaknesses. For one, the doctor has gone off the deep end."

"Which one?"

"Well, you might call it lunatic-fringe scholarship, or just plain stupidity. She's come to believe in her own subject, or at the least she's doing some curious research."

"Sticking pins in waxen images?"

"She may be, for all I know. Spiritualism, at least; and not the usual psychic bit, holding hands around a table in the dark. 'Tis a cult of some kind, with false priests and rituals. She has meetings in her house."

"Charming. I used to dabble in magic myself, in my ill-spent youth."

"Well, that's a possible lead. If, indeed, it's winning the lady's confidence that you've got in mind. . . ." He paused, his odd opaque eyes wide in pretended innocence. His companion's face became, if possible, even blanker. Sam seemed to find in this the answer he expected; his voice had a hint of satisfaction as he continued.

"To the most popular and attractive weakness of the flesh the doctor seems to be impervious. Like all these brainy women, she despises men. However"—Sam lifted one dainty forefinger and wagged it in front of his companion's amused face—"there was one weak moment, about two years back. When she fell, she fell hard. The whole town knew about it; and, my God, how the old ladies' tongues wagged. Not that Middleburg isn't as susceptible as any town to the good old human habit of casual adultery. But middle-class Americans are a hypocritical lot; they like to have the game, but not the name. Hypocrisy is not one of the doc's weaknesses; in fact she seems to enjoy rubbing people's noses in unpopular facts. Naturally, they responded by hating her guts."

"Naturally."

"Well, that's irrelevant. What may help you is the fact—mark this—that the lucky fellow somewhat resembled you."

The younger man made a rude noise.

"Not the old double routine, Sam. That isn't done nowadays."

"No, no, nothing so unlikely. 'Tis said that every man has an exact duplicate of himself walking the world; but how many people d'you know who've actually met theirs? I was speaking of a general type. Slight build, fair hair and—this is important—an Englishman."

"Why important?"

Sam leaned back in the chair and assumed the position he favored for lecturing. The sunlight had deepened to bronze; in the back of the teashop shadows gathered.

"I suppose you're too young to know these things," he said tolerantly, ignoring his companion's raised eyebrow. "You see, me boy, women aren't logical. Vessels of pure emotion they are, poor darlings; and their emotions tend to get fixed on particular types. No doubt the Freudians could explain it all in terms of father images. Unlike ourselves, the ladies—bless 'em—are not so much impressed by the important physical features as by minor characteristics like hands, voice, hair color, and so on. And you needn't be lookin' at me with your eyebrows like that. A lady friend of mine explained it all to me, once upon a time."

"A lady friend of yours?" the younger man said incredulously.

"Yes, indeed." Unoffended, Sam smiled complacently. "Didn't I say that they were illogical little creatures? It was me hands that won her heart;

me hands and the lovely shape of the back of me neck."

He rubbed the last-named feature fondly.

"How very poetic."

"Yes; I've me sentimental side, though few ever see it." Sam sighed deeply and then got back to business. "You'll see the implications. Mind, I'm not claiming the resemblance will bring the lady rushing to your arms; but you've a better chance of being well receved than if you were tall and dark and heavy-set."

"Puts me right in there with about half the men in the world," the younger man agreed sarcastically.

"A quarter," Sam said pedantically. "Tall and fair, tall and dark—"

"The redheads further confuse your categories. How many million fortunate males share my admirable characteristics, I wonder?"

"Don't forget the voice," Sam reminded him. "That's one of the things that gets them."

"Don't be vulgar. Two million instead of two billion, then."

"Well, if you want to pick flaws—"

"No, I think you've done splendidly. I shall sally forth to—what's its ghastly name?—Middleburg, and imitate a blond Englishman. I take it he wore his hair long?"

"You are the bright lad." Sam smiled sunnily.

"Too bright for my own good." His companion shoved back his chair and stood up, in a quick, abrupt movement that jarred the comatose waitress out of her dreams. "All right, Sam. I appreciate this," he added awkwardly. "Especially your seeing me personally."

"It was on me way." Sam pushed the sheaf of papers across the table. "Don't forget these. Are you just going to vanish into the Limbo, now, or will I be hearing from you?"

"Why should you be hearing from me?"

"Oh . . . sometimes these matters can't be handled by one person. If you should need any assistance . . ."

The younger man stood quite still, his hand resting lightly on the back of his chair; but his pose suggested that the slightest sound or movement might send him into flight.

"And what makes you think I'm up to anything that will require handling? Or assistance?"

Sam made a vulgar noise in the back of his throat.

"Come off it, me lad. I'll be back in about a week. You know how to reach me. The usual rates, of course," he added, with one of his unpleasant smiles.

"Of course."

There was a moment of silence, during which the two contemplated one another with expressions which were as different as they were mutually unreadable. Then the younger man said,

"Good luck, then. I expect you'll need it."

"I always do," Sam agreed calmly; and, as his companion turned, he added, "One more thing."

"What's that?"

"I neglected to mention it. The fellow you're . . . impersonating. The great lover."

"Well?"

"Well," Sam said pensively, "he's dead, you see."

# PART ONE
## *Huntsman*

# *Chapter*

## 1

MIDDLEBURG, MARYLAND, POSSESSED A POPULATION of 9300 and one of the finest small airports one descending passenger had ever seen. For a place of its size it had a surprising amount of traffic. There were several daily shuttle flights to Washington and New York, and this plane, the Friday afternoon flight from Washington, had been nearly full.

The passenger in question, a slight, fair-haired man, was the last one off the plane. He stopped at the foot of the ramp and stared across the field, noting the number of private planes and hangars. The field was miniature, but equipped with all the latest gadgetry; it looked like a rich man's toy. The setting was equally perfect. Beyond the strips of concrete and the fences a gently rolling countryside had taken on the rich colors of autumn. The grain fields were stubble now, but much of the land was wooded; the gold of maples and the crimson of oak and sumac made vivid splashes of brightness against the somber green background of firs. A faint haze lay over the land, but the day was fine, almost too warm for October. The visitor reflected that this must be what the natives called Indian summer. He shrugged out of his coat, draped it over his arm, and started off across the field toward the terminal.

It was small, like the airport, and equally perfect; built of fieldstone and timber, it looked more like a private hunting lodge than a public building. The young man joined the group waiting at the luggage counter. Only a handful of the passengers had waited; most of them, carrying briefcases, had gone directly to waiting cars. Weekenders, evidently; and weekenders who could afford two separate wardrobes and homes.

The people waiting for luggage were of the same type, and the young man categorized them with the quick impatience which was one of his many failings. The Rich. Bureaucrats or businessmen or idlers, they were all alike: people with too much money and too much leisure, so that they spent large quantities of the former trying to occupy the latter.

He himself did not fit in with the crowd, though he had a chameleonlike instinct for protective coloring. The business he was presently engaged in required another type of costume. His suit—one of his own, recently retailored to fit his reduced measurements—was old but good. His tie was modest in design, but he wore it with a slightly stifled look, as if he were unused to even that moderate formality. By the standards of the over-forty generation he still needed a haircut. He had considered horn-rimmed glasses, and had abandoned them as being a bit too much, and also as too obviously fraudulent; his vision, like Katherine More's, was twenty-twenty. But the most important part of the disguise was attitude. He had thought himself into his role so thoroughly that when the man standing next to him spoke he came out of an artistic fog with a slight jerk.

"Stupid bastards get slower every week." The man, a stocky individual, had shoulders like a bull's and a belligerent, feet-wide-apart stance. His close-cropped gray hair failed to conceal a skull as hard and round as a cannonball, or soften features which looked like something an inexperienced sculptor had roughed out and then given up as a hopeless job.

"Hmmm? Oh. I haven't been waiting very long."

"Stranger here?" The older man sized him up with a long, appraising stare, and extended a brown hand. "Volz is my name. U.S. Army, retired."

"Peter Stewart. I'm a writer." He let the U.S.

Army, retired, wring his hand, and produced a pained smile. "General, were you, sir?"

"How did you know?"

"The . . . general air," Peter murmured, and grinned modestly when the general gave a short brusque laugh that sounded like a dog barking.

"Very good. The writer's touch, eh? Have I read any of your books?"

"I very much doubt it."

Suitcases began rolling onto the rack and Volz, with an unexpurgated comment, darted forward. Peter followed more slowly. When he had retrieved his battered case he found the general still at his side.

"Going into town?"

"Yes. There are taxis, I suppose?"

"Probably taken by now. I'll give you a lift, if you like."

"That's very good of you." Peter spoke stiffly; then he reminded himself that he was being too suspicious. He knew the automatic if superficial friendliness of Americans. This loudmouthed idiot couldn't possibly know anything about him or his past—or his present intentions. He added more warmly, "I've booked a room at the Inn, but if that's out of your way—"

"No, no, got to go through town anyway. My place is on the other side. This way."

His car was just what Peter had expected: a black, shiny Lincoln with a uniformed chauffeur, who leaped out as his employer came stamping up. The chauffeur was black, six and a half feet tall, with a profile like that of the Apollo on the temple of Olympia. Even the flat crisp curls looked Greek.

Belatedly Peter tried to conceal his fascinated stare with an inane smile and a murmured greeting. The black statue responded with a stiff inclination of his head and no change of expression whatever. Chastened, Peter climbed into the back seat, and the door slammed smartly, just missing his heel.

On the way into town the general told four dirty jokes and a long tedious story about some minor skirmish during the Battle of the Bulge. Peter laughed immoderately at the jokes and made admiring noises during the anecdote. By the time they neared the outskirts of Middleburg, Volz had also extracted a major portion of Peter's biography. It was a good biography, and Peter was proud of it. He had spent two days composing it and another week gathering the documents which backed it up.

"Folklore," Volz repeated. "Thought you said you wrote fiction."

"Actually, I do write novels under another name."

"What name?"

"Ah." Peter shook his head, smiling. "That's a secret, I'm afraid."

"What?" Volz stared at him suspiciously, and Peter had to remind himself that impertinent cu-

riosity was a normal American trait. Then the
general's face broadened in a smile which was
more than impertinent; it was downright offensive. "Oh, that sort of novel. I'll bet I've read some
of them at that."

Peter returned the smile, reflecting with some
complacency on the advantages of the writer's
trade as cover for even less wholesome activities.
Anonymity was not only understandable, it was
the norm; within twenty-four hours the whole
town would be speculating on his pseudonyms
and identifying him with everybody from Norman
Mailer to Agatha Christie. He could deny all the ru-
mors with perfect sincerity, and never be believed.

Volz abandoned the question of identity as
they approached the town. He was now exhibit-
ing another notorious American characteristic—
pointing out uninteresting local sights to a visitor.
The Foundling Home, the hospital, the Catholic
Church—all new, handsome buildings, which
suggested sizable private support. Peter made
appropriate noises.

"The Club's down there," Volz said, indicating
a drive flanked by impressive stone pillars. Peter
just had time to catch the sign, which added an
emphatic "Private Drive—Members Only" to the
name of the country club.

"I don't suppose you ride," Volz said, with un-
consicous contempt.

"I used to."

"You said you'd been sick, so I figured—"

"Exercise is what I need. Healthy outdoor life, and all that. So the doctor says."

"I suppose you'll be wanting a local doctor? We've got a good man. Paul Martin."

"So I've heard. Matter of fact, I've got a letter of introduction to him. From Sir George Macpherson."

He watched, out of the corner of his eye, and saw that the name had registered.

"The British Ambassador? You know him?"

"Not personally. Just the family." He dropped it there, knowing the error of elaborating a good lie.

Volz's stare was perceptibly more friendly.

"Great guy, Sir George. When he was out with the hunt last year, he was quite impressed with my stable. Are you a hunting man?"

"I have hunted."

"Give me a call if you'd like to join us one day."

"I'd like that. But I haven't been near a horse for several years; I might disgrace myself."

"Oh, well, come out to my place someday and try my horses. I've got a new hunter, name of Sultan; cost me a pretty penny, I can tell you. Like to see you on him."

Volz grinned wickedly, and Peter made a mental note to watch out for Sultan's tricks.

"When does your season begin?" he asked.

"October; we start earlier than you people, I'm told. We meet three times a week."

"I just might join you one day. If you're sure I won't be intruding."

"Any friend of Sir George's," Volz assured him. "You'll like the other members. Important people."

"Mmm." Peter wondered how he could ascertain the one point he was most interested in. To mention Katharine More by name would be too crude even for Volz. "I understand that Middleburg has an inordinate number of nationally prominent citizens."

"Sure does. An ex-governor, several Congressmen, some of the big banking families. All friends of mine. Not that I pick my friends for that. They're all . . . interesting people. Very interesting . . ."

Before Peter could pursue the subject, Volz changed it. He leaned forward, pointing.

"Here we are. Middleburg. Not much of it, but what there is, we like."

The outskirts of the town were unusual in that the common highway deformities—neon signs, gas stations, factories—were absent. The main street was narrow, and lined with old trees whose carefully tended branches met above in a multicolored arch. The houses were set in wide lawns, with shrubbery and ornamental trees. Massed beds of chrysanthemum and aster made patches of color, from white and gold to deeper bronze and a glowing crimson. Many of the homes were white-painted wood, their size and wide verandas dating them to an era when household help was cheap, and available. Judging from the superb condition of lawns and paint,

Peter concluded that help was available, if not cheap.

"Main Street," Volz said. Peter suppressed a smile. "That's Jefferson Avenue over there, where Martin lives."

"It's an attractive town. Is it all as—prosperous as this section?"

"Yep. We're pretty proud of the place. Of course we have a few slums, like everybody else. Down by the creek is Shantytown, where the niggers live."

There was no glass partition between front seat and back. Peter glanced at the rigid back of the chauffeur and said blandly, "I'm surprised you folks haven't cleaned it up."

"You can't get trash like that to take any pride in their homes. Only way to clean the place up would be to run 'em out. And we need 'em. Servants."

"Of course."

The chauffeur's dark hand reached for the turn signal, and the car slowed. They turned left, past a white, steepled church, onto a street lined with shops. Peter frowned thoughtfully at the uniform facades, with their bow windows set in aged brick and their discreet little signs; then he remembered what the place reminded him of. Reconstructed . . . Williamsburg, was it? . . . a travel brochure, glanced at some years back, which advertised one of the restored Colonial towns of which Americans were so proud. Such places always had an air of selfconsciousness; they were not the result of slow natural growth, but of a planned effect, like a set for a film.

He caught a few of the signs, noting thankfully that there were no atrocities such as "Ye Olde Curiosity Shoppe," and then the car slid smoothly to a stop in front of a larger, more distinctive, building.

The sign read simply "Middleburg Inn," and the place looked as if it had been built as a tavern or hotel several centuries ago. A long wooden building, painted yellow, with black shutters and shingles, it had three floors, and a flat-roofed veranda, supported by black columns stretching along the length of the facade. The windows of the topmost floor were gabled. A pair of tall brick chimneys reared up from the far end; and on the left was a five-floored annex, built of the same yellow clapboard, but clearly of later date.

"Here we are," Volz said unnecessarily. "Give me a call, Stewart, about the hunt. Always happy to have a friend of Sir George's."

"Thanks for the ride." Peter accepted his suitcase from the stiffly correct chauffeur and stood watching as the car glided away. The two figures in front and back were as isolated from one another as if they had been on two different planets.

"Curious people," he said aloud, and headed for the registration desk.

His room was small and extremely Early American, with yards of flowered chintz draped here and there, and a quantity of maple furniture. The mattress was comfortable, though, and the small bathroom gleamed with gadgetry, including heated towel racks and glasses done up in paper, a custom which Peter had always considered evidence of a basically nasty mind. His eyebrows rose slightly at the rates quoted on the discreet card placed beside the telephone.

The air conditioner was going full blast. As soon as the bellboy had left, Peter turned it off and wrestled successfully with the window.

His room was in the annex, at the back; front rooms, of course, would be reserved for more important visitors. Peter had expected this, but had been prepared to find some fault with the room if necessary in order to get the location he wanted. This was quite satisfactory. Nothing faced onto the alley behind the hotel except the back doors of other business establishments; they would be closed and deserted after dark. By American standards it was a very clean alley. The trash cans were tightly lidded and placed off to one side to keep the center of the pavement free for traffic. High board fences lined both sides. And off to the right, not far from his window, was a fire escape. It was almost too perfect.

He took off his jacket, loosened his tie, and started to unpack. The domestic staff of the hotel was clearly well trained; everything was painfully neat. Even the drawers of bureau and desk had been relined with fresh white paper. That was how he knew that the singular object in the top left bureau drawer could not have been left by mistake.

It was a gold crucifix, about an inch and a half long, and distinctive in its design. The anguished figure on the cross had a simplicity of structure which marked it as modern work, but the artist had managed to suggest, in the droop of the head and the twist of the limbs, a degree of agony which reminded Peter of some of the more sadistic medieval depictions of the Crucifixion. He picked it up, conscious of an odd aversion; and as he examined it more closely his curiosity and repugnance grew. It was damned skillful work; there was no explicit detail in the beautifully modeled figure which would account for his distaste.

With an abrupt movement he put the ornament into his pocket, straightened his tie, and reached for his jacket. He needed a drink. Several drinks, in fact, if his imagination was getting that far out of hand.

He had the drinks, in a lounge which was free of the Early American touch, but which reeked equally effusively of Ye Olde English Pub, and then had dinner. The Inn, as he might have anticipated, had an excellent dining room. After dinner he went to the desk.

"I'd like to speak to the manager."

The clerk was a type: supercilious, thin, middle-aged, with a consciously well-modulated voice. It took Peter several minutes of argument, in an accent which he deliberately exaggerated, to win his point. There was more than the normal officiousness in the clerk's reluctance; Peter got the impression that the manager and owner—who was not male, but female, a Mrs. Adams—was something of a tartar. But when the clerk returned from his expedition into the inner sanctum, he was looking almost human in his surprise.

"Mrs. Adams will see you," he said in hushed tones.

Peter knew, at first glance, that he and Mrs. Adams were not going to be friends. From the clerk's attitude he had expected to find one of those frail, white-haired aristocrats whose cooing voice conceals a will as dictatorial as Hitler's. He had nothing against old ladies, even vicious aristocratic old ladies, and he had always been successful with them. He assumed the charm automatically, bending so low over Mrs. Adams' extended hand that his lips almost touched it, but he had no illusions as to the effectiveness of the performance.

Mrs. Adams was neither frail nor white-haired. Her hand showed the painfully twisted joints of arthritis, but it was still big and powerful. She had been a big-boned, tall woman, and she had not lost much of her bulk with age. Her hair was tinted an improbable shade of red, and the eyes that met his in a long, appraising stare had once been beautiful, before they sank into folds of mottled skin. They were an unusual clear green, with flecks of amber.

"I don't see people," said Mrs. Adams. Her voice reminded him of the general's; it was almost as deep and it had the same peremptory, barking tone. The habit of command, Peter thought wryly; he could picture the old lady with a whip, bullying a shivering huddle of field hands. She added, "What the hell's the idea of barging in here?"

Peter had not been invited to sit down. He folded his hands, shifted his feet, and looked guileless.

"You could have said no," he reminded her gently.

She cocked her head and peered up at him. Bad vision? Perhaps, partly, but there was a ghostly air of coquetry about the pose that reminded Peter of the fact that once, God knows how many eons before, she must have been a handsome woman. The green eyes began to sparkle and she said, less gruffly, "Sit down, I hate being loomed over. So, all right, I was curious. Hell, I'm not that old! Bennie said you were a good-looking devil, and he's usually right, if for the wrong reasons."

She burst into laughter at the sight of Peter's face.

"Relax, sonny; he won't bother you. I make damn good and sure my employees know the score. Besides, he has his own arrangements. Private ones. Now then. What's your excuse for shoving in here?"

"If I had known the charms that awaited, I'd have shoved sooner," Peter said. "And planned to stay longer. But since you force me to get to the point—"

"Don't be impertinent."

"Sorry. I found something in one of the drawers in my room. Must have been overlooked by the previous occupant. Since it appears to be gold, and may have a sentimental value, I thought I ought to give it to you personally."

Mrs. Adams took the crucifix and examined it with mild interest.

"Sentimental value?" The mass of wrinkles which was her face writhed. "That's an odd way of putting it. All right, Stewart. You've been a good little Boy Scout. Of course you could just as well have given it to Bennie. My people are honest. They know better than to try anything on me."

"I'm sure they do."

"Sentimental value." She chuckled. "A writer, are you, Stewart?"

"Yes." Peter gave the word a rising inflexion, and Mrs. Adams grinned at him.

"Hell's bells, boy, this is a small town, in spite of all the pretentiousness. And I hear everything that goes on, not only because I'm the boss here, but because I'm one of the local gentry."

"I guessed it at once, from the charming formality of your manner," Peter said.

Her grin faded, but he sensed that she was not

displeased with him. Some other thought drew her face into deeper lines that made her look centuries old.

"These new people," she muttered. "What do they know? My family goes back three hundred years in this town. Upstarts . . . carpetbaggers . . ." Then her eyes came alive; for a few seconds they had been as vacant as glass marbles. "Some of 'em aren't so bad, though. The general's a pompous ass, but he's not stupid. By tomorrow everything you told him will be all over town. Yes," she said softly, and now her grin was overtly unpleasant, "we'll know all about you, Mr. Stewart."

Peter had planned to take a walk after dinner. The night was fine, starlit and cool, with a snap of frost in the air, and he wanted to orient himself. But the conversation with Mrs. Adams had disturbed him more than he liked to admit. Certain old phobias, which he had thought to be conquered, reasserted themselves. He felt a need to get inside four walls, with a locked door between himself and the rest of the world. It might seem an unreasonable desire for a man who had spent two years staring with sick frustration and hate at another locked door; but a cell is protection as well as confinement, and freedom is not necessarily comfortable.

The window had been closed and the air conditioner turned on. Peter turned it off and opened the window. He switched off the overhead light and leaned out across the sill.

A breeze stirred the drying leaves on branch and ground, making a barely audible background rustle under the normal night sounds—the swish of cars passing on the street beyond the alley, a woman's clear voice laughing, the unmusical howl of an optimistic tomcat. Beyond the shuttered walled-in shapes of the stores in the foreground Peter could see the waving branches of trees outlined against the lighter dark of the sky, and a few cheerfully lighted windows in some of the taller houses. A nice peaceful town, Middleburg; full of nice, average people.

Under those sheltering roofs, to be sure, lay hidden all the miseries and thwarted passions which humanity brings upon itself: drugs, alcoholism, adultery, hate, frustration. . . .

The corners of Peter's mouth turned up in a smile which his friend Sam would have recognized. That was just the sort of smug superficial remark a second-rate writer might be expected to produce. Which didn't mean it wasn't accurate; the same thing could be said, without saying anything meaningful, about any nice average town anywhere in the world. In the igloos and grass huts the problems were different, but they were no less painful.

Then why did he feel that there was something particularly malevolent about Middleburg—that the peaceful-looking town was really as alert as a sleeping cat, and that the yellow windows were like slitted eyes, through which he was being studied with a concentrated inimical intelligence?

Because I'm neurotic as hell, Peter told himself. It'll take a while to get over those years, more time than I've had. Got to remember that, take it into account. Forget it. Go to bed and get some sleep.

Still he stayed at the window, arms crossed on the sill, enjoying the feel of the clean country air. It must be admitted that the inhabitants of Middleburg whom he had met so far were not attractive human beings. Mrs. Adams was not unique; he had encountered the type before, in other settings: the foul-mouthed bellowing country squiress, more at home in a paddock than a parlor, displaying an aristocrat's deliberate contempt for conventional social behavior. In her way, she was just as much a caricature as Volz was a caricature of the military man. Caricatures . . . Peter's tired brain fumbled with the idea and then gave it up. He couldn't distinguish his own neuroses from valid judgments, that was the trouble. No wonder everyone he met seemed masked.

It was while he was preparing for bed, with all the lights sanely burning, that he realized what specific point had set him off. The crucifix. There had been one inconspicuous detail wrong, besides the indefinable sense of corruption in the modeling. Such ornaments were often worn on a chain around the neck. This cross had welded to it a small gold ring through which such a chain might have been passed. But the ring was in the wrong place—at the end of the long part of the cross. If that crucifix had been worn around someone's neck, it would have hung upside down.

# Chapter
## 2

IMMEDIATELY AFTER BREAKFAST NEXT MORNING Peter put through a call to Dr. Paul Martin, introducing himself and mentioning the magic name of the Ambassador. As he accepted Martin's invitation to drop over later for a cup of coffee, he wondered whether he ought to inquire into Martin's training in psychiatry. The fantasies of the previous night had induced some singularly disquieting dreams; even in broad daylight he could not completely shake off the impression of intent yellow eyes, staring and aware.

Once he got out onto the street he forgot his mental quirks in the normalcy of the scene. The weather was so good as to be almost a legitimate topic of conversation. Dry leaves crackled pleasantly under his feet as he strolled down Adams

Avenue, past a row of shops. The stores included the usual—grocery, shoe store, cleaner's, and the like—but the effect was quite unlike that of the other small towns Peter had seen in the States. None of the buildings were garish or run down; they conformed to the imposed code, almost all being of rosy aged brick with white trim around doors and windows, and a superfluity of black wrought-iron hinges. The grocer's window displayed jars of caviar and snails and at least two vintages of wine which Peter had never seen west or south of Manhattan. There were other establishments which few villages of Middleburg's size could have supported: a saddlery, a jeweler's whose other branches were in Amsterdam and Cape Town, and a well-stocked bookstore.

On a sudden impulse Peter went into the bookstore. As he had expected, they had the book in stock; frugally he bought the soft-cover edition and tucked it into his pocket.

Martin's house wasn't far from the hotel. It was in a neighborhood of smaller but very comfortable homes, which looked newer than the old mansions of Main Street. Again Peter was struck by the well-tended lawns and shrubbery, and the fine old trees.

The doctor's office was in his home. A swinging sign by the front gate announced the office hours, and Peter saw that he had arrived at the end of the morning session. In the semi-seclusion of the entryway, which was shielded by trellises and flowers, he dealt with the book he had just purchased. He dog-eared several pages, bent the spine back ruthlessly, and rubbed the edges and the front and back covers along a concrete planter which held geraniums. A handful of dirt from the planter, applied lightly to the edges, completed the aging process. Peter put the book back in his pocket and applied his finger to the bell.

The door was opened by a plain, elderly woman in a white uniform, who showed him to the waiting room and explained that the doctor had not quite finished with his last patient. If Mr. Stewart wouldn't mind . . .

Peter said he didn't mind, and took a chair as the nurse went on into the inner office. The room was a pleasant enough place, furnished like any private sitting room except for the usual out-of-date magazines on a table; but he had a feeling he was going to get awfully sick of Early American before he left Middleburg.

Pessimistically he looked through the pile of magazines and found, as he had expected, that there was nothing he wanted to read. A more promising periodical lay on the maple-and-chintz sofa—a copy of the local paper, abandoned by an earlier patient.

The *Middleburg Herald* wasn't as pretentious as the town it served. Presumably the inhabitants got the two *Times* and the Washington papers for their main source of news; this twelve-page weekly gave only token attention to the international and national scenes and devoted the rest of the issue to burning local questions. Two pages of want ads were concerned chiefly with maids and antiques. There was a column of high-school news, written by some budding journalist of sixteen; Peter found, to his amused dismay, that he only understood about half the slang.

The Social Column was more impressive. Accustomed as he was to the unique status of Middleburg, Peter's lips pursed in a silent whistle more than once as he read through the lists of events and names. Dances, dinners, committee meetings; trips to Bermuda and Cannes—blue blood was right, dark blue. The Hunt Club was one of the more publicized groups, and its members seemed to include the most indigo of the blue blood, plus a number of names Peter didn't recognize. Local aristocracy, presumably. He was interested to note that his hostess, Mrs. Adams, figured prominently in the social news.

But the Middleburg scene was not all sweetness and light. He was just beginning the lead editorial, an indignant tirade about vandalism in the churchyard and desecration of graves, when the door of the inner office opened. A young, very pregnant woman emerged and followed the nurse to the desk. Peter got to his feet. The doctor was ready for him.

Paul Martin was not a young man, but his hair was still thick and brown, and his tall frame was in excellent physical condition. There were a few wrinkles in his cheeks and forehead, but they were lines of laughter, which deepened attractively as he shook hands with Peter. His was a generally attractive face, with candid brown eyes and a broad, easy smile; a slight Bostonian twang did not distort his soft baritone voice.

He read Peter's letter of introduction while the nurse brought in rolls and coffee. When she had left, he looked Peter up and down, without prejudice, but intently enough to make the younger man squirm internally. He had never before felt so unmistakably that he was being inspected, inside and out.

"Kind of Sir George to remember me," Martin said. "I've only met him once."

His modesty was in refreshing contrast to Volz's immediate assumption of intimacy. Peter found himself warming to the doctor.

"I gather he knows your reputation."

"Hmmm." Martin's eyes continued their inspection. "I'm not a specialist, you know; just a country GP. He doesn't mention the nature of your recent illness . . ."

Peter dropped his eyes and toyed with the coffee spoon. A mild embarrassment was, he thought, the proper reaction; and it was a relief to release his eyes from that searching scrutiny.

"Well," Martin said after a moment, "it doesn't matter. You're not in need of regular medical care now, what you want is a backstop in case of trouble. Right? It might be a good idea for me to give you a physical checkup—"

"That won't be necessary. It wasn't ... that is ..."

"Of course," Martin said quickly. "You look fit enough. Any complaints at the moment? Sleeping well? Good. You're a few pounds under your proper weight, I'd say, but that's nothing to worry about."

Still intent on the pattern of the silverware, Peter nodded mutely. The point had been made. Had it been made a little too easily? He was beginning to see why Sam had mentioned Paul Martin as a leading citizen, a man whose friendship might be important. Though the doctor lacked both money and family connections, he had an air of quiet competence and authority which inspired respect. When Martin changed the subject, Peter knew it was not because of consideration for his pretended embarrassment, but because the doctor had learned all he needed to know.

"More coffee? So you're a writer, Mr. Stewart. Interesting occupation. I gather you use a pseudonym. What sort of thing do you write about, if that question doesn't threaten your anonymity?"

"Not at all. I've done a lot of things, actually, from fiction to popular science. Popular nonfiction, pseudotechnical stuff, is what I prefer. My agent thinks just now that a book on folklore might do well. That's why Sir George suggested I spend a few weeks here. Combine rest with business, so to speak."

"Folklore." Martin leaned back in his chair and selected a pipe from the assortment on his desk. "And why, I wonder, would Sir George think of Middleburg in that connection? Why not Transylvania? Or some of the more remote areas of your own country?"

"Vampires and little old ladies pretending to be white witches? That sort of thing has been done to death, Doctor. I'm looking for something more sensational; got to think of the money, you know. Black Masses, pacts with the devil—that's the thing nowadays."

He didn't know precisely what had moved him to make that statement, unless it was the faint nagging memory connected with the reversed crucifix. Martin's reaction was somewhat unexpected. He threw back his head and laughed heartily.

"You won't find any Black Masses in Middleburg," he said. "In a somewhat more prosaic sense, though, Sir George was quite right. I just wondered how he happened to know about it; when he was here, his sole interest seemed to be pursuing a series of miserable foxes. Middleburg is a very old community, Mr. Stewart, and there are some interesting survivals. Not black magic, of course, but superstitions, traditions, old songs— even some very quaint bits of folk medicine among the old farming families. Have you visited our museum?"

"I only arrived yesterday."

"Oh, of course. Well, you may find it worth your while. It's small, but rather fine, we think. It's run by our own Folklore Society. We've a very active group. Perhaps you'd like to attend a meeting?"

"Very much."

"Then you're in luck." Martin smiled. "There's a meeting tomorrow night."

"Splendid. How many members do you have?"

"Only about a dozen. When we started out we admitted everyone, but those of us who were hard-core enthusiasts found that we were wasting a lot of time on purely social activities, so we began weeding out the dilettantes. It works much better this way. We're amateurs, but serious amateurs."

"Amateurs?" Peter repeated. "But you have at least one professional here in Middleburg. I confess I've been looking forward to meeting her."

He pulled the book from his pocket and placed it on the desk. His eyes were on the book, so he didn't see Martin's face, but he did see the sudden uncontrolled twitch of the doctor's hand. When he looked up, Martin's expression was unremarkable.

"Dr. More. Yes, she's certainly a professional. Unfortunately, she's not a member of our little group."

"Intellectual snob?"

"No, no, not at all. Well, perhaps just a bit. . . .

She's a friend as well as a patient, you see, and I don't like—"

"I'm sorry, I shouldn't have said that. I don't even know the woman. Only it seemed natural . . ."

"Natural," Martin repeated. "Yes, yes, of course. And it's natural that you should want to meet her, with your interest in the field. . . . And *The Old Religion in the New World* is a splendid book, really first-rate. I see you've studied it thoroughly. But I'm afraid Kate doesn't—meet people."

"Something of a recluse, is she?"

"Not at all," Martin said stiffly. Peter wondered at his defensiveness. Was he in love with the woman? If not, why was he so desirous of making her appear less offensive than she almost certainly was? Why didn't he simply drop the subject, as he had every right to do with an inquisitive stranger?

"You'll probably see her around town," Martin went on more easily. "She comes and goes, she's not a hermit; and if we should encounter her, naturally I'll introduce you. Be glad to. What I meant was that she isn't the sort of person who joins societies. Not a joiner," he repeated, clearly relieved to have found a nonpejorative adjective.

Peter was silent, weighing the value of what he might learn from further questioning against the disadvantage of risking Martin's friendship by boorish inquisitiveness. He was still weighing when the telephone on Martin's desk gave a discreet buzz, and the doctor reached out for it. "What? Oh, I suppose so. Tell him to come in."

He hung up the phone.

"Will you excuse me just a moment?"

Peter nodded. The door opened, and the nurse ushered in the chauffeur who had driven Peter from the airport.

"Come in, Hilary," said Martin. Peter blinked at the name. "The general wants an immediate answer? Why the devil doesn't the man use the telephone? Splendid invention, the telephone. Sit down, man, sit down; it'll take me a while to write an answer. Oh—this is Mr. Stewart. Hilary Jackson, Peter."

"I've met Mr. Stewart, sir," said Hilary Jackson.

"But not formally." Peter put out his hand. "How do you do."

Jackson gave him the cut direct, staring straight ahead and ignoring his hand.

"Very well, sir, thank you."

The man's voice was a rich bass, with no particular accent. He remained standing, hat in hand, until Martin looked up from the note, which he was perusing with a scowl, and indicated a chair.

"Sit down, Hilary, you make me nervous."

"Thank you, sir, but I'm quite comfortable."

Martin opened his mouth to expostulate, and changed his mind after a quick glance.

"All right," he muttered. "Just a minute."

Snatching a pen he scribbled a few lines on the back of the note and handed it back to the chauffeur, who took it with a slight bow which narrowly missed being a burlesque.

"Thank you, Doctor."

When the door had closed behind him, Peter turned a quizzical gaze on the doctor. Martin did not notice him. He was staring at the door, and his homely, pleasant face looked gloomy.

"Sad case, that," he muttered. "He's a bright boy—"

"Boy?" Peter said involuntarily.

"He's only eighteen."

"Oh. I wonder how big he'll be when he grows up."

Martin smiled.

"Splendid physical specimen, isn't he? And mentally just about as fine."

"What's he doing chauffeuring a . . . man like the general?"

Martin caught the slight pause; the lines at the corners of his mouth deepened briefly and then faded.

"Don't knock one of the bulwarks of our local society," he said drily. "Volz inherited money, from his wife. His ex-rank gives him even more prestige. But he's not a stupid man; don't be fooled by his manner. Why does Hilary choose to work for him? Money, my boy, filthy lucre. Volz is so objectionable that he has to pay through the nose to get any help at all. Hilary is saving for college. He'll make it, one day; but at the cost, I'm afraid, of considerable bitterness."

"But for God's sake, don't you have what-d'you-call-'ems—scholarships, grants?"

"It's not that simple," Martin explained patiently. "Hilary is bright, but he's a product of the local high school and of a home which isn't exactly an intellectual haven. Scholarships exist, but few pay all expenses. And I wonder whether Hilary doesn't . . . Well. My theories about my patients' neuroses aren't worth repeating."

"Where did he get a name like that?" Peter asked curiously.

"His mother liked it."

"Oh."

"I worry about too many things," Martin said, with a wry smile.

"And I'm taking up too much of your time." Peter rose. "You've been very kind, Doctor."

"I've enjoyed it." Martin stood up, towering over the younger man by several inches. "Come over tomorrow night for supper, why don't you? About six. We'll go on to the meeting together."

Peter went off down the street at a leisurely pace, hands in his pockets, face turned up toward the gentle breeze with a look of bland innocence. He was thinking:

Patient. A friend and patient. In what sense? Even learned sociologists get stomachaches and colds. . . . They get other things, too. If Katharine More had diabetes or tuberculosis, her doctor might not care to discuss her malady with strangers; but Martin had been more than reticent, he had been ill at ease. Odd, how the old stigma attached to mental illness still lingered, even in educated minds. . . .

It would be quite a coincidence if Katherine More really suffered from the complaint he was pretending to have had. "The doctor's gone off the deep end"; according to Sam's report she was dabbling in peculiar hobbies. But why should a woman who was successful, rich, and still young suffer from nervous complaints?

When he got back to the center of town, Peter looked for a restaurant. The Inn had lost its charm since he had met the proprietress; besides, the prices were too high. He had some money saved, the bonus for the last job; it had paid well, even if it had ended disastrously. But his resources were not unlimited, and it was beginning to look as if his present project might take longer than he had expected.

Middleburg was singularly lacking in public eating places. The fact wasn't surprising; the country club and the hotel dining room probably provided enough facilities for people who did most of their entertaining in well-staffed homes. The cheaper restaurants and lunch counters were full, with waiting lines. Seeing the number of young people and children, Peter realized that it was Saturday. No school.

They were handsome kids, taller and healthier-looking than the ones he had seen recently; in their bright, mod clothes they looked like a flock of exotic shrill-voiced birds. Peter wondered which of the ingenuous scrubbed young faces had been out digging up graves the previous week. He had passed the modest white church on the way to town and had noticed workmen replanting turf and replacing stones. All at once he felt depressed, and not only by the obvious irony of the contrast between the bright shining faces of the young and their equivocal minds. The shining faces alone were enough to make a man who had passed the fatal age of thirty feel seventy years older. Peter decided he'd have lunch at the hotel after all.

It was a near thing. If he had been ten minutes later he would have missed her.

She stood in the doorway which led into the proprietress's lair, and as Peter entered the lobby he could hear Mrs. Adams' stentorian tones, though he could not see her. The woman in the doorway answered, in a lower voice; Peter heard a reference to "tonight."

He would have known her at once, he told himself, by the pricking of his thumbs. More practically, he had seen the photograph on the back of her book—one of those carefully casual poses, like a snapshot: Dr. More in the yard of her lovely home in Maryland.

She hadn't changed much since the picture was taken. The close-cropped dark hair, hardly longer

than his, fitted her head like a black velvet cap.
Her spare figure was as slim as a boy's and as sex-
less as a statue's; its thinness was emphasized by
the clothes she wore, tight faded blue jeans and a
checked shirt with rolled-up sleeves.

Finally she closed the door, ending the conversation; and the familiar, narrow face turned toward Peter. He knew every feature—the high
forehead, with a lock of black hair falling carelessly aslant, the full mouth which was unmarked
by lipstick. The eyes were hidden. She was wearing enormous, very dark glasses, which rendered
even more expressionless a face which would not
under any circumstances have been called mobile.

For a moment the round black eyepieces
seemed to stare directly at Peter. Then something
caught the woman's attention, and she turned her
head toward the girl who was approaching her
from across the lobby.

Absorbed as he was by this first sight of his
quarry, Peter was human enough to be distracted
by the newcomer. On her, the female uniform of
the town—jeans and a tailored shirt—looked incongruous, like La Belle Dame sans Merci in a
bikini, or the Queen of Elfland in boots and a
mini skirt. The long fair hair was so fine it floated
out around her shoulders like a luminous cloud;
she moved with steps so light and quick that they
looked like dancing. The fair-skinned face was luminous too, as if a light shone within, and blazed

out through the wide-set blue eyes. She moved with joy, and shone with delight. . . .

And her figure wasn't half bad, either. Peter shook himself mentally. Ordinarily he didn't go around rhapsodizing like an adolescent. What the hell was coming over him?

More important than face or figure was the fact that this girl was undoubtedly Tiphaine Blake, the little cousin whom Sam had mentioned. ("Screwy name!!" his notes had added.) She joined Katharine More and they stood talking. Peter noticed that for all her fragile air Tiphaine was the taller of the two. The More woman was small, not many inches over five feet; her arrogance and that black, blank stare made her look taller.

After a discussion which seemed to produce disagreement, with Tiphaine indicating the dining room and Katharine jerking her head in peremptory negation, the two women moved toward the door. Always a believer in directness, Peter had considered forcing an encounter; but the plan which was beginning to shape itself in his mind made him decide against it. He moved casually out of their path. Still, he was unable to avoid the younger girl's alert eyes; she gave him a friendly smile, the smile a woman gives a man whose appearance attracts her, but warmed by something else. General *joie de vivre*, probably, Peter thought morosely; and went into the dining room in search of Chicken Maryland and beer.

According to Sam's inclusive report, the local beer was terrible, but the hotel had every imported variety.

He spent the afternoon reclining on his bed, hands under his head, staring at the ceiling. By four o'clock his plan was in fairly good shape. He put on coat and tie and sallied forth in search of a car rental agency.

As he drove the nondescript blue Falcon out of town, he had some second thoughts. Was he rushing things? Possibly. But inactivity was bad for him; the longer he waited the more impatient he became, and with impatience came recklessness. Better to move soon and avoid that danger. Anyhow, he wasn't committed to anything yet. Reconnoitering wouldn't do any harm. He had to play the hand as it was dealt to him.

He returned to the hotel at seven, exchanged comments with Bennie about the beauty of the town, and after dinner went straight up to his room.

At 11 P.M. he went out again, but not through the door.

Access to the fire escape from the inside of the hotel was gained not through a private room but from the corridor—a sensible practice of which Peter approved, particularly since it meant that he wouldn't have to pass any lighted open windows. He had to play human fly for a few feet, from his own windowsill across to the fire escape, but the handholds were numerous. The fire escape was admirably solid; it hardly creaked as Peter crept down it, stepping lightly in rubber-soled sneakers.

He hung by his hands and dropped from the landing on the first-floor level; the raised bottom flight of stairs was probably wired into some sort of alarm system. His progress down the dark alley would have been unseen, if anyone had been watching; his black sweater and slacks blended with the shadows, and he moved like a cat. Once out on the open street, though, he straightened up and walked slowly, hands in his pockets. His precautions were probably needless. But, just in case, it might be useful to have the hotel staff willing to swear he hadn't left his room. On the street, though, skulking was dangerous. A stroller out for a late walk wouldn't be noticed, but a lurker in the shadows would only arouse suspicion.

He had left the car on a side street. Five minutes after leaving the hotel he was on his way out of town. A leisurely fifteen-minute drive, with meticulous observation of the traffic laws, brought him to the estate. He had located it that afternoon, without having to ask questions. The name on the stone gateposts identified it without equivocation. "Malking Tower" was an odd name for a house, particularly when there wasn't a tower anywhere in sight, but at least it was unmistakable.

The iron gates, which had stood ajar that afternoon, were now closed. Peter left the car under a tree half a mile down the narrow country road, and climbed the wall, avoiding the gates. It was a substantial wall for these parts, where fences were intended more as a request for privacy than as physical defense; but it had no complications such as ground glass or barbed wire, and the stone of which it was built provided plenty of convenient hand- and footholds. He had checked that point during the afternoon visit.

There was a half-moon hanging in a cloudless sky; it gave just enough light to let him pick his way. As soon as he had penetrated the trees, which formed a second barrier, he saw the house before him. It was an unimpressive place, except for its size; it sprawled out over a considerable amount of territory, with wings jutting out in unexpected places. Part stone, part wood, with brick chimneys at frequent intervals, it had grown over the years from a central core which probably dated back to the early eighteenth century. Peter had been pleased to see that the landscaping was extensive; shrubs and bushes masked the foundations, affording admirable hiding places for snoopers, and some splendid old trees practically invited visitors to second-story windows.

There were gardens and outbuildings behind the house, but he was not interested in them at the moment. The front of the house faced him and he moved directly toward it, slipping like a shadow from tree to tree. The faint sound of leaves crackling underfoot didn't worry him; it blended with other nocturnal noises. The air was cold, now that the sun had fallen; it carried the faint acrid tang of wood smoke.

He stopped, paralyzed, as the air above him solidified and dropped down toward him. A faint hollow cry echoed and faded as the shape which had uttered it winged off toward the trees. Peter straightened from his instinctive crouch. An owl. Uncanny creatures. Probably the woods were full of them. Bats, too.

He reached the house without further interruption. At first he thought everyone had gone to bed. Then he caught a faint glow of light from somewhere on the first floor, and headed toward it. It was a puzzling sort of light, as ambiguous and elusive as fox fire, from behind curtained windows, possibly, but faint and oddly colored for all that.

The lighted window was in a wing north of the central portion of the house. Standing below, Peter frowned up at the source of the light. He was not puzzled as to how to reach it; the windows were on the order of French doors, opening onto one of those useless little iron balconies—useless to anyone except burglars. What was so strange was the quality of the light. The window was heavily curtained, all right, but—he noted approvingly—one of the windows had been left ajar, and the movement of the draperies let gleams and glows of illumination seep through. The light was not that of electricity, neither the yellow glow of a normal bulb nor the bluish pallor of fluorescence.

It was an ugly gray light that was almost worse than darkness.

The rim of the balcony was just beyond the tips of his extended fingers. Flexing his knees, Peter jumped, and caught the edge of the platform. As he pulled himself up, he remembered his "roommate," and the "keeping fit" routine the idiot had insisted upon, and the corners of his mouth curled up in a sardonic smile. You never knew what was going to be useful. That was one of the things that made life so interesting.

The door was open just far enough for him to get his head through; the movement of the drapes, in the night breeze, was sufficiently erratic that the additional movement caused by his careful hands would not be noticeable. In less than a minute he was crouched by the door, with a peephole at eye level.

No wonder there were no lights anywhere else in the house. The entire household was gathered in this one room, and a singular room it was. Peter realized that it must have been a small ballroom or main salon at one time, for it was of considerable size, with a high, carved ceiling and a fireplace on each of the long walls. He saw shapes only dimly in the gloom, but the room seemed to have been almost entirely cleared of furniture except for low tables set at intervals around the walls, and a peculiar structure at the far end of the room under a raised semicircular alcove that might have been a musicians' platform. A low, rectangular shape draped in dark cloth, it bore a pair of candelabra, a wide shallow bowl, and a pitcher. Bowl and pitcher were made of metal, which shone with a faint silvery luster in the dim light.

The only light in the room came from the candles, nine in all, which were neither wax nor tallow nor any other substance the unseen watcher knew. He had never seen such a light. The figures standing in a semicircle before the altar—the word was unavoidable—were barely visible, but Peter could identify them, even though their backs were turned toward him. He recognized the floating, shining hair of the girl called Tiphaine, and the rigid thinness of Katharine More. An elderly man and woman, on her left, must be the house servants. The fifth member of the group was also familiar. Dr. Paul Martin.

The sixth person in the room stood with her back to the others, facing the altar. Her robes were white, with some sort of symbol embroidered on the back in gold thread. Peter caught the glitter of it as she swayed, in rhythm to the words she muttered, in a half chant, half recitation. The candlelight focused on her lifted hands and on her frizz of hennaed hair.

Mrs. Adams turned, slowly and ungracefully, and the others dropped to their knees. Martin was the last to kneel; he turned his head to look at

Katharine, and Peter caught a glimpse of his face. Lined and frowning, it betrayed his abhorrence of the bizarre rite, and also his deep concern for the woman in the center of the half-circle.

Then the priestess's voice rose, and Peter made out the words.

"Magna Mater, mother of all, give us that boon we seek! Restore what you have taken, as your right, as part of all that which is born of woman, your heir, and comes back at last to your universal womb! Restore it, not to break the eternal barrier of your law, but to comfort your daughter, who sits in darkness seeking a sign!"

She broke into bastard Latin, and then into another language which Peter did not recognize. Hebrew?

He sat back on his heels, a slow, unpleasant smile tugging at the corners of his mouth. Was the woman really such a fool as to fall for an obvious hodgepodge of fakery like this? It wasn't even one of the well-known nut cults, but a conglomeration of half-baked scraps from a dozen different magical idioms.

The Magna Mater. Kate More, of all people, ought to know what that ambiguous cult had involved. If she was desperate enough to resort to this, she needed comfort very badly. For the intent of the service was as clear as the identity of the person for whom it was being performed. It was the same pitiful demand made of many spiritualists, whether they called themselves mediums, witches, or high priests. Communication with the spirits of the dead.

There was no pity in Peter's face, or mind, as he slowly straightened up and stood waiting.

# Chapter
### 3

HE HAD TO WAIT FOR ALMOST A QUARTER OF AN hour. It seemed longer. The cold wind numbed his motionless body and hissed drearily in the branches above, but he didn't dare retire to a less vulnerable position for fear of missing the strategic moment. The ceremony wasn't especially enthralling. Mrs. Adams wouldn't dare use any of the more exotic props with this audience and, even at their dramatic best, these affairs tended to be dull. The smell of incense made him want to sneeze. The old lady must be using the stuff lavishly if its odor wafted all the way down the room to him.

The effect of incense and ritual on the participants, who were getting the full treatment, was different. Peter's eyes narrowed thoughtfully as he saw the elderly servant woman begin to sway, slowly at first, then with a jerky, spasmodic rhythm. The older man—her husband?—was uttering low gutteral growls that sounded like a bass accompaniment to the priestess's chant. Tiphaine and the doctor stood still as statues; Tiphaine's profile, oddly shadowed by the flickering light, had a look of frozen fascination. And in the center of the half-circle Katharine More leaned slightly forward, as if in anticipation.

Peter, who had speculated cynically about drugs and too much predinner gin, realized that only the chilly air and the distance kept him from succumbing too. The old hag at the altar had power; the chanting voice, mouthing rotund syllables that had no clear meaning, began to drum hollowly inside his head. He shook the affected member vigorously, and flattened his windblown hair with a hard palm. He had to keep alert. The climax of the ceremony was due at any minute. These mass-hypnotism jobs had to be calculated carefully, so that the high point of the ceremony caught the participants at the peak of their receptivity, before they progressed to coma or fits, or the effect of the drug and ritual wore off.

Peter eased the door open a little farther. They wouldn't notice a breeze; they probably wouldn't notice anything less than a tornado. All eyes were fixed on Mrs. Adams, who was facing the altar, half-crouched, hands extended. Yes—here it came. The priestess's voice rose to an eldritch screech as she whirled, the folds of her robe flying out.

"Come! By Asmodeus and Hecate and Diana of the Three Faces, I summon you from the shades! Appear!"

All the candles went out.

Peter never learned what the next item on the program was meant to be. The cue was too good to miss, and he felt sure that the original effect wouldn't have been half so impressive. As the flames died, he grasped the heavy drapes with both hands and flung them open.

The silence in the pitch-black room was so complete that he could hear them breathing. The change in that breathing, to a harsh, collective gasp, told him that they had seen him. In actual fact they could not have seen much. His features were in shadow and his body, if visible at all against the dark background of trees and grass, was only a darker silhouette. But there was enough moonlight to give an unearthly shimmer to ruffled hair so flaxen that it must have looked silver.

Peter knew the power of imagination when heightened by anticipation. By morning, most of them would be willing to swear that they had seen a face, and recognized it. One, at least, would think so. He had never heard Katharine More speak, but he knew that it was her voice which broke the rapt silence with a short, ugly sound that was half scream and half sob.

He didn't wait for further reactions; the spell was broken, they would move now. His arms, invisible in their black sleeves, were already raised, the fingers curled over the top of the doorframe. When he pulled himself up, it must have appeared to some of the watchers as if he had floated up into the dark sky.

For an instant Peter balanced precariously, one foot on the opened leaf of the door, and then caught the rim of the matching balcony of the upper story. He reached the roof as a rush of footsteps thudded across the bare floor of the room below.

Lying flat and motionless along the edge of the sloping roof, foot and hand braced against the gutter, he heard the doctor's voice. It would be Martin who had had the fortitude to investigate.

"There's no one here," the familiar baritone, now somewhat shaken, reported. "Get some light, for God's sake."

He was answered by a glare of light—yellow, electric light—which poured out onto the balcony. Peter could see its glow from up above, but he didn't raise his head. He doubted that Martin could see him from below, the angle was too acute; but the slightest movement would attract attention.

Someone spoke from inside the room, and Martin said, "No one. How could there be? It was a hallucination, I told you. . . . Katharine. Is Katharine all right?"

"Out on her feet. Stop making like Sherlock Holmes and give me a hand with her." The voice was that of Mrs. Adams, and it sounded just as perturbed as Martin's. Peter didn't bother suppressing a grin. The old bitch wasn't even an honest nut. She hadn't expected her solemn prayers to be answered so literally.

Then a babble of sound broke out as they all started to talk at once. One woman, presumably the cook, was shrieking. Martin's voice rose over the uproar in a tone which made Peter comprehend some of his charisma.

"Stop that, all of you! Upstairs to bed, Kate, and take two of those capsules. None of your phobias about pills, that's an order. Tiphaine, go with her. Will, get a ladder and a couple of flashlights. You and I are going to have a look around."

The voices retreated, and Peter pushed himself upright.

"For a hallucination?" he jeered inaudibly. Then he shinnied up the slope of the roof, slanting toward the side of the house where he had spotted a gnarled ivy winding around the brick chimney. If he couldn't get down that before Martin found his ladder, he had really lost his touch.

Martin had a wife. Peter didn't know why this fact should have surprised him, but it did. She was such a drab, brown, self-effacing little woman that he had a hard time remembering that she existed even when she was in the same room. As he chatted with the doctor over cocktails, he wondered idly why such a popular, successful citizen had married a woman with no visible good points.

At dinner he found out. Mrs. Martin was a superlative cook. He told her so, with such enthusiasm that a faint shade of color came into the woman's pale cheeks. She glanced shyly at her husband, and Martin smiled fondly.

"I keep telling her she's wasted on me," he said. "But she thinks I'm prejudiced."

Mrs. Martin responded with a look of such intense animal devotion that Peter felt a poignant twinge. I'm getting old, he thought resignedly; must be, to consider good cooking and doglike devotion attractive qualities in a wife. He accepted a second piece of apple pie.

"Keep that up and you won't need to worry about being underweight," Martin said with a grin.

"Oh, I never gain weight," Peter said, surreptitiously flexing sore leg muscles. "I keep busy."

"I ought to be a good host, then, and urge you to keep eating. But I'm afraid that we'll be late if we don't leave now. We can get coffee at the meeting."

They walked the two blocks to the hotel through a night hazy with leaf fires and crisp enough to make ears and fingers tingle. Martin took a deep breath.

"This is my favorite time of year," he said. "Is it like this in England?"

"Much the same. But it doesn't seem quite so spectacular. Everything's on such a large scale here."

"Not Middleburg. I've always imagined that it was very much like an English village."

Peter glanced up and down the street, with its stretches of wide lawn and its huge houses.

"Something like it," he said.

Since the Folklore Society of Middleburg met at the Inn, Peter was not surprised to see the proprietress among the members who were already gathered there. She was dressed in a shapeless tweed suit and "sensible" shoes—a far cry from the fantastic robes of the previous night. Peter was amused to note a touch of coolness in Martin's greeting. He wondered if there had been words between the two that same night.

The second familiar face he saw did surprise him. Somehow he hadn't expected General Volz to be interested in ethnology. Volz, who was wearing riding attire whose flared trousers made him look almost square, greeted Peter and reminded him of his invitation. Martin nodded approval.

"Good idea, for everyone concerned. Those animals of yours don't get enough exercise, General."

"Gonna report me to the SPCA?" Volz inquired, grinning.

Martin gave him a perfunctory social smile and excused himself.

"I would be willing to wager that Dr. Martin is not a member of the hunt," Peter said.

"You'd win that bet. Like he keeps saying, he worries too much; gets into a sweat about every stray dog and dirty kid in town. He's a great guy, though, in his own funny way. Come on and meet the other members."

They were an oddly assorted crowd, Peter thought. A white-maned Senator rubbed shoulders with a local merchant, and a faded maiden lady named Device, who looked like the popular conception of a librarian, chatted amiably with two fashionably dressed young housewives.

Instead of the usual rows of folding chairs facing a speaker's podium, this room had sofas and upholstered chairs arranged before a white-framed colonial fireplace, in which flames leaped comfortably. A large round table, of the sort used for conferences, had been pushed back against the wall. A coffee urn stood on another table, and the members helped themselves when they felt the need for refreshment.

It appeared to be an informal sort of organization and, despite Martin's claims, Peter suspected that it was an organization of dilettantes. A motley crowd like this one, whose only commonality was its membership in the gentry, blooded or moneyed, of the town, could hardly produce many serious students of any subject. Yet they seemed to know one another well, and to be at ease together. One of the young matrons was telling Miss Device a funny story; the older woman began to titter, and laughed so hard she had to cover her mouth with a bony hand.

Peter eyed the hilarious group enviously. It was hard to imagine the sort of joke two such disparate women would both find amusing, but at least they were having a good time. He wasn't. Volz's only topic of conversation, except for his own wealth and social position, seemed to be those useless bums in the slums who wanted the government to support them. Peter glanced surreptitiously at his watch and swallowed a yawn. This was not only going to be a dull evening, but a wasted one. He had hoped to meet Katharine More, but—

The door opened, and all conversation stopped. Even Volz broke off in the middle of his polemic. Peter turned, and saw in the doorway the girl who had been with Katharine More in the lobby of the hotel.

She was wearing a full, very short red skirt which showed off her long slim legs, and a low-cut white blouse which did equally pleasant things for other parts of her admirable anatomy. She carried a guitar case, and her hair brushed her shoulders.

It was remarkable hair—not blond, now that he saw it again, but pure gold, with a touch of copper. She turned her head, with a grace that characterized all her movements, and the heavy mane swung out, ripples of light running down its waves. Martin had come over to speak to her. Tall as she was, she had to look up to him, and the posture showed the beautiful line of her throat and chin.

So the evening wasn't going to be a total waste after all. One of Peter's alternate plans had included Katharine's little cousin; after seeing her that afternoon, he had considered it more enthusiastically. Now it was up to him to use the opening Fate and the Folklore Society had so unexpectedly presented. He didn't have to strain his dramatic talents when Martin led her over to him; nine tenths of his fascinated stare was genuine.

"Tiphaine Blake, this is Peter Stewart." Martin gave the name only two syllables, with the accent on the last; the *i* was short, and the diphthong like a nasalized French *a*.

"When I said you were in luck, I meant it." Martin's eyes were twinkling as he glanced from Peter to the girl, and Peter damned him silently. "Tiphaine is going to sing for us. She's wonderful; we're looking forward to it ourselves."

They joined the rest of the group, who had already taken seats. Tiphaine selected a low stool before the fire. She took her guitar from its case and sat with it across her knees, head bent, striking soft chords and tuning the instrument.

Martin's voice stilled the murmur of conversation. Slouched in his chair, filling his pipe, he spoke in a casual voice but with his usual air of authority.

"We'll skip the business meeting tonight," he began, and grinned amiably as a murmur of laughter rippled through the room. "I'm sure it wouldn't amuse our visitor."

The smiling faces turned toward Peter. A private joke, clearly; maybe Martin's distaste for formal meetings amused the other members. Jolly for them.

"Anyhow," Martin continued, "it would be a shame to waste time on other matters when we could be listening to Tiphaine. My dear, will you tell Peter what you've been doing?"

She raised her head and smiled directly at Peter.

"Everything I've been doing?" she asked. Another communal chuckle passed through the room. They are a cheery little bunch, Peter thought disagreeably.

Discounting the feeble joke, her voice was as charming as he had expected it to be, a soft contralto, rich and low, but with a clarity usually found only in higher voices. She was sensitive to people's feelings; she sensed Peter's impatience, though he felt sure it had not been visible, and immediately sobered.

"As you may have guessed, Mr. Stewart, I sing folk songs. I'm not really a serious student, like these people. I just like to sing. But folk music, though a legitimate part of folklore, is a pretty big field. Paul suggested I specialize—collect particular types of songs. And since many of the members are interested in magic and superstition, I've learned some songs which deal with the supernatural. It's amazing how many there are. I'm going to sing a few of them now."

She ran her fingers over the strings and began to sing.

The soft, unemphatic speaking voice was transformed. She had not been formally trained, but she had a natural sense of pitch and rhythm, and superb control. She had something else which some trained singers lack—a fantastic range, with no awkward break between the contralto and soprano registers. Over and above the technical beauty of her voice, there was the special magic which the best folk singers have—an empathy with the song which made it come alive.

The song was of the Child ballads. "The Wife of Usher's Well." The story conformed to the theme of the supernatural which Tiphaine had chosen, telling of the return to the mourning mother of her three dead sons. Peter didn't pay much attention to the words; he was more interested in the performer. He wondered how she would come over on a recording. Her face and figure certainly didn't detract from the total effect.

The applause was enthusiastic. But when it had died away, the members of the Folklore Society plunged into a discussion which left Peter amazed. He had underestimated them; they really did know a lot about the subject. The housewife on his left pointed out that there was a variant of the song in which the boys left home for the purpose of studying "grammarie"—not grammar, but an old term for magic. The Senator asked Tiphaine to repeat the fourth verse, the mother's incantation, and she did so:

*"I wish the wind may never cease,*
*Nor storms in the flood,*
*Till my three sons come home to me,*
*In earthly flesh and blood."*

"You comprehend the reference to wind and storm," the Senator chirped, when she had finished. "Obviously the lady was no common grieving mother, but a trained witch."

"How's that?" Peter asked involuntarily.

"But these were talents attributed to witches," the Senator explained mildly. "The ability to command the wind and to raise storms at sea. You will remember, of course, the famous case of the Earl of Bothwell, who was accused of trying to kill the queen by raising a storm while her ship was at sea?"

"Oh, of course," Peter murmured. "It's just that I had never thought of it in connection with this song."

"That's what makes Tiphaine's research so interesting," Martin said, around the stem of his pipe. "Any more discussion? Next, my dear, if you please."

And so it went, through several more songs—

"The Demon Lover," "Clerk Colville," "The Elfin Knight." Peter found himself getting interested. His scanty knowledge of Black Magic was a hangover from an adolescent hobby; he had never realized it was so pervasive. He was roused from his pedantic musings by Tiphaine's next song. It was "Scarborough Fair," and with a perfectly straight face she gave them the Simon and Garfunkel adaptation instead of the original. Most of the members missed the joke; it was Miss Device, of all the unlikely pop music fans, who pointed it out.

"Trying to catch us, were you, dear?" she said sweetly.

"Not you, Miss Device," Tiphaine said with a smile. "You do know the most amazing things!"

"Well, I know why this one fits your typology," the spinster said complacently. "The herbs. They didn't use them to flavor the soup!"

"A love charm," Peter added, entering into the spirit of the thing. "I wonder whether it works."

He looked at Tiphaine; she responded with a sweet smile and a flick of her hand across the guitar strings in a strikingly dissonant chord.

"It doesn't," she said.

"All right." Martin indicated his watch. "You know the agreement, ladies and gentlemen; Mrs. Adams is kind enough to let us meet here, but we must wind up early so the guests can get some sleep. Anything else, Tiphaine?"

The girl brushed her hair back from her face.

"One more. And I bet I can baffle you this time."

She struck a slow, broken chord. Then her voice began, muted as a whisper, but so distinct that every syllable was clear.

*"Cold blows the wind to my true love,*
*And gently falls the rain.*
*I've never had but one true love,*
*And in greenwood he lies slain."*

It was the old ballad of "The Unquiet Grave," and the dead lover who cannot rest because of the excessive grieving of his sweetheart. By the time she had finished, the hairs were standing up on the back of Peter's neck. Empathy was too weak a word. She sang like someone who has herself kissed the cold lips of the dead.

He sat in silence while the babble of discussion went on. The listeners had a lot of theories, but finally Miss Device said decisively, "What's the problem about this one, Tiphaine? Of course it's a familiar superstition, that the dead are kept from their rest by the tears of the living, but—"

"It's not my idea," Tiphaine interrupted. "Katharine suggested it. She doesn't take it seriously, but she said it might be fun to throw the suggestion out and see what you made of it."

There was a long, echoing pause. Peter looked up alertly as he realized that the name which had caught his wandering attention was the cause of the general uneasiness. This was an amiable gesture, showing that Katharine More took an interest in their activities and in those of her companion and cousin. Why the chilly silence at the mention of her name?

Martin, whose smile had solidified into a grimace, was the first to recover. "You've got us all intrigued, Tiphaine. What is the suggestion?"

Tiphaine seemed unaware of the consternation she had caused. Leaning forward eagerly, she said, "The lover is lying dead in the greenwood, right? Not just dead, murdered. But the song doesn't say why, or how."

"It may be a fragment of a longer song," Mrs. Adams began, and was interrupted by the general.

"Maybe she murdered him. The girlfriend. Guilt, not grief, makes her disturb his rest."

Peter stared at Volz. It was an ingenious idea, and quite in tune with Volz's philosophy of life. He would think of murder.

"No, no." Tiphaine chuckled; it was a charming sound, like bubbling water. "Well, maybe you're right. But look at the list of things he gives her—impossible things, like water from the desert and blood from a stone. Sounds like a formula for a spell, doesn't it? Why does he want these things, if his desire is to be left in peace? Then in the last verse he says he'll see her again when the leaves are green. In the spring."

There was a blank silence when she had finished. She chuckled again and shrugged. One sleeve slid down from her tanned shoulder, and Peter momentairly lost track of what she was saying.

". . . of course it's been changed over the centuries. In some versions the true love is a woman instead of a man. But Kate says it reminds her of William Rufus, and Murray's theory of the sacrifice of the god."

Again that odd, frozen silence. It was broken by Volz.

"Murray who?" he inquired.

Laughter ended the discomfort, and Martin shook his head in mock reproach.

"Harry, you've got to read a few books or we'll drum you out of the club. Margaret Murray, an authority on the witch cult. You know her theory, that the witchcraft of the Middle Ages was simply a survival of an old pagan religion?"

"Nope," Volz said blandly.

"Well, now you know."

"Interesting," Volz muttered thoughtfully; and Peter thought he knew why such an apparent ignoramus was accepted by a group like this one. Volz was barely literate, but his intelligence could not be denied. Like other famous military men, he was simply unable to absorb the printed word. Once he heard an idea he dealt with it efficiently.

"Yes, it is interesting," Martin said drily. "But

the particular theory Tiphaine mentioned goes even further. The head of the witch cult, or Old Religion, was a god to his followers—and, *ipso facto*, a Devil to the outraged Christians. Miss Murray believed that the Incarnate God had to be sacrificed periodically to ensure the well-being of his worshipers. The notion of the dying god, who is reborn in the spring, is very ancient; you find it in Egypt and Babylonia and, later, in Greece. Death and resurrection; not only a symbol of the new life which comes forth from the earth each spring, from the quickened seed, but an assurance, through sympathetic magic, that that rebirth would surely come. A symbol and a promise."

Martin's voice was soft and slow; the rest of the group sat in respectful silence. Then the doctor shook himself and went on more briskly.

"You're aware of the significance of the one Resurrection, of course, but as students you must remember that the concept has historical precedents. It is found in many fertility cults, and if you remember the descriptions of the Witches' Sabbath you'll see why Miss Murray believes that the Old Religion was a kind of fertility cult. She suggests that Joan of Arc, for instance, was a head of the cult, and that she accepted her own execution as the inevitable sacrifice. William Rufus—for your information, Harry—was a very early king of England who was murdered while hunting.

Murray indentifies him as another witch "god,"
whose death was the cult sacrifice. Most authori-
ties disagree, but—"

"But it does fit the song," Miss Device said.
"Slain in the greenwood. And the rest of it is a
corrupt reference to the resurrection of the god."

"Very ingenious," Martin agreed. "And very
hazardous."

"I don't know," one of the housewives said.
"What about . . ."

Peter looked at Tiphaine. It was becoming his
favorite occupation. Having thrown her little
bombshell she had withdrawn again, but she was
clearly enjoying the effect, smiling as her eyes
moved from one animated face to the next. They
met Peter's waiting eyes, and were held.

He put his cup down on the table, rose, and
held out his hand.

"May I?" he asked.

She came slowly to her feet and put the guitar
into his hands. She was almost as tall as he; the
wide blue eyes met his with satisfaction and—he
had almost thought—recognition.

He motioned her back to her seat and stood
with one knee raised to support the guitar. The
others had stopped talking as they watched. Peter
turned to them with a deprecating smile.

"I have some evidence to support Miss Blake's
idea," he said. "If you don't mind."

"Of course not," Martin said quickly. "Have we

by any chance touched upon your specialty. Peter? I wish you'd warned me."

"Not a specialty, no. Just an odd coincidence. I happened to be in northern Scotland a few years ago, and heard an elderly lady sing a version of this song which I'd never encountered before. It has two additional verses which may interest you."

He felt for a C major chord and missed by a quarter of an inch. Martin gave him an encouraging nod, and Peter winced theatrically.

"I am out of practice. There, that's got it.

*'Go fetch me persil and cinquefoil,*
*Poplar leaves and rue,*
*And we will rise through the windy night,*
*As we were wont to do,*

*'When the oaken leaves that fall are green,*
*And the dying year's reborn,*
*When the seed of the withered flower swells,*
*You'll have no need to mourn.'"*

Peter ended with a flourish, and glanced up.

"She put them in at the end," he said.

Either his singing was even worse than he had imagined, or his verses were better; the whole group sat still, with faces set in expressions of deep concentration. Or was the word consternation?

Martin was the first to speak.

"Splendid," he said, patting the tips of his fingers together. "I might even say, brilliant."

Peter tried to look modest, but he was inclined to agree—in view of the fact that he had invented the new verses himself, within the last ten minutes. He looked at Tiphaine.

"Cheater," she whispered.

"I wasn't trying to upstage you, honestly."

"Bad enough that you're an expert in sheep's clothing. If I'd known you could sing like that—"

"You would never have let me begin."

The discussion went on around them; Peter paid no attention until Volz banged him on the back demanding further details, which he cheerfully supplied. His powers of invention were flourishing after that auspicious beginning. It was a good thing he had glanced at Katharine's book that afternoon. The discussion of the "flying ointment" used by the witches had interested him, and he had remembered some of the ingredients. The well-informed folklorists caught every one of them. Martin had to exert all his authority to break up the meeting. As the others straggled out, still arguing, Martin joined the performers.

"We've entertained a savant unawares," he said with a smile. "Is making people underestimate you part of your professional technique, Peter?"

"And he sings almost as well as Glen Campbell," Tiphaine murmured, with a sidelong glance at Peter's outraged face. "I'd love to sing duets with you, Mr. Stewart. How are you on the Beatles?"

Martin laughed and put an avuncular arm around the girl's shoulders.

"Stop that," he said affectionately. "I think you've hit upon a splendid idea. Why don't you two work up a program for us? And I wasn't thinking of the compositions of the—er—Beatles."

"Some of their compositions are pretty folksy," Peter said. "Or do I mean folkish?"

"I apologize," Tiphaine said, smiling at him. "I think it's a marvelous idea. Are you going to be in town long, Mr. Stewart?"

"I plan to be," Peter said, looking steadily at her.

"Good, I'll call you."

"I'll call you. Better still, I'll see you home."

She looked up from fastening the guitar case; her eyes were twinkling.

"How very conventional, Mr. Stewart! Thanks, but that's quite unnecessary. Also impractical, unless you can make like young Lochinvar."

Peter looked blank, but Martin understood. His brows came together.

"Are you riding that brute again, Tiphaine? I told you—"

"I love riding at night," she said dreamily. "With Sultan it's like riding the wind, with the stars shooting by overhead. . . . Don't be square, Paul."

"I'm going to speak to Volz. If he wants to lend

you one of his horses, he ought to pick one that's more manageable. And how does Sultan get home from your place?"

"Timmy brought him over. He'll take him back."

The doctor's face reddened.

"That makes it worse," he growled.

"Who is Timmy?" Peter asked curiously. "Your local ax murderer?"

Tiphaine laughed and did a little dance step.

"You'd think so, to hear Martin. He's just a poor, half-witted boy, the general's stablehand. I think it's sweet of General Volz to keep him. Nobody else would hire Timmy."

"I suspect he gets Timmy's services cheap," Peter said, before he could stop himself. Martin gave a sharp laugh.

"That's the correct explanation of the general's charity. Timmy is mentally retarded, but physically he's a full-grown man. I keep telling you, Tiphaine—"

"Oh, Martin!" She spun around in sheer exuberance. "I'm not afraid of Timmy. He adores me."

"I know," Martin said. His tone was so grim that Peter glanced at him in sudden comprehension.

"Maybe the doctor's right," he said. "Let me take you home. I've always wanted to try that Lochinvar stunt."

"Now you're both being square." Tiphaine bounced up on tiptoe, deposited a kiss on the doctor's cheek, and darted away. "I'll telephone you tomorrow, Mr. Stewart," she called back over her shoulder. "Just to assure you that I'm still alive and unraped!" Her laughter was cut off by the closing door.

Peter turned, brows raised, to meet Martin's thunderous glare. After a moment the doctor laughed ruefully and reached for his pipe, his usual solace in times of stress.

"I told you, I worry too much."

"You've got me worried too."

"Why?" the doctor asked bluntly.

"She's so sweet," Peter said fatuously. "So inno-cent. . . . I mean, without meaning to, she's proba-bly driving the poor devil out of his mind. What there is of it."

The doctor laughed, and clapped Peter on the shoulder.

"You sound quite incoherent," he said. "Love at first sight?"

"Second. I've seen her once before, with an older, dark-haired woman. I thought she looked familiar—the dark woman. Was it, by any chance . . . ?"

"Yes, it probably was." Martin's friendly hand fell away. "Tiphaine lives with Dr. More. They're distantly related."

The doctor's farewells were uncharacteristi-cally abrupt, and as Peter headed for his room, he was more than ever eager to meet his elusive quarry. What was there about Katharine More that caused the townspeople to react so oddly to the very mention of her name? His own phrase lingered in his mind: the dark woman. From the way people acted, you'd think she was a witch, or something.

# Chapter
## 4
_____

"I WANT TO SEE YOU," PETER SAID.

"How about tomorrow morning?" Tiphaine's voice had a musical lilt which was unmarred even by the distortion of the telephone.

"Today. This minute."

"What a pity. Because I'm going riding today."

"By a strange coincidence," Peter said smoothly, "General Volz has offered me the use of his stable. I'll meet you there—when?"

The faint laughter sounded like bells.

"Three o'clock."

"That's too far away."

"Have a good hearty lunch," she advised. "That'll take your mind off."

"Off what?" Peter asked, and heard the laughter again, just before she hung up.

She was there before him when he arrived at the general's estate. That was what Volz called it, and for once he wasn't bragging. The house was almost too new for Peter's taste, which had become accustomed to the gracious lines of the older homes of the area. Volz's house was an enormous block of concrete and glass; one wall, jutting out over the ridge of a low hill, was all windows, which caught the sunlight in a blinding glitter. Peter wondered how this anomaly had passed the Architectural Committee. Was it too far out of town to be included in the regulations; or was the answer just plain bribery?

The stables, behind the house, were more conventional; it would take a wilder mind than Volz's to come up with anything *outré* in the way of a stable. The general didn't stint himself on horses any more than he did on the other comforts of life. Half a dozen of the stalls were occupied, and the tack room, into which Peter glanced, was filled with expensive leather.

As he crossed the stone-paved stableyard, Tiphaine came out of the second stall, leading a horse which was already bridled and saddled. She greeted Peter with a dazzling smile and a casual "Hi." He returned the smile, but the horse held his attention.

He had no doubt that this was Sultan, to whom the doctor had objected, and he was inclined to agree with Martin. Sultan was big, well over the sixteen hands that was considered a good height for a hunter; a chestnut, he was one of the handsomest animals Peter had ever seen. His conformation was faultless, from the small, well-set ears to the clean, big-boned hocks. But there was something about him. . . .

Peter eyed the horse with disfavor, and Sultan's wicked rolling eyes returned the look, with interest. He strolled over and put a casual hand on the arched neck. Sultan's head whipped around. Peter didn't move; and after a moment Sultan snorted and decided to pretend he had only been yawning. He looked out over the stableyard with an air of supreme disdain.

"Terrible actor, isn't he?" Peter said, still stroking the animal's neck.

"Oh, yes, you always know exactly what he's thinking."

"I don't think I like what he's thinking. Look here, why don't you let me take this monster?"

"I'm tempted to agree. Just out of natural wickedness."

"All right. I promise to fall off a few times if that will amuse you."

"It's a deal. I'll take Starlight. Timmy!"

The name, as much as the sudden rising of her voice, made Peter start. Since his professed concern for Tiphaine had been part of the act which would, he hoped, get him into the confidence of Tiphaine's cousin, he had forgotten about the feeble-witted stableboy. But at the sight of the figure which came shambling out of one of the stalls he felt a stir of real revulsion.

Timmy was short and slender. From that point of view he didn't look very dangerous. He was also incredibly dirty, far filthier than his occupation gave him any excuse for being. His tattered shirt and shapeless trousers exuded a powerful atmosphere that made Peter wrinkle his nose, even at a distance. Or was the atmosphere pure Timmy? A shock of dusty-looking brown hair obviously hadn't been washed in weeks; it had straw, and other less wholesome fragments, stuck in it.

Timmy's features would long remain a blur to Peter. After the first casual glance he found himself unable to look at the man's face. The birthmark was incredible; Peter had seen similar marks, but never one so extensive. It turned almost half of Timmy's face into a liver-red horror. Peter was moved by an unwilling surge of pity. Talk about Job. When the benevolent Creator afflicted His creatures, He did a good, thorough job of it. To take another viewpoint, and get God off the hook, you could assume that Timmy had been something nasty in his previous incarnation. Something very, very nasty.

Apparently Timmy didn't talk. He could hear all right, responding to the girl's request with a sickening, shambling alacrity, so Peter gathered he wasn't deaf and dumb. Perhaps he didn't have anything to say. Peter watched, studying the man's bare arms—which were tanned and fairly well muscled—and his back rather than his face. But when the little silver-gray mare was saddled, and Timmy turned, hands out, to assist the girl to mount, Peter moved, out of an instinct which for the moment was stronger than any rational reason.

"Let me, Tiphaine," he said.

Timmy fell back as he approached, for which Peter was grateful; the smell of Timmy would have been overpowering at close quarters. He didn't see Timmy's expression, since he didn't look at Timmy's face. He didn't need to. The wave of hate was almost palpable. This time Peter didn't care about making unnecessary enemies, though he usually avoided doing so as a principle of good business. He was inclined to agree with the doctor that Timmy, unlike most of his afflicted fellows, was potentially dangerous; but so long as he was on guard, the miserable creature couldn't do him any harm.

Tiphaine turned to wave at Timmy as they walked the horses out of the stableyard, and then gave Peter a taunting smile.

"Welcome to the club," she said.

"The 'Hate Timmy' club?"

"The 'Timmy-ugh' club would be more like it."

"That one I'll join. Martin is right, Tiphaine; there's something wrong with that lad. And I don't mean his intelligence quotient. Most mental deficients are gentle as lambs. But Timmy—"

"There are two paths," she said blandly. "Through the fields and through the woods. Which do you prefer?"

"Stop trying to change the subject. Haven't you ever heard about the birds and the bees?"

For answer Tiphaine leaned forward and brought her crop down on the mare's flank. The little animal leaped forward. Automatically Peter's legs closed in on Sultan's sides and his hands relaxed; two years of inactivity had not dulled the reflexes acquired from earlier years of practice. But he was accustomed to riding horses, not thunderbolts; Sultan's jet-propelled takeoff nearly unseated him. His grip on the reins tightened. It was close enough to have slowed a more sensitive animal, but sensitivity, he had observed, was not one of Sultan's character traits. How the hell, he wondered, did Tiphaine ride this brute with a simple snaffle bit? What Sultan needed was a chunk of barbed wire in his mouth. Good thing he wasn't wearing a hat; he'd have lost it in that first rush.

Ahead of him Tiphaine leaned forward over the horse's neck, her blowing hair like a stream of molten copper. She glanced back over her shoulder, saw the hurricane bearing down on her, and straightened, slowing Starlight to a trot. Peter gathered his own reins in as they came abreast. Sultan hesitated perceptibly; then, gauging his rider's temper correctly, he changed to a slower gait, so abruptly that Peter's teeth clashed together. Torn between reluctant admiration for Sultan's speed, and irritation at his deliberately uncomfortable trot, he used the powerful pulley rein to bring the big animal to a sudden stop. Now he knew why Volz had bought the horse, who was probably anathema to every other hunting man in the neighborhood. With the general, flashy performance would win out over disposition any day.

Tiphaine came cantering sedately up to join him. Her hair had coiled itself around her neck and shoulders, and her face was flushed.

"You *are* a cheater," she said, grinning broadly. "You promised you'd fall off."

"Or are you under the mistaken impression," Peter said, as if the conversation had never been interrupted, "that that moldy specimen's hormones have been inhibited along with his brains?"

Tiphaine doubled up with laughter, falling forward over the horse's neck till her bright locks mingled with the silver-gray mane.

"You win," she said, raising a flushed face. "Aren't you ever distracted by anything?"

Peter let his gaze move from the V of her blouse, where a pulse throbbed in the little hollow at the base of her throat, to the slim thighs, encased in skin-tight jeans.

"Try me," he suggested.

Instead of blushing or giggling, she returned the look, inspecting him from head to foot.

"You're too thin," she said coolly. "But that's all right, I like thin men. Good shoulders. And a nice mouth—when you let it relax. Ah, there it goes, all tightened up!"

Peter grinned unwillingly; he had just remembered Sam's lecture on the foibles of the female sex. Was the old devil ever wrong?

"That's better," Tiphaine said, her own mouth relaxing. "I like your hands, too. Nice thin hands. No hair."

"No hair?" Peter repeated, fascinated.

"On your hands. Some men have big thick tufts on the backs of their fingers." She shivered delicately. "And mats of it on their chests, like bears. Or dogs. You're all right."

She extended one finger and poked him on the skin exposed by the open neck of his shirt. Peter flinched.

"You make me feel like a horse," he said lightly, trying to conceal an unexpected surge of annoyance.

Tiphaine laughed.

"Come on, I'll show you the sights. No more lectures, promise?"

"I'm speechless," Peter said.

They talked about horses, and songs, and things in general. Not about Timmy, or Katharine More, though Peter was aching to work his way into that subject. An instinctive sense kept him from doing so. This was his afternoon for Tiphaine, and a hint of any other interest might queer the pitch. It was a successful afternoon—from that point of view, and from others. Peter was beginning to sympathize with Martin's sentiments, if not about the town, at least about the surrounding countryside. Placid, inhabited, well cultivated, it still had an air of extravagance; the rolling land, the vast blue of the arching sky, the crisp purity of the air, and over all the landscape the brilliant sweep of fall foliage—it was far from the smoggy industrial America which is all many visitors ever see. He hadn't been out like this, with a good horse under him and a pretty girl beside him, for a long time. He wondered what it would be like to have these things without any reservations or hidden purpose clouding the brightness of the day, and then dismissed the thought with a brusque mental expletive. He had ridden with dark thoughts too long. It was impossible to go back now.

The sun slid westward, reddening. Tiphaine glanced at it, and then at her watch. A shadow dimmed the brightness of her face.

"Time to go back," she said. "I promised to be home by five."

"Promised your parents?" Peter said casually, as they turned the horses.

"My parents are dead."

"I'm sorry."

"Oh, years ago. I live with my cousin. Katharine More." She gave him a quick sidelong glance which was half veiled by her falling hair. "Martin said you knew her."

"I know her name, that's all." Peter guided Sultan, unnecessarily, around a heap of rocks. "I've read her book."

"She's a marvelous person," Tiphaine said, her blue eyes fixed on the horizon. "She isn't really my cousin; she's the niece of my stepfather."

"Sounds like one of those genealogical French exercises."

"What I mean is, she has no obligation toward me at all. But she took me in after Stephan died; he left her all the money, you see. I mean, he didn't make a will. So it all went to her."

It would have been fairly incoherent if Peter hadn't already known the story. Tiphaine's voice had become higher, with a slight stammer. He said casually,

"Stephan being your stepfather? It seems to me that there was an obligation. Moral, if not legal; his, if not hers."

"But that's just it," Tiphaine said eagerly. "She didn't owe me a thing."

"So she took you in. What do you do to earn your keep? Wash her socks?" The look in her eyes hit Peter hard. He added, in a smooth even voice, "Or scrub the floors, perhaps? While she paces the hall muttering, 'Mirror, mirror, on the wall'?"

He half expected her to fly to Katharine's defense; she surprised him with a splutter of laughter and a shining glance.

"How did you know? And you," she said mockingly, "only need a plumed velvet cap on those golden locks. Come around tomorrow and sing under my balcony."

"Not me," Peter said, recovering himself. "If I remember the original, the prince got thrown into the dungeon."

"You wouldn't be put off by a little dungeon, would you?"

"Too damp. Bad for my cough."

"Chicken. Oh, gosh, it's late. We'll have to hurry."

When they reached the stableyard, Timmy was nowhere in sight. Volz had returned from wherever he had been; his big black car stood in the stableyard, and his chauffeur was washing it. In shirt sleeves Jackson looked even bigger and more muscular than Peter remembered him. He greeted the man with a smile and a wave as Jackson looked up, and got a cool inclination of the head in return.

"Where's Timmy, Hilary?" Tiphaine asked, sliding off the mare's back.

"He's . . . busy," the chauffeur answered. "I'll take care of your horse, Miss Tiphaine."

She nodded casually. Peter dismounted.

"I'll drive you home. Just a second."

He started unbuckling the girth. Jackson put down his cloth and came over.

"I'll do that. Sir."

Peter straightened to his full height and stared up—way up—into the other man's face. It had the splendid blankness, and the chiseled regularity, of a granite statue's. He wondered how anyone could kid himself into feeling superior to a specimen like Jackson. He was not usually sensitive to his own lack of inches, but the chauffeur made him feel like a worm.

"Thanks," he said wanly.

There was a flicker of movement in one of the stalls. Peter caught a glimpse of rusty-brown hair and an intensely malevolent stare before Timmy ducked back out of sight. Jackson saw it too. With one hand he made a quick, twisting gesture. Then he looked guiltily at Peter, and the latter saw the first crack in the granite of his face. He grinned.

"If that means what I think it means . . ." he said. "Maybe you could show me how to do it?"

He turned away without waiting for an answer which he probably wouldn't have gotten anyway. Tiphaine was waiting in the car, and he slid behind the wheel with an apology for the delay. Tiphaine gave him directions which he solemnly followed. The drive took about ten minutes. It was the long way around, Tiphaine explained; there was a path through the woods which she took when she came on foot.

"You're back in plenty of time," Peter said, as he stopped the car in front of the house. "And please give my regards to the Wicked Queen."

Sooner or later, if their acquaintance developed—and he intended that it should—she would have to invite him into the house. Apparently Tiphaine had come to the same conclusion. She said, without any perceptible hesitation.

"Come in and give them yourself. No, really, I know she'd like to meet you. I told her about your new verses and she was intrigued. Unfortunately I couldn't remember all the words."

Peter hoped devoutly that he could.

He was a little keyed up, and therefore looking particularly casual, as he followed Tiphaine into the hall and through a door on the left.

The afternoon sunlight, pouring through wide French windows along the far wall, gave a luminous glow to the mellow brown leather of the chairs and brought out the rich reds of the huge Bokhara which covered most of the floor. Katharine More sat on the couch, stockinged feet tucked under her; the pale blue of her slacks and the white of her shirt stood out against the crimson upholstery. Curled up in her lap was an enormous black cat. The sunlight gave his plushy fur a kind of iridescence. Kate's hair was exactly the same shade of black.

Tiphaine performed the introductions with less than her usual charm, and, at her cousin's suggestion, went off to make cocktails. Peter, impaled by his hostess's considering eye, sought desperately for a topic of conversation other than folk music. He was afraid she was going to mention that damned song, and he hadn't got the words quite straight.

"I admire your house. This room, especially."

"It's very definitely a man's room." Her lips parted in a smile which did suggest the Wicked Stepmother, strong white teeth and all. "My uncle furnished it. With his usual taste, and lots and lots of money."

He understood, now, why she wore dark glasses in public. Her face was young and unlined, but the eyes betrayed her—not her age, which wasn't that great, but something worse. Whatever it was, it was eating her away inside; the result showed in the darkly shadowed eye sockets and the fixity of her look. He had seen eyes like those on men just before they started screaming and clawing at the bars.

There were other betraying signs—the jerkiness of the movement with which she turned to take a tall frosted glass from Tiphaine, the unnecessary tension of her hand around its curved surface. Peter accepted a Scotch and water, and Tiphaine sat down with her own drink. The cat had lifted its head and was regarding the visitor with a fixed feline stare which strongly resembled that of its mistress.

"I see you keep a familiar," Peter said at random. He was not prepared for the reaction. Tiphaine gasped, and Katharine More almost dropped her glass.

"He was my uncle's cat," she said harshly.

"He seems to approve of you." Peter snapped his fingers at the animal. Its eyes narrowed contemptuously.

"He approves of everyone; he's a big, fat senti-mentalist in spite of his appearance." Kate had recovered herself; there was amusement in her voice as she watched Peter's attempts to ingratiate himself. "But he has his dignity. Don't address him as 'kitty, kitty.' "

"What's his name?"

"What would you expect—for a familiar?" Her smile was strained. "Pyewacket."

At the sound of his name the cat stood up and stretched, looking fantastically like a miniature black leopard. He jumped down off Kate's lap and stalked toward the closed door, where he stood on his hind legs, wrapped both black paws around the doorknob, and twisted. There was a click. The cat dropped down, inserted one paw into the crack, and pulled the door open. He left without once looking at Peter, who was frankly gaping.

"I'd like to have known your uncle," he said.

"That's a simple trick," Kate said scornfully. "Many cats can do it."

"First time I've ever seen it."

"You're probably a dog lover. Cats are just as bright. They just don't give a damn about pleasing people. But they can learn anything they choose to learn, if it's to their advantage."

"They're uncanny beasts, though. That combination of grace and ferocity . . ."

"Which is why so many of the poor things were burned as witches' familiars. You, as an expert on folklore, know all about that, of course."

"Of course." Peter cast about for another change of subject. "Uh . . . your uncle preferred cats to dogs?"

"Pyewacket was the only exception. He didn't like other animals. Or people."

Well, well, Peter thought. Before he could inquire further into Katharine's obvious dislike of the uncle who had endowed her with a tidy fortune, Tiphaine broke her long silence.

"That's not very polite, Kate."

"To you or Stephan? It's true; he approved of you."

Her hostility was poorly concealed. Tiphaine's cheeks flushed with embarrassment, but her mouth was set stubbornly.

"He'd have to approve of you," Peter said. "Didn't he bring you up?"

"And gave me my name."

"I wondered how you came by it. I've never heard the name before."

"My real name is Melanie." Tiphaine shook her head. "Isn't it insipid? When I got to be about twelve I insisted it had to be changed. Stephan named me Tiphaine. He said it was the proper name for an elf."

"How very imaginative."

"Oh, he was certainly imaginative," Kate said drily. "You seem to be interested in my uncle, Mr. Stewart. That's his portrait."

Peter had noticed the painting, but the stiff, archaic style and the old-fashioned garb of the subject had given him an impression of greater age. As he studied it, he realized that the effect was intentional. The black suit, and the column, topped with a marble urn, on which the man's hand rested, were done with sketchy disinterest, but the face and hands came out of the canvas with a near three-dimensional effect—long cadaverous white hands, and a face set in a wide, sneering smile which showed a set of splendid teeth.

Privately, Peter thought it would make a nice decoration for the office of a dentist with morbid tastes. He leaned back in his chair.

"He looks like someone who might haunt a house, doesn't he?"

"They say he does." Tiphaine came over to sit on the arm of Peter's chair.

"Who says he does?"

"The Negroes. Of course they're a superstitious lot."

"So far as Stephan was concerned, they have reason. He was a real bastard." Katharine's voice was calm, but the word dropped like a stone.

"Simon Legree?" Peter raised an eyebrow. "I thought you people had done away with that sort of thing."

Katharine's mouth twisted, but she said nothing.

"Oh, it wasn't anything like that," Tiphaine exclaimed. "They thought he was a magician—a warlock. They were scared to death of him. Imagine!"

"Oh, I can," Katharine said sarcastically. "After

all, when a man insists on stalking around the village in a long black cape, baring his teeth at everyone . . ."

"It was a game," Tiphaine said defensively. "He happened to have two fingers which were precisely the same length. When he found out about the old werewolf stories it amused him to pretend. He even let his eyebrows grow together."

"What did he do about reflections in a mirror?" Peter asked, with genuine interest.

"He ostentatiously avoided mirrors." Tiphaine giggled. "It really was funny, Peter, watching him stalk around town swishing that cape. He'd come home and laugh and laugh."

"Sounds like a fun-loving old gentleman," Peter agreed politely.

Katharine gave him a quick look.

"I'm sure our family eccentricities don't interest Mr. Stewart."

"Oh, but they do. I hadn't realized that the interest in magic and folklore ran in the family."

"I suppose it does," Katharine said. "I remember visiting Stephan when I was a little girl. He had a fantastic library, and I was a compulsive reader. Maybe that started me on my—peculiar career."

"Library?" Peter saw the opening and dived in, head first. "I say, that must be fascinating. I know it's presumptuous of me to ask . . ."

"To use the library? Certainly. Martin said you were going to do a book." Katharine gave him another of those wide, white smiles. "And you'll sing me those fabulous new verses to "The Unquiet Grave," won't you?"

"Certainly." Peter put his glass down and rose, without haste. "Next time. I've kept you too long as it is. The charm of your hospitality made me forget the time."

Katharine uncoiled herself and stood up. Once again it struck Peter with a slight shock to see how small she was; in stocking feet she barely reached to his nose.

"It has been fun, hasn't it?" she said clearly.

When she tipped her head back to look up at him, there was not the slightest hint of coquetry in her manner. Quite the contrary; war had been declared. But in her direct gaze there was something else, considerably more basic. The feeling was mutual. And Peter knew she disliked it as much as he did.

According to the radio, a storm was on its way. After sundown the temperature dropped sharply, and when Peter slid out of his window into the night, the sky was spotted with sly little clouds. He dropped his chin into the high neck of his sweater and walked faster. What a climate! Well, he wouldn't suffer from the cold tonight. He'd be moving too fast.

His next supernatural appearance was going to be even more dramatic than the first. He had acquired the necessary paraphernalia at a pharmacist's in the next town, twenty miles away. It fit nicely into the briecase he carried.

He had taken careful mental notes on the arrangement of Volz's place that afternoon. It ought to be an easy job. The biggest potential fly in the ointment was the problem of the dogs. There hadn't been any.

Since Volz was Master of the Hunt, it was reasonable to suppose that he had some foxhounds around somewhere. In Peter's experience, dogs did bark in the night, at friend or foe; he had to know where the general's hounds were kenneled, if he wanted his nocturnal presence to be unannounced. But he had neither heard nor seen any sign of canine life that afternoon.

Guiding the car with one casual hand, Peter decided that maybe Volz just didn't like dogs. An infallible sign of character, liking or not liking dogs. From what he knew of the general he wouldn't expect Volz to like them.

Timmy was another potential problem, but a minor one. Peter assumed that the repulsive young man sometimes slept in the stables; he certainly smelled as if he did. But surely, on a cold night even a half-witted stableboy would be entitled to four walls and a fire. Peter was prepared to deal with Timmy, though, if he had to. He wasn't expecting any trouble from that quarter.

Volz was remarkably careless about protecting his property. The wall around the stableyard was a flimsy wooden affair, and the gate didn't even have a padlock. In a spirit of fair-mindedness Peter had to admit that horse thieves were pretty much out of style. He suspected that the house was loaded with bolts and chains and burglar alarms, but that was fine with him. He had no designs on the house.

The wind whistled through the trees and tugged irritably at his hair as he approched the back of the house, moving silently but with no attempt at concealment. One set of windows in an upper floor was alight. Presumably Volz was about to retire to his bachelor bed. Peter wondered idly how he spent his evenings. The man couldn't read. Watching television, probably.

He checked the tack room and the stalls and found them, if not empty, at least empty of Timmy. So the man did sleep indoors. That made life somewhat simpler. He found Sultan's stall and stopped the incipient snort with a handful of sugar. While Sultan was munching, he got to work. He was crouched on the floor, tying the second of the cloths around Sultan's near fore, when the roof fell in on him.

It was instinct that saved him, the reflexive spasm of a hunted creature who has learned he must fight for the privilege of breathing. He twisted himself out from under the falling bulk just before it mashed him flat, and swung his clasped hands down on the back of the other man's neck. The next movement brought him to his feet, headed out. Timmy was one thing, and dogs were another thing. This lad was something else.

But Sultan's massive posterior blocked the exit, and Sultan's sudden cupboard love was his undoing. The big head butted him in the chest and snuffled down the front of his sweater looking for more sugar. It caught Peter off balance for a moment, and while he was trying to wriggle past Sultan's tail a hand wrapped around his ankle. His feet went out from under him and he landed flat on his back with a thud that knocked the breath out of his lungs. Before he could get it back, the other man was on top of him.

Jackson was no judo expert; he didn't need to be. His wrists pinned by two big hands, wheezing for breath, Peter looked up at the handsome black face staring down at him, and sighed. He blew up out of the corner of his mouth, trying to get the hair out of his eyes, and said mildly, "Would you mind shifting weight just a bit? You're sitting on my diaphragm."

To his surprise Jackson obeyed, leaning forward so that most of his weight rested on his knees. It was a naive move; he was now in an extremely vulnerable position, and Peter rapidly reviewed three different dirty tricks by which he could free himself. But the very innocence of the gesture disarmed him—that, and the fact that Jackson had a head like cast iron and a reach like a python's. He produced his most disarming smile.

"What happens now?" he asked. "Do you march me up to the house and deliver me to the boss man?"

Jackson's lower lip went out and his brow furrowed. He wasn't stupid; he was just confused. Peter could see his difficulty. When you hate everybody, it's hard to decide whom to fight.

Peter waited patiently, practicing breathing. His wrists hurt. He had a feeling that the circulation was being cut off. But he didn't mention it. Jackson was capable of seeing the subtler points. Most kids his age wouldn't be; he was not only smarter than most kids his age, he had had more experience—all bad, probably.

"Okay," Jackson said finally. He released Peter's wrists and leaned back.

Peter tried to keep his face straight; he wasn't entirely successful. Jackson caught the flicker of expression in the dim light from the door, and a grudging half-smile touched his mouth.

"You think I'm pretty stupid, don't you?" he said.

"Just trusting," Peter said. He pantomimed the move, in slow motion, so Jackson wouldn't take offense. "Not that you'll ever need tricks like that," he added, as he rolled himself out from under Jackson's body. "You scare the hell out of most people just standing there. If I'd known you were the watchman, I'd never have tried this."

"I need all the tricks I can get," Jackson said.

"Maybe you do," Peter agreed. He sat down,

with his back up against the wall, and reached in his pocket. "Cigarette?"

"Not in here."

"Where?" Peter shoved at the equine head which was bruising his chest. Sultan had misinterpreted his gesture toward his pocket. "Damn this animal. I'd like to talk to you."

"And I want to talk to you," Jackson said grimly.

They found a sheltered spot in the pasture, behind a rock that gave some protection against the chilly wind. Jackson was in shirt sleeves, but he didn't seem to notice the cold. He squatted, his back against the rock, and fixed his eyes intently on Peter.

"Whatchu up to in there, man?"

"Spare me the dialect," Peter said, cupping his hands around a match, and extending it toward Jackson's cigarette.

"And you spare me the stalling." Jackson took a drag and blew out smoke. The vapor was torn to tatters by the wind. "What were you doing in the stables? I've got a good imagination, but I can't think of any legal reason."

"How about illegal?"

"Quite a few. But none of them seem to apply."

"I felt like a midnight ride," Peter said.

Jackson's fist shot out toward Peter's throat, and then dropped as if it had been amputated. Still sprawled comfortably on the grass, Peter lowered his hand and said mildly, "Don't shove, Jackson. I don't like it any more than you do."

The boy rubbed his forearm.

"Where did you learn that one?"

"I watch a lot of television."

"No, come on. Show me."

Peter started to remonstrate, and then reminded himself of several not so extraneous factors. He glanced at his watch. The luminous dial showed eleven forty. He had time.

"All right," he said, rising to his feet with a groan. "Do that again, slowly, and I'll show you."

The next ten minutes were strenuous. Peter ended the demonstration by letting Jackson hook his feet out from under him, and gave a realistic grunt as he fell. From a prone and slightly theatrical position he smiled affably up at the boy's grinning face.

"Now do I get that horse?"

"Nope."

"Why not?"

Jackson sat down beside him and pulled out a crumpled pack of cigarettes. After a slight hesitation he extended it to Peter.

"You're crazy," he muttered, his head bent over the match. "I never spent such a crazy night. I catch you trying to steal a horse, and ten minutes later you're teaching me judo, or whatever the hell it is. Crazy."

"I impress some people that way," Peter agreed,

still prone. The ground was cold, but not quite as cold as the upper air.

Jackson scowled at the glowing end of his cigarette. He didn't find conversation easy, probably because there were so many ideas burgeoning in that well-endowed head of his, and too few people to whom he could express them. Peter wriggled into a more comfortable position, hands clasped under his head, and pensively contemplated the firmament. He had plenty of time. It was beginning to look as if the evening's performance would be called off.

Finally Jackson mashed his cigarette out.

"Who are you, anyhow?"

"Just a peaceful tourist."

"Peaceful like a bomb. But you know what you remind me of? You remind me of old Daniel in the lions' den. The lions stand 'round, smiling and showing all those pretty white teeth. But those teeth bite, friend. And Daniel knew they were lions."

Peter turned his head. This wasn't what he had expected.

"You speak in parables, my son. Was that a warning?"

"Forget it. I said more than I should have. Don't expect any help from me. I don't stick my neck out for anybody."

"Especially for Whitey?"

The boy glanced at him. Peter thought he had never seen a look so devoid of emotion. It was not hostile, merely set in an intensity of purpose which negated feeling.

"Some of the boys get their kicks out of name calling. Me, I'm not that stupid."

"That must make you unpopular in certain quarters," Peter said.

"It makes me unpopular in all quarters." Jackson gave him a sudden ferocious grin. "That's why I collect all the dirty tricks I can find."

"Thanks for the warning." Peter stood up. "Well. No more tricks, dirty or otherwise, from me. I've got to have something in reserve for the next time you jump me."

"Don't try it."

"Another warning?" Peter braced himself; Jackson had risen, and was looming.

"What you're up to is none of my business, Stewart. If you can pull something on that bastard up at the house, I'll cheer you on. But from the sidelines, mister—from way out on the sidelines. And if I can make a buck by acting like a big faithful watchdog, I'll make it. At your expense."

Peter shrugged.

"Fair enough. Can I collect my belongings? I left them in the stall."

They walked back in silence through the windy night. Still in silence Jackson watched Peter stuff his possessions into his bag. After the third item he couldn't stand it any longer.

"I would sort of like to know what you were going to do."

"I'll bet you would."

"Luminous paint; that stuff around Sultan's feet—black cloth—"

"It'll give you something to think about during the long nights." Peter straightened, bag in hand. "No dice, Jackson. I'm going home in a huff. You won't let me steal your horse, I won't let you play. You're better off not being involved, really."

"Sure, sure," Jackson muttered.

Peter left without a formal good-night. As he turned the corner of the stable, he heard something rustle, and he whirled, dropping his bag and raising his hands. There was nothing to be seen. Not at first. His back flat up against the rough wooden planks, he saw a slim dark shadow scuttle across a patch of moonlight and disappear as the moon hid behind a cloud.

# Chapter
## 5

THE PERFORMANCE PETER HAD PLANNED WAS USE-less without Sultan. He went back to the car, wondering about alternatives; so long as he was out, it seemed a pity to waste the evening. The night was perfect; scudding clouds, flickering moonlight, a wind keening high in the trees. Still cogitating, he drove the few miles to the other house, parked in his former spot, and climbed the wall as before.

As soon as he got through the belt of trees he realized that something was going on. The house was a blaze of light.

By now it was well past midnight. Knowing Katharine's habits, he would not have expected her to be entertaining. The absence of cars in the driveway confirmed the assumption. He wondered what had happened.

He investigated the downstairs rooms first, and found lights shining in rooms which were uninhabited, except for the kitchen. The two elderly servants were there; both had on night attire, with robes over pajamas. The cook's graying hair was done up in pink curlers. Something was boiling on the stove, and the cook was preparing a tray. She looked sleepy and disgruntled. Her husband sat at the table, elbows propped, blinking groggily into a cup of coffee. Peter watched them for a few minutes, and then decided there was nothing to be gained by waiting. With the windows shut he wouldn't be able to hear anything even if they spoke.

The upstairs window he selected had two things to recommend it. Its frontal location, above the room in which the séance had been held, suggested that it might be the master bedroom, and an old oak tree provided a convenient ladder to the small balcony. He swarmed up the tree with only one broken branch to mark his progress; the snap was lost in the general uproar of the wind. At least he hoped it was. When he stood on the balcony, outside the French doors which were the counterparts of the doors below, he saw that he had struck pay dirt.

It was Katharine's room. He would have recognized it from its air of austerity, plain furniture, and walls lined with bookcases, even if the woman herself had not been sprawled face down across the bed. Tiphaine was bending over her, one hand on her cousin's shoulder. Every light in the room was on—the overhead chandelier, the desk and dressing-table lamps, two bed lamps. Tiphaine's molten hair threw the light back like a polished bronze mirror, and swung down, half hiding her face. She wore plain white silk tailored pajamas and looked good enough to eat.

As Peter moved in closer for a better look, some slight sound must have reached the older woman's ears, for she sat bolt upright, both hands going out in a spasmodic gesture.

"What was that?"

"The wind. Only the wind. Kate, it's all right; try to relax."

Katharine nodded. She looked like hell, Peter thought clinically. Her eyes were sunken and a muscle at the corner of her mouth beat frantically, like a tiny pulse. He was sardonically amused to note that the woman who dressed in tailored slacks and shirt during the day had a less Spartan taste in nightwear. Her gown was pale green; the full skirt spread out across the bed in agitated ripples the color and opacity of seawater. One slender strap had slipped down off her shoulder. She was definitely too thin. Still, the general effect would have been arresting, if it had not been for the face—a study in sheer terror, unmasked . . .

"There's someone out there," she insisted.

Peter took one noiseless step backward and stood poised at the rim of the balcony. But Tiphaine shook her head and did not stir.

"Kate, I looked. When I first came up. There never was anyone there. It must have been a dream."

"It was his voice. Saying . . . saying . . ."

"Saying what?" Tiphaine sat down on the edge of the bed.

"Saying he wanted . . . that I should . . ." Kate shivered.

Tiphaine put her arms around her cousin, and Kate caught at her with frantic hands.

"Don't go away," she muttered. "Don't leave me alone . . ."

A soft knock sounded at the door, and she started violently.

"It's only Mrs. Schmidt," Tiphaine said soothingly. She called, "Come in."

The cook entered, carrying a tray. The pink curlers looked like some barbaric hair adornment.

"This is too hot," Tiphaine said, taking the cup. "I'll put some cold water in."

She vanished into the bathroom. Katharine was quiet now, her hands and face controlled; putting on a good front before the servants. It was hard to believe that she was the same woman who had been cowering and moaning a few moments earlier.

"Did Will search the house?" she asked.

"Yes, miss."

"Was there—anything?"

"Not a sign of anything, miss."

Having seen Will dozing over his coffee in the

kitchen not five minutes before, Peter knew the woman was lying. It was fortunate for him that the household had grown accustomed to Kate's hallucinations; he could come and go without too much fear of being seen by the Schmidts. Old Will was not the man to prowl the grounds on a cold autumn night unless he had to. And it was becoming clear that he would have to pay Kate More several more visits. The damned woman had nerves, not of steel, but of rubber; they bounced back after every shock. But not all the way. A few more surprises . . .

Tiphaine came back with the cup of tea. Over Kate's bowed head a significant glance passed between the two other women, and Peter deduced that Tiphaine had added some sort of sedative to the tea. Kate certainly needed something. Despite her control, her hands shook so badly when she took the cup that tea slopped over onto the bedspread.

The cook left, taking the tray, and Tiphaine switched off the overhead light.

"Leave it on," Kate gasped. "Don't leave me. . . ."

"You can't sleep with all the lights blazing. I'll be here, Kate. All night, if you want me."

"Kind . . ." Kate slumped back against the pillows; in her exhausted state the drug had taken quick effect.

The room was now dim except for the circles of light shed by the lamps on the desk and bedside tables. Now, before she sank into drugged sleep, was the time for the next move.

Peter climbed onto the roof. It was within arms' reach of the top of the balcony rail. Hanging head down, held by his knees and one hand, he twisted around so that he could see into the room. It was an uncomfortable position, but he didn't have to hold it long. Just long enough to give the knife the proper flip, that would make it curve down from a high point that was above normal eye level. To a mind already attuned to the supernatural it would seem to have materialized in midair. That was the explanation of the poltergeist legend; careful misdirection by the person responsible for the flying objects, so that no one noticed where they originated.

One quick movement of his wrist and it was done; he saw it thud, the carved hilt quivering, into the wooden footboard of the bed.

He twisted himself up and caught the gutter with his other hand. Much as he would have liked to see the results with his own eyes, he couldn't spare the time. There must be no sign of a material agent, or the game was spoiled; this time old Will might actually be moved to look around.

He was half way across the roof when the scream began, and it went on for some time, even after he had descended to the ground and was running toward the wall.

Peter slept the dreamless sleep which is erroneously attributed to the just. There is, after all, nothing like exercise in the fresh air before retiring. When he awoke, he lay still, blinking in the daylight, and planning his next move.

The first part of his project was easier than he had expected. Thanks to Katharine's own overactive conscience, she was already in a state of extreme nervous tension. The next step wasn't going to be so easy. He had never had any hard-and-fast scheme for getting invited to the house, though he had considered possible openings. One potential means of entree was definitely out. Katharine was not only unimpressed, she was hostile and suspicious. Tiphaine was a more hopeful prospect, but Peter's personal vanity was not so exaggerated as to make him believe he could sweep the girl off her feet within the next few days. The very success of the initial phase made haste essential. If Kate went on the way she was going, she might crack up fairly soon. He had to be on hand when the moment arrived, and that meant residence in the house, not casual lurking.

Maybe, after all, the hoary old tricks were the best.

Without rising, he stretched out one arm for the telephone and ordered breakfast. Then he asked for a local number.

Volz sounded as if he had been up, swinging from the trees, since dawn. Peter moved the telephone three inches away from his ear. He was in luck. The hunt was meeting next day.

His second outside call was less productive.

Mrs. Martin's feeble voice informed him that the doctor had gone out on a call late last night and wasn't back yet. Peter said he would stop by later that afternoon, and hung up, smiling nastily. He didn't have to ask where Martin had gone.

He amused himself for the rest of the morning by a visit to Greer's Saddlery. He had been tempted to appear next day in old slacks and sweater, but that would have been indulging his sense of humor too far. At Greer's he contemplated himself in the mirror with a grimace of amusement. The uniform was as archaistic as tights and a doublet, and much more uncomfortable. The white stock tickled his chin, and the black derby hat gave him a headache. He tapped the shining boots with the crop, fingered the chaste gold bar that adorned his stock, and bought the lot, over the moans of Mr. Greer, who insisted that everything needed taking in at the waist.

"I'll tighten my belt," Peter said shortly, and left, after paying out a sum which made him grimace again, but not with amusement.

He went to Martin's house just after three, and had to wait. Martin had a backlog of patients from that morning. When Peter was finally shown into the sanctum, he found Martin pouring himself a shot from a bottle which normally lived in the bottom drawer of his desk.

"Join me?"

"No, thanks." Peter sat down, looking concerned, and Martin shrugged.

"I don't ordinarily do this. But today has been one of those days."

"Not much sleep?"

"None." Martin swallowed his dosage, made a wry face, and then glanced keenly at Peter. "How did you know?"

"The word gets around," Peter said vaguely.

"God yes." Martin sighed. "What are people saying?"

"Rather peculiar things. It depends on whom you're talking to, of course."

"Of course," Martin said mechanically. "It's good of you to be so discreet, Stewart, but there's not much point in discretion when the whole damned town is whispering. You've met Dr. More?"

"Yesterday. And professional reticence is unnecessary with anyone who's seen her. What's wrong with the woman? Drugs? Guilty conscience?"

"What makes you say that?"

"You mean, what business is it of mine? Because Tiphaine is out there, two miles from the nearest neighbor, with only a pair of doddering old servants. Drug addicts aren't precisely the safest companions."

"It isn't drugs."

"I don't give a damn what it is. The woman is unstable. She might—hurt Tiphaine."

"Take it easy," Martin said. "You're interested in Tiphaine?"

"I'm in love with her," Peter said, and met the doctor's eyes with one of his best candid stares.

"Does she reciprocate your feelings?" Despite his furrowed brows there was a hint of amusement in the doctor's voice.

"I know it sounds ridiculous," Peter said shyly. "But sometimes it happens that way. . . . No, of course she doesn't. Not yet. If I had time . . . but in the meanwhile, what's happening out there? The situation is unhealthy, whatever the cause."

"The situation is even worse than you think," Martin said, and then fell silent. Peter waited, while Martin filled his pipe; the doctor's own concern was warring with his professional caution, and as Peter watched he could almost see the other factors being weighed—his own respectable introduction and exemplary behavior, plus the fact that this wasn't really . . .

"It isn't really a question of professional ethics," Martin said. "Of course the problem may be one of hallucinations—visual and auditory—but she isn't the sort of woman who is ordinarily affected in that way. I'm afraid, Stewart, that someone has been playing some malicious and dangerous tricks."

Peter widened his eyes and looked baffled.

"Why would anyone do a thing like that?"

"I can't imagine." Martin made a sweeping, frustrated gesture. "It can't be personal enmity, so

I can only conclude that someone here in town has it in for the family. You may have heard some of the stories about Stephan . . ."

"Tiphaine told me about his werewolf game."

"It wasn't exactly a game," Martin said. "He was always good to Tiphaine, so naturally she takes his part. But Stephan had a mean streak. He enjoyed frightening people, and he dabbled in some of the nastier magical practices. Katharine herself isn't popular; she's never done the town any harm—quite the contrary, but her charities are, at her own insistence, anonymous, and there are wild tales among the more superstitious older residents that she's inherited Stephan's talent for magic. Black magic."

"It's unbelievable," Peter murmured.

"You know better. You've traveled in backward country areas, must have, to collect your songs. How many witches have you met?"

"A few. But that was England and Scotland, little country villages. This is a modern, sophisticated town."

"Science and sophistication don't kill superstition," Martin said heavily. "Look at the newspapers—ads for palmists and astrologers, fortune-telling columns. You can find a section "Spiritualists" in the Yellow Pages. Add to that a long tradition of superstition, and you're in trouble. You've met Mrs. Adams, at the hotel? Fine horsewoman, canny businesswoman; but she's a member of some wild cult that calls on Mother

Earth. Not," he added quickly, "that I think Mrs. Adams is behind these tricks that are being played on Kate. I visualize someone simpler and more easily frightened. Someone who is suffering from illness or financial trouble, and blames it on Kate."

"But, look here!" Peter sat up, gripping the arms of his chair. "If some madman thinks she's put a spell on him—the most effective ways of canceling such a spell is to kill the witch!"

"That's what I'm afraid of." Martin knocked out his dead pipe. "At first it was simply malice, no physical threats. But last night someone threw a knife. It just missed Tiphaine."

Peter's look of dismay was genuine this time. Unless Tiphaine had moved at the last moment, he didn't see how the knife could have come anywhere near her. What was Martin trying to prove? Or had he gotten a hysterical version of the story from two frightened women?

"You have a nice, neat theory, Doctor," he said. "But isn't it also possible that Dr. More herself is playing the tricks?"

He expected a bellow of protest. Instead, Martin's shoulders sagged.

"I don't know why I'm discussing this with you," he murmured.

"Because you're worn out and worried sick. Look here, Martin, it's Tiphaine I care about. Doesn't my interest in her give me a right to be concerned?" Martin nodded heavily, without looking up, and Peter went on earnestly, "I'm not trying to build a case against Dr. More. I don't know what to think—except that Tiphaine may be in danger, either from her cousin or as one of those innocent bystanders who are always getting clobbered by careless assassins. I'm as anxious to find out the truth as you are."

"Calm down, Peter. I agree completely." Martin looked at him with a faint, haggard smile. "I must admit, it's a relief to share this with someone I can trust."

"We'll think of something," Peter said confidently. "What about a hired guard?"

"I suggested that. There isn't a man in the house except old Will, and he's as timid as a rabbit. Superstitious, too; his family has lived here for three hundred years. But Kate refused."

"She did, eh?"

"Yes, but I may yet convince her." Martin's tone was less assured than his words. "I'm going out there tonight myself."

"I wish I were. Well, if you're going to be up all night again, I'd better leave so you can nap this afternoon." Peter rose. At the door he turned, as if some sudden idea had come to him.

"Martin, I wonder . . ."

"What?" The doctor looked at him hopefully.

"I haven't quite got it worked out yet. But I may need your cooperation."

"Anything. Anything that will help."

"This might help," Peter assured him.

He left the office with the smug feeling that for once he had told the simple truth. He simply hadn't specified who would be helped by his plan.

"One of the reasons why I always hated hunting," Peter muttered, "is that you have to get up so early in the morning."

His companion, one of the plump matrons whom he had met at the Folklore Society meeting, giggled nervously. She had an improbable name—Marlene, or something like that—and teeth that looked as if they had been meant to protrude slightly before an orthodontist got his hands on her.

"It's a nice day for it, anyhow," she said. "For hunting, I mean. It's not a nice day really . . ."

Peter wiped beads of moisture from his boot. The weather was foul. In Scotland it might have been called a mist; fog shrouded the lower patches of ground, and moisture collected on every possible surface. Marlene assured him earnestly that the fog would lift by ten, and that it would be a marvelous day. Peter gave her a glance of hatred. Her riding habit was too tight; the buttons at her middle were strained. At least he wouldn't have her beside him once the hunt got underway; she sat her horse, a timid-looking filly, like a blob of jelly, and her hands were nervous on the reins.

"The unspeakable chasing the uneatable," he muttered, and gave Marlene a bland smile as she glanced at him uncertainly.

"What did you say?"

"I was admiring your horse."

"She was very expensive," Marlene said complacently. "My husband *raved* when he saw the bill."

"He doesn't hunt?"

"He doesn't do *anything*," said Marlene. "Except make money."

"Well, that's not such a bad occupation. It allows you to buy very expensive horses."

"Not all that expensive," Marlene said perversely. "Sultan cost four times as much. I sure do admire your nerve, riding that mean animal. He always tries to bite me."

As if he had understood the words, Sultan stamped and glared. His feeble wits had completely forgotten Peter's sugar the night before, and twice he had absentmindedly started to nibble his rider's boot. Peter dealt with that problem the second time. Now Sultan sulked and bided his time. Peter felt fairly sure that the noble steed would head for the first tree he saw, and try to scrape his rider off.

"He tries to bite me, too," Peter said truthfully. "Oops." He jerked in the saddle and gathered the reins closer. "He seems edgy today. Hope I haven't taken on more than I can handle."

A cacaphony of excited barking announced the

arrival of the MFH and his canine entourage. Peter studied the square, squat figure, which looked like a toad in a top hat, with disapproval.

"Volz isn't his own Huntsman, I see. How did he get to be Master?"

"It's a lot of work. He has the time and the money. He doesn't like dogs, but there's no rule that says he has to be Huntsman."

She trotted off, bouncing emphatically, toward the other riders. Peter pushed his hat back off his aching brow and glanced around. Most of the other members had arrived by now. Mrs. Adams was one of them; she was at her best in the masculine garb, and the hunt colors she wore testified to her skill. Peter recognized some of the others, from the Folklore meeting. Martin was conspicuously absent, but everyone else who was anybody seemed to be present. All the white folks, that is. Middleburg had its town Negro, a distinguished State Department official, who lived in a particularly isolated house outside the town limits, but the only black face visible here was that of Hilary Jackson, and Hilary was busy trying to hold the pack of yelling hounds.

Peter had seen Timmy's fleeting form, but the half-wit kept out of sight except when actually called upon to perform some service. At the moment, he was invisible, which suited Peter fine; the shambling, secretive form looked absolutely eerie sliding along through patches of mist. He touched Sultan's side and walked the horse over to where Hilary stood, feet braced, magnificent muscles taut against the pull of the leads. He hadn't planned to start a conversation, under the eyes of the town gentry; but he was unprepared for the hostile look Jackson gave him. The boy deliberately looked away, leaving Peter feeling rebuffed.

Two hours later he was still feeling rebuffed. He was also bored. They had killed once. As a guest, Peter kept behind, and he made a show of Sultan's wildness as they stood around the miserable remains of the fox. Sultan reared, in response to a surreptitious jab, and Volz turned from his contemplation of the bloody mess on the ground.

"Having trouble, Stewart?"

"No," Peter said. "He's just a little—oops!—nervous."

"Better go back and change mounts."

"Oh, no, that's not necessary."

"All right. Just don't get in the way."

Hounds and riders were off again. The next chase went as Peter had hoped, into the woods. It was a messy sort of forest, overgrown and thick with fallen trees; he lost himself without any trouble. He got rid of his hat along the way and loosened his stock; a few swipes with a handy bramble branch gave his face that extra touch of verisimilitude. Then he set off at a leisurely pace toward the edge of Katharine's property.

The wooded area ended about a hundred yards from the stone wall which marked the back boundaries. The wall was lower here in back, easily within a horse's jumping ability.

He reined the stallion in at the edge of the wood. Even from that point he could hear sounds of activity on the other side of the wall. They were odd sounds—a regular, monotonous thunk, thunk, like someone beating a rug. From his early investigations Peter was able to identify the sounds. There was an archery target back here, a good safe distance from the house. He was in luck. Now he wouldn't have to play his little drama right up under the kitchen windows.

He sent Sultan plunging out of the woods at a gallop and put him at the wall. He learned then another reason for Sultan's high price. The big animal jumped like Pegasus, soaring so lightly that it almost hurt Peter to spoil the picture. He came back into the saddle too hard and too soon; Sultan came down practically flat-footed, and Peter didn't have to pretend when he lost one stirrup and slipped sideways, like Tom Mix ducking Indian arrows. When he straightened up, he saw that the analogy was only too apt. He was being covered by a pair of steely eyes and an even harder steel point.

Katharine wore her usual costume, with a sweater instead of a shirt, and very dirty sneakers. Her sleeves were pushed up to the elbow to leave room for the leather archer's guard. The pose showed her slight figure to its best advantage, erect, balanced, and straight as the arrow she was aiming at the center of Peter's chest.

Peter sat very still. The black-and-red-feathered arrow had a field point, not one of the deadly broad-bladed hunting points; but it was steel, for all that, and the arms that held it had an unmistakable look of competence. Her stance was that of a professional, wrist and arm perfectly straight but not rigid. The bow was equipped with a sight, which confirmed his suspicion that she had done a lot of target shooting. The point of the arrow dropped as he watched her warily, but he was not reassured; from the point of aim, it was clear that she was pulling an unusually heavy bow for a woman of her size—thirty or thirty-five pounds, maybe.

"Out," she said succinctly. "Turn around and go back where you came from."

"Over that?" Peter nodded at the wall. "I barely made it the first time."

"You shouldn't have tried."

"I couldn't help it."

She squinted, studying his scratched face and general dishevelment.

"I'm afraid Tiphaine is too impressionable. She raved about your riding."

"Sultan seems a little nervous," Peter said defensively. He raised one hand to brush his hair back, and Sultan danced.

"So he does. How unfortunate. Out."

"But, look here! I'm sorry about intruding, but it was an accident."

"I don't allow hunting, or any other sort of intrusion. If you want to see me, come to the front door."

"But, Dr. More—"

"Out."

Peter started to expostulate, then closed his mouth and shrugged. He wasn't at all sure she wouldn't shoot him. He turned Sultan. They were not far enough from the wall for a good approach, and both he and the horse knew it, but by that time Sultan was so annoyed he didn't care. He flung himself up and barely made it, his heels scraping the stone; and Peter, releasing reins and stirrups at the same moment, slid ungracefully out of the saddle.

He landed on the outer side of the wall, with a crash and rattle of shrubbery which was as spectacular as he had hoped, and lay as he had fallen, with one eye cocked toward the wall. Katharine's startled face appeared above it, and Peter closed the eye. He heard her scramble down and approach. He was sprawled on his back, one leg twisted under him. A cold hand touched his forehead, brushing the hair back and lingering on a rising lump. He heard a soft intake of breath and got ready to respond, with pathetic weakness, to cries of feminine distress and pity.

"Damn it to hell," Katharine said to herself. "The stupid fool's killed himself."

* * *

An hour later Peter was reclining in bed upstairs, with a splitting headache whose discomfort was mitigated by the knowledge that Phase Two of the plan had been successful. Martin had come and gone; he had given Peter a reproachful look, but one which was tempered by amusement and relief, and he had spoken gravely of possible concussion. In view of the fact that the poor chap was living at the hotel, where service, though splendid, was not designed for the sick . . .

"What about the hospital?" Katharine interrupted.

Peter looked up at her from under his lashes as she stood by the bed, fingers tapping impatiently on the footboard. Her mouth was a tight slit and her eyes were narrowed with a fury which the doctor's diagnosis had only slightly calmed.

"You know how crowded we are, Kate. Besides, moving him would be ill advised. If you need help, I might be able to send a nurse. . . ."

"From your overworked hospital? Oh, all right, Martin. I can't very well throw him out bodily, can I? But I wish you weren't so damned *nice!*"

She flung out of the room, closing the door with exaggerated care. Peter grinned at Martin, who answered with a wink and a slight nod toward Tiphaine, who stood by the door.

"Just stay in bed and take it easy," Martin said casually. "Tiphaine will keep an eye on you, you don't really need a nurse. Child, you know what to watch out for—bleeding from ears or nostrils, drowsiness, nausea. . . ."

"I know." Tiphaine glided forward, giving Peter a smile that made his abused head swim. "Don't worry, Paul, I'll take care of him."

When the doctor had left, she sat down on the edge of the bed and took Peter's hand in both hers. She was very lovely, with her vibrant features and that unbelievable hair, between gold and copper. Peter was wondering how soon he could reasonably recover from a slight concussion when she spoke.

"What happened, Peter?"

"I fell off," Peter said literally.

"You forget, darling, I've seen you ride. Did someone—do something to Sultan?"

"Now what," Peter said, "would make you think a thing like that?"

"Stop it." Color flamed in her cheeks; she looked beautiful and rather alarming. "The whole town is gossiping about what's happening here. Paul knows. You've been talking to him, haven't you?"

"Well, yes. But . . ."

"So you decided you were going to rush in and rescue us." The blue eyes were blazing; the fine hairs lifted about her face as if electrified. "The big hero. Prying and prowling and . . . Why don't you leave us alone? Everything was fine until you came. . . ."

Peter, who had been trying ineffectually to get a

word in, decided that there was only one way to shut her up. He caught her clenched fists and pulled her down, so hard that several hitherto unnoticed bruises complained; but after the first twinge Peter was in no state to notice. For the first second or two she twisted like an eel in his grasp. This stage was succeeded by one of enthusiastic cooperation. But as soon as his grip relaxed she was up, and out of his arms, in one lithe movement. Peter was left with his mouth open and his arms out. He closed the former, dropped the latter, and looked reproachfully at Tiphaine.

She was still flushed, but not with anger; after a moment her wide mouth curved up and she sat down again.

"Bad to worse," she said, a little breathlessly. "Is that any way to calm a girl's suspicions?"

"I'm sorry." They contemplated one another solemnly for a moment. Then Peter said, "I'm also a liar."

"I guess I should apologize." There were lines in her face that shouldn't have been there, and Peter felt an emotion so unfamiliar that it took him some time to identify it. He felt like a heel.

"I was answering your suspicions," he said, drowning out the small voice of his conscience. "And explaining—in pantomime, that is—why I'm here."

"That's sweet of you. But unnecessary. There's no reason why you should worry about me."

"Yes, there is. What's wrong with Kate?"

Tiphaine was silent, scrutinizing him with an intensity which was almost as uncomfortable as the doctor's had been. But her questioning eyes were harder to face than Martin's. Finally she gave a long sigh.

"It's Mark. That's what is wrong with Kate."

"Who," Peter said carefully, "is Mark?"

"Someone we—Kate used to know. Her . . . well, he was . . ."

"Mmmhmm," Peter said.

"She was in love with him, and he died."

"How?"

"He was out with a gun. Alone. The gun went off, somehow, and killed him."

"I see. And he's the one she wants—" Peter caught himself just in time. He wasn't supposed to know about the cult of Mother Earth. "To forget," he ended lamely.

Tiphaine didn't seem to have noticed the tiny pause.

"That's the trouble, she can't forget him. It's been almost a year, but she's still—haunted."

Peter leaned back against his pillow.

"He must have been quite a guy."

"He was," Tiphaine said softly, "quite a guy."

"You liked him too?"

"Liked him? Mark?" She considered the question, smiling faintly, eyes remote. "You didn't like Mark. You hated him or you were crazy about him." She smiled suddenly, mockingly. "Most men hated him."

"Oh, that type."

"No, not that type! Well, I guess he was . . . sort of. Women adored him. That was enough to make other men dislike him," she added with a worldly air. "And he could be pretty sarcastic. One look, and one comment in that drawly voice of his, and people just shriveled."

"I don't think I'd have liked him," Peter said.

"Probably not. Though you reminded me of him, at first," she said thoughtfully; and Peter thought, hell, not again. "Until you kissed me," she added.

"I gather you have a basis for comparison," Peter said coolly. He had been wondering why he was so ridiculously jealous of a dead man.

"Mark kissed all the girls. No offense, no hard feelings." Smiling, she put out a delicate finger and ran it down his face from temple to cheek to mouth. "You're dying to know what the difference is, aren't you?"

Peter took her hand and put it firmly down on the spread.

"What are you up to now. Distraction?"

"But there's nothing else to say," she exclaimed. "I don't know any more."

"I think you do."

"Then—if I do—I can't tell you." She stood up and started for the door. With her hand on the knob, she turned to look at him. "But I'm glad you're here, Peter," she said softly.

# Chapter
## 6

AS SOON AS THE HOUSEHOLD HAD GONE TO BED, Peter prowled. No incidents were scheduled for that night—it would be too suspicious, on his first night in the house—but he wanted to get the interior geography of the place clear in his mind. After an hour of sitting in the dark, his night vision was complete. He couldn't risk even the smallest light, not with the household in its present state of nerves.

Like the downstairs, with its wings and additions, the upstairs was a rabbit warren. Luckily only one wing was in full use, the one over the huge séance room he had seen the first night. It had one corridor with rooms on either side. Katharine's rooms, the master suite, occupied the entire end of the wing. His room was as far away from hers as possible, next to the staircase. Tiphaine's smaller chamber adjoined her cousin's, and there were two other rooms, empty guest chambers.

Peter approved the thick carpeting of the corridor, which muffled footsteps, and was happy to find that door hinges and knobs were well oiled. He discovered this by looking into the two unoccupied rooms; he would like to have ascertained whether Katharine locked her door, but was afraid to try it. Ten to one she was lying awake, staring into the darkness; the slightest sound, at door or window, would set her screeching.

If he were in her shoes, he wouldn't know what to do about locks. Do you lock the door against intruders, or leave it unlocked so that help can reach you quickly? After all, ghosts aren't hindered by locks and bolts.

The room across the hall from Tiphaine's was as dark as the proverbial cow's interior, once he had closed the door. Shades and curtains were drawn, and he had to inch his way across the floor, feeling with hands and feet. He didn't pull the drapes back; they were on rings, which might rattle. Instead he slid between them, raised the blind, and pushed back the bolt that kept the window locked.

The first gust of wind set the drapes swinging and produced a slight rattle from the rings. Peter pulled his head back in and got the window shut in a hurry, though he doubted that the sound had been loud enough to rouse anyone. He had seen enough. The window ledges were wide and the wall was covered with vines and trellises. A careful climber could get around from this room to Kate's balcony. He was on his way out of the room when another idea came to him, and he investigated. As he had hoped, the bathroom adjoining his room was meant to serve this room too. The connecting door was closed, but the bolt on this side was not drawn.

Peter studied it for a moment, and a slow smile spread over his face. Yes, it was definitely an idea; and a nice effect it would make, too, if he could work it properly.

He spent the next half hour practicing, with a shoelace and a drawing pin—they called them thumbtacks here—which had held back the curtains in his room. The shoelace was too thick, naturally; he would have to get another kind of twine, white, or transparent plastic, that wouldn't show against the white paint of the door. Plastic fishline, that was the stuff; strong enough to do the job, and thin enough to slide easily through the crack between door and doorframe. He could pick that up in town tomorrow, along with some white-head thumbtacks. At least he had the positions of the latter figured out, along the minute cracks in the inner molding of the door, so there wouldn't be any betraying holes after the pins were removed.

He returned to his room through the bathroom,

and went on through into the hall. The servants didn't sleep in this wing, and it would be a good idea to locate their bedrooms, so he would know how to avoid them.

The Schmidts slept at the other end of the house, over the kitchen; Peter identified the room some distance away by the resounding duet of snores. A good safe distance from the gentry, near the cook's domain; still, if he had been Kate he would have gathered them in closer. He doubted whether they would hear a machine gun, let alone a scream, over the sounds of their own snores. He wanted to explore the downstairs, particularly the library. He fancied he would find Katharine's working desk there, and he was curious to see whether papers, such as her bank receipts, would contain any interesting material. But he decided not to risk the trip. Give her one quiet night, to calm her nerves. Then the next performance would hit her even harder.

Peter spent the morning in bed, catching up on his sleep. It was a very comfortable bed. The cook brought him his lunch, but refused to be inveigled into conversation. Philosophically Peter turned his attention to food. It was excellent. All the homely women he had met so far in this peculiar town were splendid cooks. He wondered if the converse was true.

After lunch he decided that he had loafed long

enough, and got dressed. The sound of guitar music led him to the living room. Tiphaine was wearing stretch pants and a striped jersey in an electric shade of green that made her hair blaze like a fire. She looked up from the guitar in her lap with some surprise.

"Should you be up?" she asked.

"No bleeding from the ears, no excessive drowsiness, no—"

"I haven't been a very good nurse, have I?" Her smile was just a little sarcastic. It did not become her, Peter decided.

"I haven't been a very good patient," he admitted, dropping into a chair. "I got bored, I'm afraid. Sing something."

She did some of the familiar ones, "Venezuela" and "Barbara Allen"; then she began "The False Lover Regained," and Peter obligingly joined in. They did several other songs together, but Tiphaine's voice had lost some of its sparkle; before long she put the guitar down and leaned forward, chin on her hands.

"Peter. How much longer are you going to stay?"

"I'll leave today, if you want me to."

"You will?"

"I'll leave the house. But I'll be sitting out there tonight, watching your window. Probably in a patch of poison ivy," he added more lightly. "That's the sort of thing that generally happens to my grand gestures."

She gave him a slow, bewitching smile.

"Then you really meant it, about being worried about me?"

Peter decided, against his will, that his lady love was a bit laborious.

"Yes, I really meant it."

"And I meant it when I said I was glad you were here. I wanted to tell you—look out, someone's coming. . . ."

She struck a chord at random. Peter leaned back, hands clasped around his raised knee.

"If you sing 'Greensleeves,'" he said in a loud voice, "I'm leaving."

"How did you know?" Tiphaine played up beautifully, raising her own voice just a little.

"That old familiar E minor chord. Not that you don't have the voice for it. It's just that I've rendered that cursed song, and heard it rendered, at every school and village concert since I was three years old. It palls. It's beautiful, but it palls."

He turned his head casually, and then started to get up.

"Don't stand," said Kate, framed in the doorway. "I'd feel bad if gallantry made you swoon at my feet."

After that, of course, he had no choice but to rise.

"If that really worries you, you'd better sit down yourself."

Kate dropped onto the sofa and reached for a cigarette.

"Don't let me interrupt you. Maybe now I'll hear those famous verses."

"Glad to oblige," Peter said. He had spent some of his spare time that morning polishing the said verses. Silently Tiphaine handed him the guitar.

"Interesting," Kate said when he had finished. She blew out a cloud of smoke which hid her expression, but her voice held a note Peter didn't like at all. It was amused, and a little respectful. Still, it was the most pleasant tone he had heard from the lady so far.

"I've been thinking, Tiphaine," she went on casually, "that perhaps Mr. Stewart ought to attend the meeting tonight."

The silence was so thick it could have been cut with a knife. Tiphaine sat motionless, hands clasped on her knee.

"It's up to you," she said finally. "But do you think . . . ?"

Kate's hand moved to her mouth; she took a deep drag on her cigarette.

"Oh, I definitely do think."

Tiphaine turned her head so that the waves of hair veiled her face, and Peter said easily, "What's the meeting about? More folklore?"

"A little experiment," Kate said. "I shan't tell you about it in order not to prejudice you. Unbiased observers are so important, don't you think?"

"Definitely," Peter murmured. Their glances locked, and once again he was aware of that strong, physical pull which had nothing to do with likes and dislikes. To cover his confusion he ran his fingers over the guitar strings, and Kate said sweetly.

"You have such a pleasant voice, Mr. Stewart. Sing something for me, won't you? Some other gem from your own private researches."

Dinner that night was as good as the meals Peter had been getting on trays, if not better. They ate this one in the formal dining room downstairs, *en famille*. His hostess had said nothing about dressing for dinner, so Peter was surprised to see her sweep into the room in what was almost formal evening attire—a long red skirt, which rustled and flared as she walked, and one of her favorite tailored blouses, silk this time, with wide sleeves caught at the wrists by jeweled links, and a barbaric tangle of gold and colored stones around her neck. Tiphaine wore something blue, pale and flowing. In her case, one noticed the girl rather than the clothes.

Conversation was spasmodic. Toward the end of the meal Kate fell into a frowning silence and didn't even pretend to follow the talk of the other two. Her hands were restless, toying with the silverware, and with her wineglass. They waited on themselves, and Kate kept her glass filled.

They were still at the table, and Kate was pouring coffee when Peter heard the doorbell chime. A few minutes later Martin entered, pulling off his driving gloves. His face was ruddy and his hair windblown.

"Colder tonight," he announced, putting his hand on Kate's shoulder. "Thanks, I would like some coffee. My heater seems to be on the blink."

"You ought to trade that old wreck in," Tiphaine said.

"Can't afford it." Martin sat down at Kate's left and accepted a steaming cup of coffee. "No self-respecting dealer would offer me more than a couple of hundred on a trade-in, so I might as well wear it out."

A casual conversation, over coffee, with old friends—but it wasn't even a good performance, Peter thought. The women were both tense as horses before a storm, and Martin's eyes kept coming back to Kate's face. All pretense ended when Kate broke into a discussion of American cars versus foreign cars.

"Mr. Stewart is sitting in tonight, Paul."

Martin couldn't be much of a poker player, his face was too mobile. It registered first surprise, then pleasure.

"Good," he said emphatically. "We need a skeptic."

"But I'm not," Peter said blandly. "I believe in everything. Ghosts, and werewolves, and succubi—"

"We'd better go," Kate said, starting to her feet. She was white to the lips.

Mrs. Adams was already in the séance room when they got there, and Peter wondered uneasily whether the woman had the run of the house, and her own key. She was squatting, in an ungainly fashion, tracing some design on the polished floor with a piece of chalk. In her trailing robes she ought to have looked absurd; but when she straightened up and turned her hard green eyes to him, Peter had no desire to laugh.

"Evening, everybody. Mr. Stewart."

"You don't seem surprised to see Peter," Tiphaine said.

"I knew he'd be here."

"How?"

"They told me." Her voice was brusque, almost impatient, quite unlike the mystical whine in which Peter had heard similar announcements made. Somehow this effect was more chilling.

Peter inspected the room with the sort of interest he might be expected to display on seeing it for the first time. It looked much the same as it had that other night, except that now it was brilliantly lit by two crystal chandeliers. The altar was in place, with fresh candles in the holders. The only difference was the odd diagram which Mrs. Adams had just finished inscribing in the middle of the floor.

It consisted of four concentric circles, of considerable size; the innermost was about four feet in diameter, with each additional circle adding another foot or so. In the center was the familiar six-pointed star, each point ending in a cross, with cabalistic signs occupying each outer angle. The three outer circles had crosses alternating with mystic names; from where he stood Peter could make out a few of them: Jehova, Adonai, Agia.

"Agrippa's circle," he said. "So it's a good spirit you're summoning, is it?"

The listeners were visibly impressed, and Peter thanked his encyclopedic memory and his childhood interest in the macabre.

"Is that what it is?" Martin said. "I'm afraid this particular aspect of folklore has never interested me."

"Since you are an adept," Mrs. Adams said, "perhaps you would like to perform the ceremony?"

"I'm no adept, not even a humble practitioner of the Art. Nor is it my specialty. I'll leave the witchcraft to you, Mrs. Adams."

Tiphaine chuckled softly, but Mrs. Adams was unmoved.

"The Art is not witchcraft—as you know quite well, Mr. Stewart. All right, we've got to start pretty soon. The hour is propitious after eight and before nine. Where are the Schmidts?"

As if on cue, the Schmidts made their appearance, and Mrs. Adams moved to the altar.

"Lights," she said—for all the world like a bloody film director, Peter thought disgustedly. Will Schmidt found the switch, and the room plunged into darkness.

Darkness complete and without alleviation.

The drapes covering the windows were drawn tight. Then a faint glow of light appeared. Mrs. Adams had lit the first candle—by second sight, Peter presumed. The other candles followed, and in the sickly half-light the priestess turned and genuflected toward the altar. She turned the wrong way, though, and a genuine chill ruffled the hair on Peter's neck.

Agrippa and the good spirits be damned; if this old hag wasn't a witch, and a black one at that, he would eat his shoes.

He didn't believe that she was going to summon up any spirits, good or evil. But in a sense she was just as much a witch as the poor bedlamites who were burned for that crime during the ghastly witch hunts of the Middle Ages. She thought she was. The atmosphere was already curdling; his first instant distaste for Mrs. Adams was intensifying into full-blown repulsion.

Mrs. Adams poured some of the liquid from the pitcher into the basin. The liquid was hot; the effect of the steam rising around the old woman's wrinkled features and barbaric hair was enough to set a nervous person screaming. From somewhere in her ample robes Mrs. Adams pulled out a little bag and threw a pinch of its contents into the steaming bowl. A sharp acrid smell of something nasty rose up. Peter coughed.

With peremptory gestures Mrs. Adams beckoned them into the circle, cautioning them in sharp whispers not to scuff out any of the lines.

Peter doubted that, in the darkness, the precaution could have been observed. He wasn't particularly worried about it. The magic circle was for the protection of the magician and his friends, in case the spirits summoned got out of hand. Either Adams was a true believer in which case no spirits were going to materialize, or she was cynic enough to provide a material "ghost"—in which case chalk lines wouldn't be much protection. Peter didn't know what to expect, but he wanted to be prepared for anything; he spent the next few minutes of the ceremony removing his shoes.

The witch was now holding a short stick or baton—her magic wand—which she had produced from among the folds of her robe. Raising the wand she intoned the words, "Raphael, Rael, Miraton, Tarmiel, Rex."

The circle was crowded, with all of them in it, but no one moved. It was also far enough from the dull candlelight so that Peter found it hard to tell who was who; he was surrounded by dark, heavily breathing shapes, and for a mad moment it seemed to him that there were more such shapes than there had been at first. Then he caught a faint gleam from Tiphaine's hair, and felt a warm hand fumble and slip into his hand. He gave it a reassuring squeeze and let it go.

The priestess spoke again, this time in English. "Infernal powers, you who carry disturbance into the universe, leave your somber habitation and render yourselves to the place beyond the

Styx. If you hold in your power him whom I call, I conjure you, in the name of the King of Kings, to let this person appear at the hour which I will indicate."

The voice stopped, and Peter raised his drooping head. Damn the woman; the words were prosaic, almost pedantic, but the tone was hypnotic as hell. Again he speculated about drugs. Something in the coffee at dinner? Something in that vile-smelling liquid in the bowl?

Adams stepped back out of the circle and Peter took advantage of her movement to shuffle out of Tiphaine's reach. He could see why she wanted to hold hands, and he would have enjoyed it himself, for other reasons. But if he decided to take a walk, he didn't want any clinging fingers holding him back.

Crouching, Mrs. Adams sprinkled something over the floor, something that pattered faintly, like sand or fine birdseed. Peter knew it wasn't either one. Then she rose to her full height, stretched out her wand, and shouted, "May he who is dust wake from his sleep. May he step out of his dust and answer to my demands, which I will make in the name of the Father of all men."

Nice, ambiguous invocation, Peter thought, trying to keep his critical sense awake under the bombardment of gibberish. Sounded like an appeal to the Christian God; but the witches used the same terms for their dark Master. What a voice the woman had! She bellowed like a bull.

But her shrieks were spookier than the usual medium's shivery whisper. And, in a dreadful fashion, they made better sense. The voice that summons the strengthless dead must carry a long, long way.

Mrs. Adams squatted again and flung two small objects down among the scattered dirt on the floor—white, hard objects, that contacted the wood with a brittle click.

*"Exurgent mortui et ad me veniunt! Ego sum, te peto et videre queo!"*

She made a series of rapid gestures with her hands. All the candles went out.

Momentarily impressed, Peter realized that it had been expert legerdemain. He had seen good stage magicians do that with candles. The smell of hot wax did not overcome the pungent smell of the liquid, which now seemed overpowering. Peter felt his head spin. The room was closed in, and dead; yet he had a sense that somewhere, someone was waiting. After the first startled gasp the others had fallen silent, but Katharine's breath rattled in her throat.

If anything was going to appear, it would appear now. The ceremony was complete, the adjuration had been made. More practically, the total darkness was very useful to the appearance of nonspiritual spirits. Pete left his shoes and slid away. It was so dark he couldn't see his hand in front of his face, so he felt sure his absence wouldn't be noticed immediately. Only his sense of location told him where he was; he knew where he was going. The door or the window, both at the far ends of the room. He suspected the latter. It was a convenient spot for materialization, as he knew from personal experience.

Something was happening, down there by the windows. The curtains were moving, back from the center. He heard the rattle of the wooden rings and saw a pale rectangle appear, and widen. The light seemed bright after the intense blackness. Only one problem. There was no one in sight who could have pulled those draperies.

The figure did not appear in the window, as he had. They—whoever they were—had had more time to plan their effect. It was a good one, too. The figure that rose slowly up from the floor was featureless, only a black silhouette—a man's silhouette, that of a young man, erect and slender.

Peter, halfway between the stunned, huddled group in the circle and the "materialization," stopped short as a sudden suspicion fired his brain. That silhouette was oddly familiar. It looked . . . it looked like . . .

"God Almighty," he said in a whisper which echoed through the hushed room. Then he launched himself in the longest tackle he had ever made in his life.

He was so relieved when his outflund arms met solid, human flesh that he almost lost his grip.

"Lights," he yelled and added an expletive as a pair of very material teeth found his hand. The creature he was holding had turned into an animal; wriggling, writhing, kicking, biting, it kept him fully occupied till the lights finally went on. Blinded, Peter fought off one final spasm; then his opponent subsided into a sobbing heap, and Peter, slightly nauseated, rose to his feet.

It was Timmy, of course; he was unique, though the marred face was now hidden in his bent arms. Martin was the one who had responded to Peter's demand for light. He came trotting down the length of the room, reaching the spot just as Timmy flung himself over in a violent spasm. His body stiffened, his eyes rolled back into his head, and a trace of foam appeared at the corner of his distorted mouth. Peter stepped back, and Martin dropped to his knees by the writhing body, mercifully hiding the ghastly face.

"Epilepsy?" Peter asked.

"Yes. Poor devil, that on top of everything else." Martin shifted slightly to one side and Peter saw, before he hastily averted his eyes, that the doctor had jammed a folded handkerchief into Timmy's mouth. "That's all I can do now; the attack should pass off in a few minutes. No, Kate, don't look at him, he's not—a very attractive sight."

Kate stopped where she was, a good ten feet away. Her face looked like a death mask, skin stretched whitely over the bones; but under her pallor there was a look of pitiful relief.

"Timmy?" she said. "Only . . . Timmy?"

"Only," Peter said bitterly. He had unconsciously been scrubbing at his hands with his own handkerchief; looking down at it, he was surprised to see that it was stained with red. Katharine's eyes followed his.

"You're hurt," she said; and Peter, fascinated, watched a new trickle slither down from under his cuff.

"He's got a knife," he said urgently, turning to the doctor. "Find it before he wakes up, for God's sake."

"Here it is." Martin pulled it out from under the body, whose spasms seemed to be subsiding. "Lucky he didn't fall on the blade."

"Lucky for whom?" Peter asked nobody in particular. He pushed back his sleeve and found a slit in shirt and skin which ran for several inches along his forearm.

Martin took his hand and pulled it down to eye level.

"Had a tetanus shot lately? That's good; the knife is an ordinary switchblade, looks new, but anything that's been in contact with Timmy is bound to be filthy. It's just a cut, Kate can handle the first aid. I've got to get this boy to the hospital right away."

Peter nodded, distracted by this description of Timmy. He couldn't be very old, at that; but it was hard to think of him in terms of anything so normal as years old. Now that he had had it brought to his attention, the cut was beginning to sting. In the excitement he hadn't even noticed when it was inflicted.

"Shall I call an ambulance for you?" Katharine asked calmly. Martin shook his head.

"No, no, he'll be all right when he comes out of it, just a little shaky. I'll drive him myself. There—it's passing now."

Timmy's legs were flat, except for an occasional twitch. As the doctor lifted his patient's filthy head, Peter turned away.

"Come upstairs, Mr. Stewart, and I'll find a Band-Aid for you," Kate said. "I'd leave the TLC to Tiphaine, but she'll be busy soothing Bertha for some time yet."

Peter glanced at the group that was still huddled in the circle. Tiphaine, white-faced and tight-lipped, had her arms around the cook's heaving shoulders. Will Schmidt wasn't being much help; he looked as if he wanted to run.

Peter followed Katharine's rustling skirts to the door and then stopped.

"I don't want to bleed all over that Persian rug."

Turning, she took him by the wrist and raised his arm.

"Your shirt's ruined anyway," she said unconcernedly. "Drip down into your sleeve."

Her fingers were firm and cold as ice. The contact, the first physical one that had occurred between them, startled both, and for a second Katharine stood motionless, staring at their joined hands. There was blood on her fingers now, and when she turned away and started up the stairs, she kept her right hand out away from her body, holding her skirts with the other. At the top of the stairs she stopped with a sudden startled intake of breath and whirled, so abruptly that she almost bumped into him.

"Peter. I just realized—"

"What?"

"It was Timmy. Only Timmy."

"Yes. Just a crude, cheap trick," Peter said soothingly.

He had underestimated the lady; this time she was not seeking reassurance. She shook her head impatiently.

"No, no, that's just it. How could he have done anything so stupid? We'd have recognized him."

"It was pretty dark. . . ."

"It wouldn't have been." From a pocket hidden in the sweeping folds of her skirt she produced a small flashlight.

Peter's lips pursed in a silent whistle, and he studied her resolute face with reluctant admiration.

"Timmy didn't plan this," he said thoughtfully. "He hasn't the wits. And if someone else put him up to it, that someone would have taken precautions. Timmy's face is unique. He would have been supplied with—is that what you're thinking?"

"A mask, yes. You didn't search him?"

"I didn't even know he had a knife," Peter said ruefully; and her face softened, minutely.

"I'm sorry, I forgot. Come along."

Ten minutes later she surveyed her handiwork critically, and nodded.

"I'll ask Martin to have a look at it in the morning, but that should do. You're looking a little green. Have you any other injuries?"

"No," Peter said, trying to ignore the various areas which Timmy's feet and fists had contacted.

"Do you need any help getting to bed?"

Peter looked at her. After a moment the corners of her mouth turned up, stiffly, as if not used to such exercise, and she said, "I'll send Will up."

"Never mind," Peter said sadly. He wondered what she would look like if she really smiled. The sardonic grimace that passed for that expression wasn't really a smile; it never reached her eyes.

"While I'm thinking about it . . ." Katharine reached for the telephone by the bed and dialed a number.

"Is Dr. Martin there yet? . . . Yes, please. I'll wait. . . . Paul, it's Kate. Everything all right? . . . Good. I want to ask you something. It occurred to me that Timmy might have been prepared for a masquerade. Could you check to see whether he had any sort of disguise, a wig or a mask, tucked away? One of those thin plastic masks would fit into a pocket. . . ."

She listened, and her face changed. "Oh. I see . . . No, that's all right. Good night, Paul."

She hung up.

"They looked through his clothing when they

undressed him. Paul says he plans to burn the foul stuff."

"No mask?"

"No nothing. Good night, Mr. Stewart. Thank you."

"You called me Peter before."

"A momentary aberration."

She went out, closing the door emphatically.

Richard is himself again, Peter thought. At least she had the grace to say thanks. Damn the woman, she had a brain like a razor. She wasn't thanking him for the damage he had incurred on her behalf; that had been pure bad luck, and she gave it precisely the value it deserved. She was thanking him for helping to restore her slipping grasp on reality.

He slid between the sheets with a muffled groan. He was going to have a few sore spots tomorrow. Damn Timmy, too. . . .

That same keen brain of Kate's wouldn't miss the other implications of this evening's fascinating performance. It had worked out fine, just as well as anything he could have engineered. Give her another day or two, to relax—and to think. To realize that, by no stretch of the imagination, could the figure she had seen on the balcony have been that of Timmy. To wonder why anything so unconvincing as Timmy had been presented at all. To begin to imagine horrors all the worse for being unknown. One more day, then a quick, hard blow straight to the core of the problem. That ought to do it.

# Chapter
## 7

"YOU LET HIM GO?" PETER REPEATED INCREDU-
lously. The news took his mind momentarily off
his aches and pains; Martin was rebandaging his
arm, and was being unexpectedly heavy-handed
about it.

"What else could I do with him?"

"I can think of several things."

"He isn't aggressive," Martin said. "He fought
back when you attacked him, as any animal
would."

"Attacked him!"

"Oh, you had to, I'm not blaming you. But
that's all he is—an animal, barely functioning beyond instinctive behavior. What else could I do,
Peter? The state institutions are overcrowded, and
pretty horrible. Volz knows how to handle

Timmy. I've told him about the knife, and he's promised to keep a closer eye on the poor devil. Of course, if you insist on preferring charges . . ."

They were in Martin's office. Peter had driven himself to town instead of waiting for the doctor to make a house call, so that he could pick up his belongings from the Inn. Kate had indeed been thinking. She had come in with Peter's breakfast tray and asked him to stay on for a few days. She mentioned his desire to do some reading in Stephan's library, but neither of them was fooled by that excuse. Timmy's downfall had convinced her, if not of Peter's *bona fides*, at least of his usefulness.

"Oh, the hell with it," Peter said. "Why should I prefer charges?"

"That's decent of you," Martin said gratefully. "Wait a minute, you'd better have a sling for that arm, for a day or two anyway."

Peter started to protest and then thought better of it. He had no objection to publicity, nor to appearing more helpless than he was. Beneath his satisfaction at the way things were working out, a small ugly doubt festered. Since he hadn't engineered the Timmy episode—who had?

"I suppose Mrs. A. is keeping quiet this morning," he said casually.

"I had a few words to say to her," Martin admitted, with a faint smile. "Of course she denies putting Timmy up to it."

"Who else could have done it?"

"The evidence certainly seems to point to her.

Still . . ." The doctor stepped back to inspect his work, and nodded. "Still, I was frankly surprised. She's a genuine fanatic; really believes in all that nonsense. I wouldn't have thought she'd descend to trickery."

"Isn't that one of the odd vagaries these people have? I've heard of séance mediums caught in the most flagrant deceit, who stoutly maintained that the rest of the phenomena were genuine."

"I know. As you say, it's a psychological quirk and we just have to accept it. But I think I put the fear of God into Mrs. Adams. She won't be trying anything else."

Peter didn't voice his skepticism. Mrs. Adams was a tough customer—too tough, he suspected, for the mild doctor. Still, Martin had a way with him and perhaps he could be forceful when he got angry enough.

As he went along the hall, trying to keep his coat from falling off the shoulder whose sleeve wasn't occupied, a dim little figure darted out from under the stairs.

"Oh . . . Mrs. Martin." Peter relaxed. "You startled me."

"You ought to button that coat," she said faintly, and did so. Then she looked up at him, her hands still on his coat front.

"Mr. Stewart," she whispered, "how much longer are you staying in Middleburg?"

"I don't know. I thought—"

"Sssh." Her hands covered his mouth. "Please,

not so loudly. You must go away. Go away now. And take her with you."

"Who?" Peter obediently lowered his voice. "Tiphaine?"

"No, no. No. The other one. Today, go today. Next week will be—"

The office door opened and Mrs. Martin froze.

"Oh . . . my dear. I see you had the same thought I did," Martin said affectionately. "Have you persuaded Mr. Stewart to stay for a cup of coffee?"

She shook her head mutely.

"Mrs. Martin was kind enough to come to my rescue," Peter said. "I must have looked like a contortionist coming down the hall."

"Oh, I see. Should have thought of it myself. How about that coffee, though?"

"I'd better not. Got a few errands to do. Will I see you later?"

"Tomorrow, if not this afternoon. I'll be out."

"Good. Thank you, Mrs. Martin."

At the door he hesitated for a moment, looking back into the semidusk of the hall; but Mrs. Martin had already disappeared. Timmy wasn't the only one who was a little off. But the cause of Mrs. Martin's distress was only too obvious, and too normal. Martin had been spending a lot of time with a younger, richer, more attractive, woman. Even without the millions, Kate's physical attraction was enough to—

Peter stopped himself right there, none too pleased at the direction his thoughts were taking.

It was almost the end of October, and if he stayed around much longer, he was going to start liking this part of the world. The sunlight was warm and seductive, with just enough snap in the air to be invigorating. A carpet of colored leaves covered streets and sidewalks and lawns, but many of the trees were still spectacular in gold and red.

As he strolled down the street, he passed children rolling in leaf piles, shrieking with pleasure. The busy rakers were almost all black, and as Peter walked on he noticed something. As soon as they saw him coming, they retreated. It wasn't just his imagination. One man, who had worked his heap of fallen leaves almost up to the sidewalk, literally dropped his rake and fled.

On impulse he turned right, onto a side street, instead of continuing toward the shopping area. This was a block of smaller houses, and there were fewer hired workers. Peter went on at a deliberately leisurely pace, like a visitor admiring the well-tended gardens and neat lawns. Then it happened again. The yardman, a young fellow of about Jackson's age, took his rake with him when he retreated, but the intent was the same.

Peter proceeded, frowning. Small incidents, both of them, but they were disturbing, because they recalled other incidents and impressions which he hadn't wanted to contemplate. That first night in Middleburg, when he had thought of it as a cat-town, pretending to sleep, but watching through slitted eyes . . . maybe it hadn't been just a neurotic fancy. Maybe his busy subconscious mind had been formulating data which he hadn't consciously noticed.

When he roused himself from his musings, he realized that he was in a part of town which he hadn't explored. He couldn't be far from the center of town; it was ridiculous to get lost in a hick town the size of Middleburg. He turned right, went on a few steps—and found himself facing a big white house, built in the gingerbread style of the 1880's. It looked like many of its neighbors, except for one thing—a sign which read "Middleburg Historical Association and City Museum."

There must be someone in the museum who could give him directions. He turned up the walk.

On the front door another sign gave the hours: 9 to 5 weekdays, 1 to 5 Saturdays and Sundays. The door was unlocked. There was no one in sight when Peter stepped into the hall, which was furnished like that of an ordinary dwelling house except that the antique furniture bore neat labels, and the walls were covered with old prints and paintings.

A door on the right opened, just a crack, and a face peered out, a thin spectacled face crowned with an untidy coil of gray hair. Peter recognized the woman who had been introduced to him at the Folklore Society meeting. Miss . . . Device— that was it; he remembered the name because it had struck a familiar note, though he couldn't remember offhand where he had heard it.

Either Miss Device needed a new pair of glasses, or she was preoccupied; it was several seconds before her thin lips cracked in a smile of welcome. She came out of the other room in sections, first an arm, then a leg modestly covered by heavy stockings and a skirt which reached three inches below her knee, then the rest of her body.

"Mr. Stewart, is it not? We've been hoping you'd pay us a visit."

She looked as if she meant it; the greedy gleam in her gray eyes reminded Peter of other faces, those of guards and curators in various unpopular tourist attractions which he had had occasion to visit. The poor devils got bored, sitting around all day with no one to talk to, and when an unwary visitor did appear, they leaped on him like ghouls.

Peter sighed, but not audibly. It would be gauche and unkind to tell the woman that he had only been looking for directions. It would also be useless. He wasn't going to get out of here without the full tour.

First he heard the interminable, dull life history of every town worthy whose portrait adorned the walls of the entrance hall. The contents of the next room were no more enthralling. The objects lovingly preserved in glass cases were just as boring as the ones he had viewed in little local museums abroad: old letters, receipts for tallow and wool and tobacco, corroded tools, patched coarse pottery.

Without Miss Device, he would have passed straight through the next room. But this exhibit, which filled half a dozen case, was clearly her pride and joy, and a blush colored her thin cheeks as she admitted that she had done the work with her own hands.

"It took me over ten years," she said.

Peter murmured something appreciative, and gave the contents of the nearest case a closer look.

They were clever, if you cared for that sort of thing: dolls, dozens of dolls, dressed with meticulous attention to detail in the costumes of the various historical eras since the founding of the town. Bearded courtiers of the time of James I, in cloaks and ruffs; little-girl dolls in homespun gowns and caps; a court lady dressed in satin, with a diminutive lace collar and curled ringlets. Intrigued, Peter bent over the case. The lady's curls looked like real hair, and the face, modeled out of clay or—no, something finer—wax, perhaps, was so individualistic as to suggest an attempt at portraiture.

He turned to the next case, which contained costumes of the eighteenth century—workmen in leather aprons, ladies in towering powdered wigs, gentlemen in embroidered waistcoats. These were no ready-made dolls, dressed by a clever seamstress; the figures themselves had been individually modeled and painted.

The exhibit was an impressive piece of work, and Peter said so; this time, for a change, his good manners paid an unexpected dividend. Miss Device became so flustered that she excused herself and left him alone.

Peter glanced again at the dolls. His unexpressed opinion would not have pleased Miss Device; he was brooding on the sterility of ten years spent on such a hobby. The ancient and no doubt honorable line of the Device family was ending with the conventional whimper. Once again the name struck that odd note of familiarity, but try as he might he couldn't place it.

He had had enough of dolls and shy spinsters, and just about enough of the prim little museum. He might as well go on through the other rooms—at a fast walk—and try to sneak out without Miss Device's seeing him.

But the next room was something of a surprise. The contents were familiar enough, but they seemed out of place in this tidy Victorian house. Not so incongruous to the room was the figure which stood, hands clasped behind its back, staring at a particularly elegant example of a pillory.

"Hello, General," Peter said. "I didn't know you liked museums."

Volz turned.

"So you're up and about, are you? What's the idea of damaging a perfectly good stablehand?"

He snorted. Evidently this was supposed to be a joke.

"You people amaze me," Peter said. "Back in the old country we have our share of village idiots, but we don't accept their iniquities quite so casually."

"Like hell you don't. Old Sam, who beats his wife to a pulp whenever he gets drunk; little Mamie, who sets fire to things . . . You just don't expect to find the same tolerance here. Damned British arrogance," he added, and went off into a paroxysm of grating laughter.

Feeling himself at a slight disadvantage—the old so-and-so definitely had a point—Peter joined him as he turned his fascinated gaze back toward the infernal device before him. The wood had weathered over the years, but was still intact. Rusty chains dangled from the cross bars, and the holes were suggestive, even now.

Flanking the pillory were the stocks, with holes for hands and feet instead of for the head, and an object which Peter was slower to recognize. Somehow—damned British arrogance?—he hadn't expected to find one here. Pillory and stocks were common punishment in the Colonial period, but a ducking stool? Then he remembered that it had been used to rehabilitate shrews and nags as well as to test witches; for some reason the recollection made him feel better.

"Where's the Iron Maiden?" he asked facetiously; and was decidedly taken aback when Volz bobbed his head at the other corner.

Peter turned. They were all there, the objects he had seen in the musty dungeons of Nuremberg and the Tower of London—the rack, the boot, thumbscrews. They looked even worse set against the clean-painted walls of this sunny room than they had in the stone-walled grimness of the fortresses.

Volz watched his face with ugly amusement.

"Why so surprised? This stuff goes back to the seventeenth century. That's when the colony was founded. The boys brought along some little bits of home, that's all."

"But I thought the colony was founded on the basis of religious freedom."

"Too much freedom," said Volz, not so cryptically. "I can see you don't know much history, Stewart. Thinking in terms of the Inquisition? All this stuff was part of the normal interrogation process, for criminals of various kinds. Heresy and witchcraft were crimes, sure; but we had our share of that here too, you know. Remember Salem?"

"Certainly. But I thought it was an isolated instance. The last flowering of a vicious belief."

"No, no. Just the most publicized. Look here."

He indicated a glass case in the center of the room. At first glance its contents were a refreshing change from the rusty horrors which filled the rest of the room. They were, for the most part, old books and documents. Peter's attention was caught by the central exhibit, a badly executed but evocative drawing of a woman's face. The features were uncannily familiar, from the pale thin mouth to the untidy gray hair; but the style of the drawing dated its subject to a far earlier century than the one Miss Device now graced. Yet the contrast jogged that one hitherto elusive memory. Peter didn't need the identifying label to recall the affair, with all its ugly details.

"Elizabeth Device," he muttered. "Good God, of course! The Lancashire Witches. Sixteen . . . thirty-something? Old Demdike, the head witch of the coven, her real name was Device. The whole damned family were witches. Oh, no. Don't tell me—"

"Oh, yes." Volz gave a hoarse shout of laughter, and one of the vile gadgets caught the vibration and whispered rustily. "Our little lady is the last descendant of one of the most notorious families in the history of witchcraft. Funniest thing I ever heard of. Especially when . . ." He added a description of Miss Device which, while probably accurate, was unquestionably defamatory. Peter grinned unwillingly. Volz had a mind like a sewer, but he also had a gift for pungent description.

"I didn't know any of the family emigrated," he said, turning back to the glass case.

"It wasn't publicized," Volz said dryly. "The boys—two brothers they were—denied the family. But they made the mistake of bringing along a gossipy aunt—that one—and it wasn't long before the town found out. Those"—his nod indicated the moldering documents in the case—"those are the records of the trial."

Peter studied the long wrinkled face and squinted eyes. Not a pretty face, no; but still . . .

"What did they do to her?"

"She died during the ducking procedure. Third time down."

"Drowned?"

"Probably a heart attack, from terror," Volz said indifferently. "The men who handled the stool were experts; they didn't want the suspects to drown. It must have frustrated the hell out of them when the old lady died on their hands." He chuckled.

Peter looked at him in distaste, and had a sudden, horrific vision of Volz's stocky form clad in the doublet and ruff of the period he was talking about. Black doublet, of course, and cropped hair; he'd be a Puritan, and a great little prosecutor. Studying Volz's pouting mouth and beady eyes, Peter amended the description. A witch pricker, that's what he'd have been, enjoying the shame of the exposed witches as much as the money he received for sticking pins in strategic parts of their bodies.

Volz was not completely insensitive; his eyes narrowed at Peter's unconcealed disgust, and he said, "Let me show you the Iron Maiden. It's a particularly good one."

"No thanks. I'm weak already, and I don't want to spoil my appetite."

"Yes. Too bad about last night." Volz's eyes lingered pleasurably on Peter's sling.

You little bastard, Peter thought. Aloud he said, "Someone put Timmy up to that performance.

Aren't you even slightly curious about who is corrupting your servants?"

"He might of thought of it himself. Who knows how these crazy people think?"

Peter gave him a sweet smile; his accompanying thoughts were better not revealed. Whatever the mess going on in this town, Volz had to be part of it. He wasn't even bothering any longer to conceal his hostility.

"I didn't see your car in front," he said. "Or I'd ask for a lift."

"Having a little trouble with the carburetor, left it at the garage." Volz puffed out his chest. "Great exercise, walking. Be good for you."

"Mmm." Peter said. He left Volz in rapt contemplation of the rack.

At the corner of the next street he caught sight of the church steeple, and knew where he was. He also knew where he was going. To the gentry of Middleburg, only one of the town's three garages was The Garage. Tom and Mack's, not far from the hotel.

Volz's shiny Lincoln was parked in the lot, but there was no sign of Jackson. Peter found him in the alley behind the garage, having a cigarette with two young men about his own age. At the sight of Peter, the two boys simply melted away. Jackson stood his ground, tossing his cigarette butt to the ground, but his expression was sullen.

"Got time for a cup of coffee?" Peter asked.

"Where? In the Colonial Room?"

"Anywhere you say."

"Ain't you scared you'll get in bad with my boss?"

Peter, who was already exasperated by his most recent encounter with Volz, made a grimace. Jackson's face did not relax.

"Leave me alone," he said. "I told you before, I'm not sticking my neck out."

"Jackson, why don't you get the hell out of this town? This isn't all the world, not even all the country. This place—"

"Stinks. So how do I get out? You gonna adopt me? Listen, Stewart, you're trouble. It was bad enough before, now you've had the sign put on you." Jackson's voice dropped to a whisper. He glanced uneasily over his shoulder; and Peter's nerves tightened. The signs of fear, which would have been disturbing enough in an ordinary man, were unnerving coming from Jackson.

"What sign?" Peter asked; unconsciously, his voice had also become lower.

"I've already said more than I should. For God's sake. Stewart, I told you, you're poison. Do you really want to drag me down too? Then stick around; that's all you have to do to finish me, just—stick around."

There was only one possible answer to that agonized plea, Peter turned on his heel and walked away.

On his way back to the hotel he stopped in several shops, to pick up odds and ends such as toothpaste, and a gift for his unenthusiastic hostess. The drugstore still retained its small town apothecary atmosphere; as Peter stood brooding darkly over the brightly colored rows of toothpaste, the proprietor spoke from behind the counter.

"Looking for something in particular, mister?"

"Just trying to make up my mind." Peter selected a package at random. "Is there any difference, really?"

"Not much. It's kind of confusing, I guess, for a furriner." Peter glanced up, eyebrows raised, and the man said, "You must be the writer fella who's staying at the Inn. English, ain't you?"

Peter admitted the fact, and the man extended his hand.

"Olivetti's my name."

"Stewart."

"Oh. Then you ain't related to that other young fella who used to come in here. English, too, he was."

Peter pocketed his change.

"Was?"

"Yep, he's dead. Shot hisself."

"Shot . . ." Peter turned back. "Suicide?"

"Well, the coroner *said* it was a accident." Olivetti leaned both elbows on the counter and prepared to enjoy himself. "But everybody knew he wasn't the careless sort. Got mixed up with that female, old Stephan's niece. She's poison, she is."

"Killed himself for love?" Peter leaned his elbows on the counter too. When in Rome . . .

"Well, now, he didn't seem like that kind neither."

"What kind was he?" Peter asked.

Olivetti turned and spat neatly into some invisible container behind the counter. A melodious echo sounded, but Peter was too absorbed in the conversation to appreciate this survival from America's past.

"Owed me fifty bucks," Olivetti said briefly. "I wasn't the only one, neither. You figure it."

A fussy old lady hobbled up, demanding advice, and Olivetti turned away, with an invitation to drop in any time. Peter left.

There were, actually, several ways of "figuring it." Peter considered them as he did his other errands. His conversations with the shop attendants were not so casual as they seemed, and the comments he heard interested him very much. The languishing lady who ran the flower shop remembered Kate's dead lover as a "sweet boy, with the most sensitive eyes"; the grocer referred darkly to ruined village maidens and irate fathers; the high school girl behind the counter in Woolworth's had never met him, but she remembered him, "you bet your sweet life, mister, you couldn't forget a guy like that." Loaded with parcels, an inappropriate bunch of red roses, and a mass of vital but indigested information, Peter headed hotelward.

His room was neat and airless; it was odd how even a few days of nonoccupancy could remove the lived-in look of a room. Peter collected his clothes and tossed them into his suitcase. Habit, born of years of transient lodgings, made him recheck all the drawers.

He found it in the bureau, in the upper drawer, the same one in which he had found the crucifix. The meaning of this object was not so ambiguous.

It was a doll. No, Peter thought; the old word came, unsought and unwelcome, into his mind. A poppet. The old word, which sounded so cute and innocuous, and which had such a deadly significance.

This was no crude clay image bristling with pins. It was a work of art, a miniature model, barely eight inches high, dressed in tiny slacks and doll-sized sweater; there were even little leather shoes on the feet. The features were modeled with loving—no, scratch that word—with care. And—this was the detail that really got him—the shaggy cap of blond hair was not only a good imitation of his, it *was* his. Real hair.

Peter picked the doll up. As he studied the features more carefully, a wry smile touched his face. Clever; yes, clever as hell, but there was a hint of caricature which was reassuringly malicious and, therefore, human. Was his nose really that long?

The eyes—he couldn't judge them. They were covered with a narrow wisp of black cloth tied around the head like a blindfold. The miniature hands were bound together at the wrists.

Peter weighed the image in his hand. It wasn't very heavy. Just cloth, from the look of it, stuffed with cotton or some similar material. Except for the head. The intent was clear enough, but puzzling in its very lack of violence. No pins. If his memory served him correctly, they usually used pins.

"They" being the witches and warlocks who fashioned little images of their enemies, using the principle of sympathetic magic to give them the identity of the would-be victim, so that any indignity or harm perpetrated on the image would be suffered by the living man or woman.

So, no pins. It was a warning—perhaps a threat—and a hindrance. The bound hands and blinded eyes—ignorance and impotence, that was what they had wished upon him.

They, again. The doll certainly suggested one specific person. But if he hadn't happened to pass the museum, by pure accident, he wouldn't have known about Miss Device's pretty little hobby.

Mrs. Adams, and the cult of Magna Mater; Miss Device and her dolls; Volz's filthy mind and overt antagonism; Timmy . . . How many of them were there? Or had one person employed a variety of devices to incriminate the innocent and blur the picture?

It certainly seemed that some other person in Middleburg besides himself had it, as they said, "in for" Kate More. Now he had got the sign, as Jackson put it. Why? Did the unknown view him as an ally of Kate's? Possibly. The doll had not turned up until after the Timmy episode, in which he had openly supported Kate. On the other hand, he didn't know when the doll had been put in the drawer; he hadn't been in his room for several days. A complicated image like that one would take some little time to make.

Another possibility was that he was interfering, somehow, with the unknown plotter's purpose; that his subversive activities against Kate had been observed, and disapproved of. But that didn't make sense, because the end result of the series of supernatural happenings, his own and the others, must be the same: the annihilation of Katharine More. Unless . . . unless the other person (or persons) wanted the same result, for a different reason. A hypothesis slid sneakily into his unreceptive mind, and he considered it sourly. No use thinking about it; he would have to do some more investigating before he had enough data to work with. It was only one of a number of possibilities, after all.

Peter shelved that idea for future consideration, and went on to his third possibility: that Kate Ross herself was the perpetrator of the other tricks, including the ones which had been aimed against him. So far as he knew, nothing had happened which she couldn't have engineered herself, from the phony nightmares to the involvement of Timmy. Why she should want to make herself look like a budding psychotic he didn't know. Again, there were a few possible explanations, but no proof. But that was the trouble with all his ideas: nobody, except himself, had any obvious motives.

One thing was clear—and it was just about the only thing that was. He had to know more. Unknown quantities were always potentially dangerous; in this case the danger was no longer merely potential.

He looked down at the doll and moved by a wild impulse, began to pluck at the string that bound the small hands. He felt a crazy reluctance to damage the image; it took him some time to unwind the string without hurting the inanimate wrists. As he did so, something sharp pricked the ball of his finger. Maybe he'd been wrong about the pins. . . . But when he located the almost invisible end of the sharp object, and pulled it out of the stuffed palm, it was not a pin. It was a fingernail clipping, curved and thin and pointed.

His fingernail clipping, just as it was his hair—parts of himself, added to the image, which gave the sympathetic identification greater force. The last time he had performed that particular hygienic ceremony had been—here, at the hotel? Or at Kate's house? He couldn't remember. The hair must have come from the barbershop. Or had someone sneaked in while he was asleep, and raped a lock? Either notion was impossible. He had a mental image of Miss Device scuttling into the masculine confines of Alfie's Barber Shop and snatching a lock of hair from under Alfie's broom. His mind reeled.

It would be difficult to imitate one of Miss Device's dolls, but not impossible. The blind, helpless eyes bothered him. He plucked at the blindfold, but it didn't move. Sewn into place, perhaps. He turned the doll over to look, and his lips pursed in a silent whistle.

Not just a hindrance; a definite warning. On the back of the image was a tiny white patch; the color made its shape quite distinct against the black fabric. It was in the shape of a heart, and it was sewn, or glued, slightly to the left of center, just under the shoulder blade.

Symbolic, not anatomically accurate. But clear. The heart is just as easily reached from the back as from the front. Peter had the distinct impression that the symbolism was not that of a love charm.

When he left the hotel, the doll was in his suitcase. He told himself, ironically, that he was getting quite attached to the thing—even if its nose was too long. He wasn't quite willing to admit that he wanted to keep it safe—away from any sharp objects which just might be inserted into that target on its back.

# Chapter

## 8

PETER HAD LUNCH IN TOWN AND GOT BACK TO THE house at a time when he knew half the inhabitants would be taking naps. Kate usually slept after lunch; no wonder, with the disturbed nights she had been having. The Schmidts would be in the kitchen or in their room, and Tiphaine was probably out somewhere. At any rate, she wouldn't be looking for him in the library.

Like the living room, it was definitely a man's room, but not that of a man whose acquaintance Peter would have been keen on having. The deep leather armchairs and dark, heavy furniture were all right; so were the fine oak paneling and the walls lined with books. But there was a suggestion of feminine luxuriousness about the embroidered cushions and soft hassocks scattered about; and who in his right mind would want to live with those pictures? Hans Baldung's "Witches at the Sabbath"; the Durer engraving of the four beefy females—who might simply have been having a girlish chat, *au naturel*, if Peter hadn't known the title of the picture; a set of medieval woodcuts, crude in style and even cruder in subject, showing executions of various kinds—hanging, burning, the headsman's block . . .

Dear old Uncle Stephan, Peter thought, and turned his attention to the books.

Magic and witchcraft, sorcery and alchemy; volumes in German and French and Arabic, scholarly works such as Murray and Frazer; the classics, Reginald Scot and James I; the screwballs, such as Montague Summers. It was the most complete collection of books on the occult Peter had ever seen; fifteen years ago he would have rubbed his hands together and sailed in. Now he felt bored and slightly disgusted. It was a hell of a hobby for a grown man.

But everything he might need was here. He found a number of references to the poppets, or dolls; the idea of waxen images was old, very old, and distributed through many cultures. Sympathetic magic, according to Sir James Frazer. Used for love charms, ritual murder, even curing illness. And probably quite effective too, in a culture where people believed in its efficacy. But the books only confirmed his vague memories; they told him nothing new.

He put the *History of Magic* back on the shelf and went to the ornate mahogany desk that stood in front of the windows. A cursory investigation told him that he was wasting his time. Kate didn't work in this room; none of her papers, scholarly or financial, were here. He could see her point.

For want of anything better to do, he selected a book at random and sat down in a chair. It was a comfortable chair—almost too comfortable. It didn't feel like leather, but like some softer, more yielding, substance, and Peter was unpleasantly reminded of a horror story he had once read about furniture which embraced its owner. He grimaced, and settled himself firmly. Jolly old Uncle Stephan . . .

Two hours later there were books all over the floor around the chair, and Peter was still reading. A watcher, if there had been one, might have deduced that he was not at all happy about what he was reading.

Katharine remained invisible the rest of the day. She didn't appear for dinner, and Peter asked about her.

"No, she's all right," Tiphaine said. "Just resting. She often has a tray in her room when she's working, or just feeling antisocial."

They served themselves, as was the household

custom; Mrs. Schmidt put a savory-smelling casserole and a salad in front of Tiphaine, and left the room.

"Smells good," Peter said, accepting a full plate.

"Mrs. Schmidt is a marvelous cook, even if she isn't the most cheerful companion in the world. She grows her own herbs. Fresh seasoning makes a tremendous difference in cooking."

"Parsley, sage, rosemary and thyme," Peter murmured, poking at the heap on his plate.

"And savory, dill, basil and tarragon," Tiphaine said mockingly. "They are used for just plain ordinary cooking, you know. Have some salad. Basil and dill in that."

Peter sampled the salad.

"You're right; the woman's a witch at cooking."

Tiphaine put her fork down and looked exasperated.

"Peter, just for once, can't you—"

"The subject seems to be on my mind."

"The trouble is you're fighting it," Tiphaine said shrewdly. "You don't want to believe that things like that can happen."

"That's probably true. Which is not very rational of me; I know perfectly well that people do believe in the occult. What I can't understand is how a woman like Kate could fall for such rot. I could see the first time I met her that she was under an abnormal strain. Ordinarily I'd have thought of blackmail, anonymous letters, the usual things."

"Anonymous letters?" Tiphaine shrugged. "You don't know Kate. Her reaction to a poison-pen letter would be a shout of laughter and a clinical analysis of the mental state of the writer. You've heard people say that they don't care what the rest of the world thinks. Mostly they're lying. But Kate really doesn't care."

Peter nodded. He was remembering Sam's comment: "She takes a kind of pleasure in rubbing people's noses in facts they don't want to face."

"You mean she does whatever she pleases, and to hell with gossip."

"Not exactly," Tiphaine said. "She doesn't do things for the hell of it. But if she felt she had a good reason for behaving in a certain way, she wouldn't let gossip bother her."

"And that," Peter pointed out, "is why her present state of nerves is so surprising. I agree; she isn't susceptible to blackmail or threats for the ordinary peccadilloes that terrify most people. But there's a difference between fear of losing one's reputation and fear of—death, shall we say?"

Tiphaine's head jerked up. For a moment her face was unguarded, and Peter saw that the idea was not new to her.

"Not necessarily death," he went on. "But every human being has some weakness. Every one. Remember *Nineteen Eight-Four* and Room One-oh-one. That was where they took the stubborn ones, the rebels whom nothing else could break. And the thing that waited for them in Room One-oh-one was simply the worst thing in the world. The one thing that they couldn't endure. Different for every person; but for every person there was something. What is it for Kate? What one thing is it that she can't endure?"

"Loss?" Tiphaine said softly; chin propped on her hands, she had listened intently. "Mark?"

"You've been singing too many folks songs," Peter said rudely.

" 'Cold blows the wind to my true love, And gently falls the rain . . . ' " She sang it, unselfconsciously, in an eerie little voice that was hardly more than a whisper. "It would be . . . funny . . . wouldn't it, if it were true . . ."

"Funny is not precisely the word." Peter didn't care for the look in her eyes. "Snap out of it, Tiphaine. Kate is no simpleminded romantic. How do you know she isn't inventing her apparitions?"

"Pretending, you mean?"

"She may not be doing it deliberately," Peter conceded.

"Deliberate or not, that's not possible. I've seen things myself, Peter."

"That doesn't mean Kate couldn't have engineered them."

"Oh, that's absurd. Why on earth should she?"

"How the hell should I know? None of it makes any sense. It's you I'm worried about. If I could be sure you were in no danger . . ."

His hand slid up her bare arm. She was wearing

something sleeveless and low-cut, of a pale ivory that set off her tan. After a moment Peter removed his hand.

"Sorry again."

"Mrs. Schmidt will be bringing in the coffee at any moment," she murmured. "Peter, I can tell; you have something in mind. What is it?"

"Just a tentative scheme for catching the person who's behind these tricks. If it turns out to be someone other than Kate, at least I'll know that the malice is directed against her. I don't mean to sound callous, but you're my chief concern."

"That's very sweet."

"Not so sweet, no. Look here. Sooner or later, some night, if not tonight, another incident will occur. Whoever it was who prompted Timmy, he'll have to act again, to destroy the confidence Timmy's capture gave Kate. And I think he'll act soon."

"Soon? Then you think—"

Peter drew his chair closer to hers.

"Tonight . . ."


When Tiphaine came out of her cousin's room Peter was waiting in the hall. She put her finger to her lips.

"I slipped one of the pills Paul left into her tea. She'll be asleep in minutes."

"Martin prescribed them?"

"Do you wonder? She has a thing about drugs,

that's why I have to sneak." Tiphaine grimaced. "I hate doing it, but—"

"You have to. I know. Then you're sure she won't be walking around anymore tonight?"

"Yes."

"Any luck with locking the doors onto the balcony?"

"No. I tried, but she told me to leave them open. She likes fresh air."

Peter had been fairly sure of that, but he was relieved to hear it.

"Never mind. I strung thread all over those bushes under the window. If anything goes up that way, we'll know about it. Now for the inside of the house. Got the stuff?"

"I'll get it." Tiphaine went into her room and came back with a box of talcum. Peter sprinkled it lightly but thoroughly over the hall carpet, beginning at Kate's door. When the whiteness reached down to the door of the adjoining room, he stopped as if struck by a sudden thought.

"My bathroom. Doesn't it communicate with this room?"

"Yes. But what—"

While she stood in the doorway watching, Peter crossed the spare room and slid the bolt in place. The white-headed pins and the plastic twine were completely invisible from where she stood, but she saw his ostentatious manipulation of the bolt.

"Door's bolted," he said, coming back. "On this side."

"Right. What does that prove?"

"I hope it will prove something, if anything untoward occurs. She's suspicious of me, and if you're not, you ought to be."

"What do you mean by that?"

"I mean you shouldn't trust anyone."

He finished sprinkling the hallway, leaving Tiphaine marooned in her own doorway. She watched while he finished the job, backing into his own room like a painter who has painted himself into a corner. He waved the near-empty can of talcum cheerfully at Tiphaine, who responded with a faint smile. She closed her door, and Peter followed suit. Now no one could enter the hall without leaving traces in the even coating of powder.

Peter read for an hour. Then he turned out his light and sat in the dark for another hour. By this time it was nearly 1 A.M., and he decided it was safe to proceed.

Most of his precautions were already made: the rumpled bed, the mechanism on the bathroom door, the chair under the doorknob of the bedroom door. Changing clothes was unnecessary; his gray slacks and shirt would be better camouflage against the pale facade of the house than dark clothing. He had already removed his shoes.

He went to the door on the other side of the bathroom and took hold of the left-hand pair of threads. The plastic fishline was made for the job;

invisible against any surface, it was stronger than twine. He pulled slowly and steadily, and felt the bolt slide back.

The adjoining room was dark, and he didn't dare turn on the light. A small pocket flashlight, gripped uncomfortably in his teeth, let him re-arrange the device which controlled the bolt. He removed the pair of thumbtacks to the right of the bolt, and the length of fishline which had passed over them, from the head of the bolt, back through the crack between door and doorframe. He tested the tacks on the other side, and the piece of fishline which would shoot the bolt again after he got back into his room. Perfect.

So far so good. He opened the window, and got out as quickly as he could. The wind was stronger than he realized. It tore at him as he moved crab-wise along the window ledge and groped for a handhold among the tough vines to the left of the window. It was a cold wind. "Cold blows the wind . . ." The plaintive little melody Tiphaine had sung began running through his head. "And gently falls the rain . . ." No rain. Thank God for that, he couldn't have tried this stunt in wet weather. He must appear at the strategic moment looking as if he had just been summoned from a warm, dry bed.

"I've never had but one true love . . ." He couldn't get the tune out of his head. His toes jammed painfully into a crack in the stone. Peter fumbled for his next handhold. "Funny if it were true," Tiphaine had said. The Unquiet Grave. No . . . not funny at all.

His reverie ended when he reached the corner of the wing and the only really sticky part of the trip. The ivy was old and solidly entrenched; it was climbing a cargo net. But there was no ivy on the end of the house, near Kate's balcony.

Clinging like a chimpanzee to the drainpipe on the corner, Peter eyed the six-foot gap between his perch and the edge of the balcony. It was an easy jump, if there had been any solid ground from which to launch himself. He had seen the problem before, but there wasn't really any sure solution to it. Getting to the balcony wasn't so hard; it was getting back that bothered him. Shinnying up the pipe a few feet, he hooked his heels into the space between wall and pipe and fell forward, arms extended and body straight. His hands caught the edge of the balcony with inches to spare, and in a moment he was climbing over the rail.

What he saw brought him to a dead stop. There was a light inside the room.

Peter stood on the balcony, stockinged toes curled up against the chill of the flooring, and swore under his breath. All his work was for nothing if she was still awake. Hell of a doctor Martin was; he couldn't even prescribe sleeping pills that worked. But when he peered through the curtains he framed a mental apology. She was asleep all right, and breathing heavily. But she had left a night light burning. He ought to have expected that.

Holding the curtains slightly apart, he studied the situation before he ventured in. She was sleeping soundly now, but she hadn't dropped off easily; the bedclothes were twisted into knots and pushed down toward the bottom of the bed. She slept on her side, curled up protectively; her arms were wrapped around the pillow which she held close to her, like a baby—or a shield. The nightgown was black lace this time. Clearly she was no sunbather. The tan on her legs faded above the knees. . . .

Peter's cold feet reminded him that he had no time for that. She wouldn't hear anything short of a yell, that was the important thing. He slid into the room and got his second surprise when an object popped up from among the tumbled bedclothes. It was small, round, black, and had pointed ears, now pricked inquiringly.

Peter and Pyewacket contemplated one another. The cat was curious but not perturbed. Peter glowered at it. He knew how unpredictably a sleeper's sense of hearing functions; people can snore through a parade of fire engines, and waken at a child's whimper. The movement of the cat's heavy body might be enough to rouse Kate. He went about his business as quickly as he could.

By the time he had the arrangement set up, Pyewacket hadn't moved. His ears were still pricked, though, and his head was cocked at an inquiring angle. Peter decided to risk one more delay. He had set up his display on top of the small desk which was conveniently close to the window. He wanted very much to see what was in the drawers.

He found Kate's checkbook in the top center drawer, and a quick glance at the register of checks told him what he wanted to know. So she was impervious to blackmail, was she? A series of sizable withdrawals, made out to cash, over the past nine or ten months, might be for some innocent purpose; at the moment he couldn't think of one. Ten thousand was the highest amount, five thousand the least. They added up to a formidable sum.

Peter put the checkbook back precisely as he had found it, and closed the drawer. Everything was set. But for the best effect, that light ought to be out.

It was on the bedside table, within arm's reach of the sleeper. A risky business, especially with that damned cat staring at him, ready to jump. But it had to be risked. If the sudden darkness, or a shriek from the cat, woke her—well, she had to wake up pretty soon anyhow.

Peter started the tape recorder. One of the new, small casette types, it made only a whisper of noise. He crossed the room on tiptoe. Hand poised, he looked at Kate. She hadn't moved. Sleep wasn't knitting up any ravels for her; the long dark lashes veiled the circles under her eyes, but there were two vertical lines between her brows, and the full mouth was drawn down at the corners. The lines in her forehead deepened and she stirred, murmuring. Peter's hand slammed down on the light switch, and the room went dark. He heard a rustle of bedclothes and an inquiring meow; but by that time he was sliding through the window.

He had to make sure she was awake before he went any farther. The taped voice had begun, and grown louder; the candles were due to burst into flames at any second. It would be better if she saw them light up. Crouching, peering through the slit in the curtains, he heard, over the muttering voice on the tape, the solid thud as Pyewacket hit the floor and wandered over to see what was making all the noise. Still no movement from the sleeper.

A paw, sheathed, but ready to erupt into claws at the slightest encouragement, patted hopefully at Peter's fingers. He slid his other hand down the seductive, trusting slope of Pyewacket's back, located the waving tail, and gave it a sharp tug. An anguished cry of trust betrayed rent the night, and Peter jerked his hand back just in time to avoid an incriminating set of scratches.

He heard Kate sit up, so suddenly that the bed squealed. The candles chose that auspicious moment to light; and he had one glimpse of an ashen face and staring black eyes before he went over the edge of the balcony. The recorded voice was loud enough now to drown the sounds of his movements, including, he hoped, the only loud noise he must make.

The recording sounded good. The voices couldn't be much alike, but the tormented whispering tone concealed differences in timbre, and the accent was convincing. Good old Sam— always right about the important things. When Peter had made the recording that afternoon, in the seclusion of his bathroom, with the shower streaming, he had thought of Sam. Even the background rush of running water came through nicely. If you didn't know what it was, you'd think it might be a wind howling eerily—or the crackle of flames, maybe.

Poised on the outer edge of the balcony, Peter began his return trip. This was the only bad part. If that drainpipe wasn't sturdy enough to bear the impact of his body, or if his hands missed its narrow circumference ... He compensated for the second difficulty by letting himself fall parallel to the wall with his shoulder actually brushing it. The pipe sagged, but held; grasping it with one hand, Peter pulled the string wound around his waist and heard the series of tiny bumps as the recorder bounded onto the balcony, hit the rim, and came up over the rail. He reeled the string in as fast as he could, but the recorder swung against the wall as it fell. It didn't matter; he probably wouldn't need it again.

With the tape recorder dangling from his belt like a scalp, Peter slithered across the side wall and in the window. He was moving fast, unbuttoning his shirt and unwinding string as he dashed across the spare bedroom. Recorder, socks, and shirt went into the bathroom hamper. Time was getting on; he could hear interesting sounds from the hall. His hand tugged gently on the remaining length of fishline; an extra sharp tug, after the bolt was drawn, dislodged the thumbtack, and the twine's full length came through the crack into his hand. Tugging at his belt, Peter ran across the room, threw the chair aside, and opened the door.

The hall was brightly lit; Kate had turned on the switch outside her door. She was standing in the doorway, arms out and braced; only their pressure on the doorframe held her erect, he could see the sag of her knees under the sheer black skirt. Her face was as white as paper, but a queer relief came over it as her eyes fell on Peter. Tiphaine, in her own doorway, had stopped to slip her arms into a robe. Following Peter's instructions, she had not stepped onto the floor of the hall, where the white powder lay virgin and unmarked.

"What happened?" Peter asked, blinking. The light hurt his eyes; it gave a fine air of verisimilitude to the picture he presented, that of a man abruptly awakened from peaceful slumbers, who has delayed answering the cries of the maiden in distress only long enough to assume his trousers.

He finished rebuckling his belt and stepped carefully out into the hall.

Kate's lips parted, but no sound came out. Tiphaine was studying the unmarked surface of the talcum. She looked up, caught Peter's eyes, and nodded; and Peter made a dash forward just in time to catch Kate as she fell.

She couldn't weigh much more than a hundred pounds. The taut limbs, which looked so hard and competent when she was awake, felt thin to the point of fragility now. Tiphaine was at his shoulder when he laid Kate down on her bed. He turned her and repeated the question.

"What happened?"

"I don't know. I heard her call—look!"

She pointed.

On the desk the twelve black candles burned, the flames flickering in the breeze from the window. There was an additional effect which Peter hadn't planned: Pyewacket, fascinated by the dancing lights, sat like a black Egyptian statue between the candelabra, tail wound around his sleek flanks. But Tiphaine's eyes were focused on the small object that lay before the cat, between the candlesticks.

"Where did that come from?" she asked breathlessly.

"What is it?"

She walked to the desk, picked the object up, and held it out to Peter.

"A rabbit's foot." She added, in a flat, even

voice, "Mark carried one, as a lucky piece. Some uncle from America gave it to him when he was a little boy."

"What happened to it?" Peter took Kate's hand and felt for a pulse. It was faint but steady; she'd be coming to in a minute.

"It was—buried with him, I suppose."

"There are thousands of the things around. How do you know this was his?"

"I don't. But—what point would there be to this unless it was—is—Mark's?"

"Who knew about it?"

"Most everyone. He showed it to people." She dropped the talisman back on the desk and rubbed her fingers together, shivering.

"Get it out of sight," Peter ordered. "And the candles. She's coming around. You don't want her to see that macabre arrangement again, do you?"

Tiphaine obeyed, but she moved so slowly that Kate's eyes flickered open before she had finished clearing away. From her prone position Kate could look straight across the room at the desk. Her mouth twisted, and Peter felt the hand he held tighten around his fingers.

"The voice," she muttered. "It was yours. Had to be . . . yours."

Peter was silent, partly because it was a reasonable reaction, partly because he was struck momentarily speechless. Damn the woman; what did it take to break her down, gibbering phosphorescent wraiths and skeletal fingers on her throat?

She had been frightened into a fainting fit, but that subborn core of strength had led her straight to the only rational answer. Now he was glad he had taken those seemingly unnecessary precautions.

"You heard a voice?" he said calmly.

"In the darkness . . . the candles flared up . . . A voice like . . . yours."

"It wasn't Peter." Tiphaine had swept the candles and rabbit's foot into the pocket of her robe. She came swiftly back to the bed, leaving a disappointed cat behind. "We sprinkled powder on the floor, Kate; there wasn't a mark on it when I came to the door.

"Connecting bath," Kate muttered. Incongruously, through all her accusations, she retained her desperate grip on Peter's hand.

"It's bolted. On this side."

"Go look."

Tiphaine gave Peter an expressive look and a shrug. She was back almost at once.

"Still bolted. Kate, even if he got into the next room, how could he have reached yours? Footprints would have shown in the hall; he can't walk on the ceiling, you know."

Kate's teeth began to chatter. The room wasn't particularly cold.

"That's enough for now," Peter said. "Tiphaine, you'd better call—no, I'll do it; you stay with her."

He went out, flexing ostentatiously empty hands. Kate's next thought would be for some sort of mechanical recording device; she'd insist that

Tiphaine search the room. Just to be on the safe side, he'd better get rid of the tape recorder. The trip downstairs, to admit the doctor, would give him an opportunity, and it was logical that he would stop off in his own room to put on more clothes. With Katharine More you couldn't take too many precautions. But as he closed the door gently behind him, he knew he had struck a damaging blow. The last thing he heard was her admission of defeat.

"Then it was Mark. Mark's voice . . ."

"Is she still pacing up there?"

"Yes." Tiphaine was doing some pacing of her own; she swung around on her heel, bright hair flying. "Martin says he can't give her anything more. Old maid, that's what he is! I think I'll go out of my mind if she doesn't stop!"

"She ought to get out of the house," Peter said.

"She won't go with me." The strain was telling on the girl; irritability sharpened her voice and flushed her cheeks.

"Let me see what I can do."

"I wish you luck."

Peter expected he would need it. He wanted to get Kate off by herself, preferably out of the house, where she couldn't yell for help, but he didn't expect her to acquiesce. But Kate agreed without a struggle when he suggested a walk. Apparently Tiphaine's report last night had cleared him.

They went across the yard and through the gate into the woods, Kate leading, Peter trailing like a watchdog—or keeper, he thought. He didn't try to talk. She couldn't keep up her present pace very long. After a while her steps slowed and stumbled; but when Peter took her arm she shook his hand off.

"I don't need any help."

"Like hell you don't," Peter said unemphatically.

She glanced up at him and then looked away. Her eyes were unfocused and dilated to blacker blackness than usual.

"Let's get off the path," she said. "Someone might come, and I don't want—"

"Lead the way."

"There's a place I go to sometimes." She pointed up the trail, to a spot where a coil of wickedly beautiful scarlet leaves twined around a tree, and a broken branch stuck out from a tall oak.

Between the oak and the poison ivy a faint path went off into the underbrush, but Peter would not have seen it without guidance. Clearly it had not been used for some time; honeysuckle and poison ivy made a thick treacherous matting underfoot, and climbed to strangle trees and bushes. Kate wiggled her way through and Peter ungallantly let her lead. He was scratched and perspiring by the time they broke through into a final tangle of thorned bushes into a small glade.

A brook ran rippling across the cleared space and vanished between trees to the right. Tall trees ringed the clearing, shading it. Some pines; the ground was covered with a thick soft carpet of browning needles, which had triumphed even over the omnipresent honeysuckle. At the far end of the clearing, to the left of the path by which they had come, stood an unusual object—a massive block of stone about ten feet high and almost as broad. Its color was dark, almost black; granite, possibly. The top was flat, like a platform, but it bore no trace of man's hand.

"A meteorite?" Peter hazarded.

"No, just a chunk of rock. The local people call it the Devil's Pulpit." Kate crossed over to the rock and dropped down beside it. She fumbled in her pocket for her cigarettes. "They avoid this place, particularly around Halloween. That's why I like to come here."

"Halloween?" Peter sat down beside her and declined a cigarette with a shake of his head. "Oh, yes, your local Allhallows. Jack-o'-lanterns and—what is it? Trick or treat."

"Haven't you ever seen it?"

"No. Sounds like a combination of Guy Fawkes and Carnival."

"When I was small, there used to be farms around here." Kate propped herself on one elbow and stared absently at a shaft of sunlight jabbing down through the trees. "The children came trick or treating to our place. Once."

"Once?"

"Uncle Stephan met them at the door," Kate

said dreamingly. "I was there on a visit. He'd worked awfully hard on his costume. When they rang the bell he answered it. They were dressed . . . oh, rabbits, and little witches, and Superman. He'd painted his face dead white, except for his mouth. It was red. His canine teeth were particularly long and they shone in the dark. He made . . . noises."

Peter was silent. Comment was unnecessary.

"Two of the fathers came next day," she went on, in the same voice. "They didn't stay long."

She put her cigarette out very carefully, pinching the ends to make sure no spark remained. Then in one convulsive movement she slid down flat onto the ground and hid her face in her arms.

"Go ahead and cry," Peter said gently. "It'll do you good."

"I'm not crying." She rolled over onto her back and lay still, staring fixedly up at the blue circle of sky. "I'm trying to think. Whether I should see a psychiatrist. Or move away from here. Or do what he wants. Or just kill myself and get it over with."

"That's no solution," Peter said. The moment he had been waiting for had arrived, and he didn't quite know what to do with it.

"That's what I'm afraid of." She gave a sudden dry laugh, like a stick snapping. " 'For in that sleep of death, what dreams may come . . . ' My dreams are bad enough now. That leaves three choices, doesn't it?"

"Who," Peter said, "is 'he'?"

"Someone I used to know." She rolled onto her side, looking at him through half-closed eyes.

It took Peter several seconds to recognize the look, not because it was new to him, but because he had never expected it from her. Yet the pull was there, he had been aware of it for some time. She looked so much smaller when she wasn't standing. He put out his hand and traced with his fingers the curve of her cheek and throat. Then her arms were around him, pulling him down.

She lay on her back, eyes closed and face lifted, her arms lax and white against the brown pine needles. Peter propped himself up on one elbow and studied her face. It hadn't changed. The tension was still there, tightening the corners of her mouth and hollowing her cheeks. Her sudden, unpremeditated try for temporary amnesia hadn't worked. She hadn't made any pretense about it; no soft murmurings about love, only wordless sounds of pure physical pleasure. Still . . . even from that point of view, it had been quite an experience.

"Want a cigarette?" he asked.

She shook her head without opening her eyes.

"Help yourself."

Peter reached across for her shirt and felt in the pocket. His hand lingered on the return trip, and a faint smile curled her mouth, but she kept her eyes closed. . . .

She must have felt the change in the pressure of his fingers, for her eyes flew open and she tried to sit up. Peter straightened his elbow, and she fell back.

"You're hurting me . . . What is it? What are you staring at?"

The signs were faint, but they couldn't be missed. On a fair-skinned blonde like Tiphaine, maybe; but Kate was dark.

From a tree high above, a mocking bird sang a long trill. It sounded miles away. Peter shook his head dazedly. Of all the unexpected . . . How the hell had Sam ever missed this? He felt her shrink under the painful pressure of his hand, and looked up to meet eyes wide with terror, and as easy to read as a page of print.

"So it's true," he said stonily. "What happened to it?"

Her answer was barely audible, even in the dead silence. The bird had stopped singing.

"She lived for eight months. It was pneumonia."

He knew what need had driven her to the cult of Mother Earth, and the resurrection of the dead.

# PART TWO
## *Quarry*

# *Chapter*
## 9

KATE KNEW SHE HAD BETRAYED HERSELF WITH THAT
one simple change of pronoun. Not only the fact,
but what it had meant to her. . . . A chink in the ar-
mor, a break in the wall; a weakness through
which she could be attacked. She closed her eyes,
wondering idly whether the hard hand would
move up to her throat and tighten, and knowing
that she didn't really care any longer.

He had betrayed himself as well; but she had always known, in some remote corner of her mind,
who he really was. They weren't much alike, actually, only in superficial features like the shape of
their heads, and the unruly fair hair. Mark's delicate nose and mouth and boyishly rounded face
were nothing like Peter's features. But when Peter's eyes narrowed and his mouth went tight, she

could see him—Mark—in one of his rages. Mark . . . one long year in his grave, and still haunting her, in no figurative sense. Against the blackness of her closed eyes the picture formed again, the same scene that had fought its way past her will on countless other days and nights.

He always carried himself so arrogantly, walking on the balls of his feet with his head thrust forward. In the moonlight, that last night, he looked like one of Milton's fallen angels—poised as if about to lift in flight, a thin diabolic smile on his youthful face. It was October, and cold—October, almost exactly one year ago—but Mark was coatless, and that, too, was typical of Mark. He expected even the elements to conform to his requirements. When they didn't conform, he behaved as if they had.

First she had tried to reason with him. It didn't work; it never had. Then she had tried to hurt him. The stinging words hadn't bothered Mark; they bounced back off the barrier of his fantastic ego like tennis balls off a brick wall. He couldn't believe any woman could resist him. But he had cause to think himself irresistible; once she had responded to the boyish charm and the words which seemed so much wittier and less trite than conventional wooing. Witch woman he had called her, enchantress, weaving spells. . . . Succubus, that was one of his favorite endearments—the supernaturally beautiful seductive spirit, preying on human lovers who cannot resist her deadly charms.

The epithets had palled even before Mark did; that night, in the cold passionless light of the moon, they made her angry. Mark had tried every trick in his considerable repertoire: threats, charm, even tears. Everything except reason, because that was a quality beyond Mark's comprehension. When all his devices failed, there was only one thing left. And somehow the gun was in her hand, and he was coming toward her. . . .

Katharine forced her eyes open. Peter was standing with his back to her, buttoning his shirt. The discarded sling lay on the ground at his feet.

"Your arm," she said dully. "I forgot about it."

"So did I." Peter turned, with a smile that reminded her of an archaic statue's—curved, remote, and terrible. "You're very skillful. Practice, or natural talent?"

His eyes moved over her body with an inhuman contempt, and Kate snatched at her clothing.

"Don't," she whispered.

"Mark was something of a connoisseur. I'm sure he appreciated you even more than I could. Until you tired of him."

Her head bent, Kate began to dress. But she could not close her ears to the remorseless voice.

"It must have been the final blow to him when he found out why you really wanted him. Not as a husband, not even as a lover. Just for breeding stock, like a healthly thoroughbred dog. Because it wasn't carelessness, was it? Not with a woman of your intelligence, not these days, when every gum-chewing adolescent knows how to take precautions. That's the only thing I find hard to believe: that a cold-blooded bitch like you could have one normal instinct. But then it is an instinct, isn't it—a matter of uncontrollable hormones. A sick, sentimental substitute for—"

"Stop it!" Kate clutched at her ears.

He caught her by the elbows and forced her to face him.

"What did you do to him? What happened? I've always known it wasn't an accident, Mark knew too much about guns. He killed himself, didn't he? Didn't he? And you drove him to it."

Shaken in his grasp like a doll, Kate stared up at him from under her loosened hair.

"Killed himself?" she gasped. "Himself? Mark?"

She began to laugh. It surprised her. She hadn't meant to laugh, and once she started she couldn't stop. Through a haze of dreadful, shaking mirth she saw Peter's face alter, saw his hand swing back; and then the red haze faded into a lovely blackness, a cold blackness that swallowed up the laughter and the sting of the blow across her face, and all other sensation. She fell into a deep dark hole, embracing the blackness. Maybe, if she was clever and careful, she would never have to come out of it again.

* * *

Martin's voice brought her out of it, and she hated Martin. She hated the pressure of the bedclothes on her body and the familiar smell of fresh linen and the smooth feel of it on her cheek. All her reluctant senses fought at being awakened; she curled herself up tighter inside and tried to go back into the dark.

Almost . . . She hovered on the rim of the blackness. But the hateful voice wouldn't be still.

"What the hell happened? Goddamn it, don't shake your head and look blank at me; something must have happened, something cataclysmic; she's in a catatonic state, I can't even reach her."

"Let me try." That voice. That one was worse. Kate hated it, it meant disaster; but it jabbed and prodded like a needle, sliding in past defenses that kindlier voices could not pierce.

"Kate, wake up. You can't hide, it doesn't work. Kate . . . Answer me, Kate. . . ."

Oh, now—now she was feeling more—the hand on her shoulder, the bedsprings sagging as he sat down. Tears of fury welled up and slid down from under her stubbornly closed lids; and Peter said, with a queer relief, "She's crying."

Then it was nighttime, and that seemed strange, because it was as if no time had passed at all and the same voices had been talking without interruption.

"Hasn't she been asleep a long time?"

"The injection should be wearing off soon. But if she does withdraw again—well, you brought her out of it once."

"She didn't need me. She'd have come out of it herself."

"She's tough, yes, but everyone has his breaking point."

"Wise remark number forty-two."

"I haven't had an easy day myself, Stewart."

"Sorry. You're quite fond of her, aren't you?"

"I wanted to marry her," Martin said.

Kate lay very still, her eyes closed; with that vital sense cut off, it seemed as if the others were strengthened. She could almost feel Peter's reaction, and Martin's response to it.

"I know," Martin said, after a moment or two. "I already have a wife. But that doesn't prevent a man from dreaming."

"What did prevent you?" Peter asked pleasantly.

"She was in love with someone else."

"So I've heard. What was the fellow like?"

"Rather like you. Nothing specific; but that first day, when you came into my office, there was a look. . . . I think," Martin added, "that Kate's seen it too."

Kate opened her eyes a slit. They stood at the foot of the bed, facing one another. Peter leaned wearily on the footboard; his hair looked as if he had been running both hands through it, and his face was haggard. Paul looked tired too. Poor Paul; he had probably been working over her all day.

"I don't care what he looked like," Peter said sharply. "What was he like?"

Martin took his time about answering. When he did, his comment was concise and his tone savage.

"Treacherous, arrogant, selfish."

"Mmm." Peter rubbed his chin thoughtfully. "Well, but he's dead. Has been, for almost a year. Since conventional considerations don't prevent you from—er—dreaming, why haven't you tried again?"

The smooth, sneering voice was so like Mark's that Kate made a little movement of withdrawal. Neither man noticed. Martin stiffened and Peter straightened up. The air was electric with antagonism.

Kate pulled herself to a sitting position.

"Stop it," she said. "Paul, stop it, stop it, stop—"

"It's all right, Kate." He was beside her at once, pushing her back onto the pillows. "Be quiet now, calm down. You don't want another injection, do you?"

His hands were hard against her shoulders, and she was weaker than she had thought.

"No," she muttered; all at once she felt as limp as a rag doll, as limp as a little wax figure held over a fire, softening, melting. . . .

"Don't want . . . that," she said, with an enormous effort. "Want . . . I want . . ."

"What? What is it you want?"

"My lawyer," Kate said. "I want . . . make my will."

That was right, that was the right thing to say. She knew at once, from the heavenly feeling of lassitude that was beginning to fog her senses.

Martin sat back, lifting his hands. He looked up to exchange glances with Peter, who had come around to the side of the bed.

"I thought you'd made your will," Martin said in a puzzled voice.

Kate felt a sharp pang of anxiety. He was going to argue, he wasn't going to do what she asked.

"My lawyer," she insisted. "Tomorrow. Promise, Paul . . . promise. . . ."

"All right, all right," Martin said. "I promise, Kate. I'll call him this evening. It can't do any harm," he added, as if to himself; but Kate knew he was speaking to Peter, who stood staring down at her with his brows drawn together in a frown. It didn't matter what he thought. She let out a long sigh. Paul would keep his promise. He always kept his promise.

She was still a little weak next morning, but she insisted on getting up to meet the lawyer. Somehow that was important, that he shouldn't find her helpless in bed. Martin didn't argue. He wasn't arguing about anything. Kate knew why he responded to her slightest suggestion with such suspicious alacrity, why he watched her when he thought she wasn't looking. Deep down inside she laughed, and hugged herself with a secret joy. He didn't fool her. No, she was the one who was tricking them, all of them.

The lawyer didn't seem to notice anything unusual when she rose to greet him, slim and poised in a black suit she seldom wore except for business meetings like this one. Her instructions were simple and concise; he nodded with grave approval when she explained them. The only time he looked taken aback was when she asked him to have the will ready next day. Lawyers were like that, she told herself, and smiled tolerantly at him. They liked lots of time to quibble about nonessentials.

"You said yourself it was quite straightforward," she reminded him, and smiled her best smile. "I know it's an imposition, but—as a favor to me?"

And because I'm your richest client, she added silently. She knew he would agree; everything was going the way she wanted it to now.

"Very well, Miss More. I'll bring it out in the morning, since it's so important to you. Is tomorrow an anniversary of some sort? October—let me see, it will be the thirty-first." He laughed. "Of course, the thirty-first, Halloween."

"Yes," Kate said softly. "It's an anniversary—of some sort."

* * *

For the rest of that day her feeling of dreamy contentment persisted. In some far-off corner of her mind Kate knew the mood wouldn't last; people couldn't live their whole lives feeling as if they were wrapped in invisible cotton which insulated them against the touch of the outside world. But the feeling was so pleasant, after the long months of tension, that she wanted to enjoy it as long as she could.

Her new mood affected everyone in the house. Even Mrs. Schmidt was seen to smile as she carried in the tea tray. Tiphaine was brilliant, flushed, dancing. Martin relaxed so far as to go home in the early afternoon, announcing with a wry smile that he did, after all, have other patients. He took Kate aside to assure her that he would be back that night.

The only person unaffected by the new regime was Peter Stewart. He kept out of sight, as if he expected a dismissal once his presence was noted; but Kate caught glimpses of him, prowling the halls and peering in at windows. His expression was glum.

In the afternoon it began to rain, and when the two women sat down to dinner, the patter of water against the windows sounded like thousands of little running feet. Martin had not yet returned, and Peter was also missing. Kate didn't ask about him.

They made trivial conversation during dinner; afterward they went into the living room. Kate picked up a book and Pyewacket came purring in and settled himself on her lap. His considerable bulk made reading difficult, since the owner of the favored lap had to keep elbows out at an odd angle to avoid jabbing the black back; and tonight the cat seemed restless, never settling in one position but turning and rearranging himself like a grumpy arthritic old man. Finally he sank his claws deliberately into Kate's thigh, responded to her exclamation with a growl, and jumped down. He stood in the center of the floor, his long black tail waving like a whip, and then stalked off, pried the door open, and vanished.

Kate watched him go with mingled amusement and irritation. His restlessness had affected her; she couldn't concentrate on her book. She turned her head to look at Tiphaine, who was draped over an armchair, feet dangling across the arm. Her pretty face was set in a frown of concentration and her hands moved in quick motions, manipulating a long piece of string.

"More cats' cradles?" Kate asked. "That looks like a new one."

"Damn." The string knotted and caught, and Tiphaine began to untangle it. "It's new, and awfully complicated. I keep forgetting— There."

She put her hands inside the loop, stretching it wide, and began again.

"Funny colored string," Kate said lazily.

"Just ordinary red twine. I found it in the kitchen drawer. It must have been on a package. You know how Mrs. Schmidt is about saving things."

Again the string caught. Tiphaine shook her head and tried a third time.

Kate watched for a while. She was really too sleepy to do anything useful; even the patterned movement of the string, and the flash of Tiphaine's white fingers, made her drowsy.

"I think I'll go to bed," she said finally. "Listen to the rain. Sounds as if we're in for a spell of bad weather."

"Ah." Tiphaine made a soft sound of satisfaction and jerked her hands apart. The string slid and held, forming a pattern too complex for Kate's blinking eyes to see clearly; there seemed to be a double set of seven strands raying out from the center.

"No more rain," Tiphaine announced with a grin. "I've conjured up a wind. It should clear before morning."

"You mean you listened to the weather report," Kate said, but the words lacked her usual snap, and Tiphaine looked at her intently.

"You do look tired. Want me to come up and tuck you in?"

"Certainly not. Are you going to sit up much longer?"

"Not much longer."

"Good night, then."

Once upstairs, Kate found that she was no longer sleepy. Her bones ached with weariness, but after she was in bed, with the bed lamp turned down low, sleep would not come. That silly string game of Tiphaine's obsessed her; whenever she closed her eyes she seemed to see the pattern outlined in bright streaks of reddish light against blackness. After a period of restless tossing and turning—just like Pyewacket—she gave up, turned the lamp to a brighter setting, and reached for a book.

She had read only a few pages when she heard footsteps in the hall. They were very soft, as if tiptoeing; they sounded like a man's step.

Before she had time to become frightened, she remembered Martin. He had promised to come back and he always kept his promises. Probably he thought she was asleep and was tiptoeing in to look at her. The doorknob turned, and she looked up with a welcoming smile—a smile which froze as she recognized Peter Stewart.

He had been outside; rain flattened his hair and darkened the shoulders of his coat. While Kate stared, he raised one finger to his lips in a gesture for silence.

"I want to talk to you," he said in a low voice.

"I don't want to talk to you," Kate said childishly. "Go away."

His hand moved, so quickly that she had no chance to avoid it. The stiffened fingers struck her twice across the cheeks, sharp blows that stung the skin without rocking her head.

She gasped and clawed at him with both hands. He caught her wrists and held them. The corners of his mouth lifted in a parody of a smile which was all the more unpleasant because the cold watchful eyes did not change.

"That's better," he said. "You've been in a fog all day. What are you taking, some sort of tranquilizer?"

"I don't know. Martin gave me an injection—"

"Don't let him give you any more. You've had enough happy medicine." He released her hands and sat down on the edge of the bed. "We never finished our conversation, did we?"

"We aren't going to finish it. Get out of here. Pack your things and get out of the house."

"Not until I've found out what I came here for." He leaned forward. "What happened to Mark?"

The name was a blow, a sharp jab with a heavy implement that jarred even through the thick cotton insulation, an insulation already weakened by Peter's presence. She shook her head.

"No. It's all over. I don't have to talk about—him."

"It's not over. Quite the contrary." His hands reached out for her again, gripping her shoulders and pulling her up till their faces were only inches apart. Her treacherous body betrayed her; she went limp, held erect only by the painful grip of his hands, her head fallen back. But she could not avoid his eyes. They held hers hypnotically.

"But I did it," she whispered. "I did what he told me to do."

"Who?" The intent blue eyes widened. "Mark?"

She moved her head feebly.

"Did . . . what he told me. Now he'll leave me alone."

"Leave you . . ." His grip relaxed, and Kate fell back bonelessly against the pillows. "Not an accident," he said, as if to himself. "Not suicide. You killed him, didn't you?"

The words had been there so long, buried deep in her consciousness, but always beating against the barriers that held them in.

"Yes," she said, and her voice was suddenly strong and steady. "I killed him."

His eyelids flickered, but he showed no other reaction, except for the slow draining of color from his cheeks. There was no time for anything else; the door burst open, and Martin came into the room.

"I was afraid of this," he said grimly. "Kate. What has he done to you?"

"Nothing," Kate said vaguely. "I told him. About Mark."

"Good God," Martin groaned. He turned on Peter, who hadn't moved. His lids had drooped, hiding his eyes. His lashes were darker than his hair, and very thick; Kate had noticed them on another occasion, and the memory of it must have shown in her face as she looked at him; for Martin's mouth tightened as he glanced from Peter to Kate.

"Get out, Stewart. If you try to approach Kate again, I'll call the police."

Peter stood up, stiffly. He did not speak, but when he raised his head and looked at Martin, the doctor stepped back.

"Will!"

The handyman materialized in the open doorway. Peter looked from him to Martin, and shrugged.

"You've made your point," he said, and sauntered toward the door. Will stepped back to let him pass; he left without another word or backward glance.

"Make sure he leaves the house," Martin ordered. He closed the door and came over to the bed, taking both Kate's limp hands in his.

"My poor darling. What have you done?"

Witchcraft or weather report, Tiphaine was right. Kate didn't hear the wind rise and howl around the house; she was deep in drugged sleep. She woke next morning to a bright, cold world, as brilliantly polished as a jewel. She lay unmoving for a few moments, trying to grasp the vague memory that made her uneasy; then she recalled what had happened the night before. But the recollection wasn't as painful as it might have been.

Fatigue and the aftermath of shock had dulled her memories of the later part of the night, but she remembered Martin's soft voice, repeating reassurances. There was no proof; it was Peter's word against hers. She could deny ever saying it. Confessions under duress weren't evidence. It was all right. Everything was all right. . . .

Evidently Tiphaine had heard of Peter's visit, for her expression when she greeted Kate at the breakfast table was anxious.

"Mr. Watts called," she said tentatively. "He said he'd be out at ten, if that wasn't too early. I'm to call him back if you—"

"That's fine," Kate said. "Ten o'clock is fine."

She patted the younger girl's cheek and saw her face brighten at this unusual demonstration of affection.

At ten Mr. Watts duly appeared, and she signed the will. He had brought two of his clerks with him as witnesses. Common courtesy demanded that she offer him coffee, and she managed to conceal her annoyance when he accepted. Luckily he was too busy to linger long. By eleven he had left, and Kate went out of doors. The day looked so bright and fair that she was caught unawares by the strength of the wind; it swooped at her and sent her staggering. At the sound of the door being opened, Pyewacket came darting toward her like a black streak of lightning. His morning nap in the sun had proved too uncomfortable with the wind plucking at every hair. Naturally he blamed Kate for the weather; he spat at her when she held the door for him.

Kate walked around the side of the south wing, bending over to pick up fallen branches which had been blown down by the wind. That must have been a real gale last night. She found the cold air refreshing; it seemed to blow a few of the cobwebs from her brain.

When she reached the kitchen door it opened and Tiphaine came out. She was wearing a bulky cable-knit sweater of off-white over her black slacks, and she carried Kate's jacket.

"Here you are. Out in this wind without a coat?"

"I was just about to go in."

"It's too nice a day." Tiphaine held the jacket for her. "Want to beat me at archery?"

"I thought you hated it."

"I feel like doing something violent." Tiphaine grinned and clutched at her hair. It was lifting straight up off her head, like a bright flame. "Come on, it'll do you good."

"All right. But you won't even hit the target in this wind."

Her prediction proved to be correct. Tiphaine hadn't had enough experience to allow for the wind, and her arrows sailed blithely in every direction. The girl was in one of her giddily cheerful moods this morning; she laughed at each blunder. Kate shot with her usual methodical care, finding the challenge of the wild gusts interesting, and managed to get a reasonable number of black-and-red-feathered shafts into the inner circles of the target. On Tiphaine's next turn the wind, which had been playing with her hair like a lover, wrapped the whole length of its ruddy gold around her face, and her shot went so wide that Kate jumped back, even though she was standing, as prescribed, behind the archer.

"That's enough of that," Tiphaine said, muffled. She unwound herself and unstrung her bow. "I'll shoot myself if I go on this way. Coming in, Kate?"

She had to repeat the question. Kate was staring off, across the lichened gray stones of the wall, toward the woods. The brilliant colors were beginning to fade now; last night's gale had stripped many of the remaining leaves from the trees. But the effect was still glorious, and it seemed to draw her.

"What?" she said. "No, I think maybe I'll go for a walk."

"It's almost lunchtime," Tiphaine said. Kate turned to answer, and was just in time to see the look of calculation, quickly veiled, which had narrowed the girl's eyes. "Maybe there is time for a walk," she went on, too quickly. "I'll come with you. I can't after lunch; I promised Miss Device I'd help her with some sewing."

"Let's skip the walk, then," Kate said casually. "I'm getting hungry."

She waited until Tiphaine left for town before she got up from the chaise longue on which she had promised to nap. Looking out the window, she saw the car slow at the gate and then spin sharply to the right. She collected shoes, jacket, and a scarf for her hair, and went out.

She found herself tiptoeing on the stairs and listening for sounds. There should be none; Mrs. Schmidt would be busy in the kitchen, and Will always disappeared after lunch—for a nap, she suspected, though she had never caught him at it. And what difference did it make if anyone saw her? She was the mistress of the house; she was going out for a little walk. Nevertheless, she was very careful in closing the heavy front door, and she didn't put her shoes on until she was outside. As she set out across the lawn she was almost running.

She had to cross the stubble of Mr. Goldberg's cornfield to reach the wood from this direction. Walking was hard among the stiff short stalks, and she took care not to fall on any of them. Goldberg had planted a few vines of pumpkin along the edge; the big orange globes looked like fallen moons, but not pretty golden moons—more like the swollen red monsters that hang above a smoky horizon like goblin faces. Speaking of faces, the children had been busy among the pumpkins. Presumably they had carried the successful carvings off with them, but a few botched jack-o'-lanterns lay among litters of seed and pulp. One had been almost finished when the knife slipped, making a long, twisted gash of a mouth. Its big round eyes stared up at her, hollowed and empty with blackness.

Kate shivered. The jolliness gone wrong, the sinister merriment, reminded her that Halloween had originally been Allhallows' Eve, the night when the dead walk and the powers of evil have strength to work their will. That's the sort of thing we do here, she thought; we try to hide horror with a painted clown's mask. Our funerals, and embalming, and . . . She shook herself mentally and went on at a faster pace. Of all the morbid trains of thought . . .

Once inside the woods she felt better, but even the familiar, friendly terrain seemed changed. It was a wild wood, which had never been cleared; she liked its tangled freedom, even when her ankles were scratched by shoots of wild holly and fir, and trapped by the ubiquitous honeysuckle. It was a bright, vivid place even in winter; the orange berries of bittersweet stood out against the green of the pines, and blue jays and cardinals swung from graceful bare branches. There were always animals about, and she knew many of them personally; hours spent sitting, in perfect stillness, on a fallen log or rock had accustomed many of the shy wood dwellers to her presence. There was an old striped badger, who lived in a bank farther back in the woods, and a family of woodchucks, who trundled out to sun themselves on warm days. But today nothing seemed to be stirring. The woods were uncannily quiet. Once a jay shrieked, and the harsh note broke off in mid-call, as if the sound of its own voice had frightened the bird.

She was on the bridle path when she heard hoofbeats coming toward her. The rider was still out of sight, and Kate looked about for a side path she could duck into. She didn't feel in the mood for people. Then the horse came into view. She recognized both horse and rider, and dashed toward the trees.

In her haste she picked a spot where honeysuckle made an almost impenetrable curtain between two pines. Tearing at the resistant stems, Kate watched his handling of the horse and knew for certain what she had only suspected before. That fall of his had been a fake.

He slid down off the horse and came toward her, and Kate abandoned her attempt at flight. Better to meet him here, in a semipublic place.

He was dressed even more carelessly than usual, in a dark sweater and slacks which needed pressing; above the black fabric his face looked bleached and spectral, the skin drawn tightly over the high cheekbones, the eyes faintly shadowed.

"I tried to see you this morning," he said. "They've got the place too well guarded."

"Naturally. You realize that what I said last night—"

"Forget about that. I'm interested in this morning. Have you signed that will?"

Kate gaped, not knowing whether to be more surprised at his casual dismissal of her admission, or at his knowledge.

"How did you know about the will? I mean, that I was signing it this morning?"

"Snooping," Peter said briefly. "Have you signed it?"

"Yes."

"Damn." He ran his fingers through his hair so that it stood up on end like a rooster's crest.

"It's none of your business, anyhow," Kate said, and tried to pass him. He caught her by the arms.

"I'm not going to struggle with you," she said distantly. "Nor argue, nor even talk. So you may as well let me go."

His fingers tightened and then relaxed, though he did not release her.

"I've been up most of the night, thinking," he muttered. "But I suppose there's nothing I could say to you, now, that would make you believe . . . Tell me something. You've been paying blackmail. For Mark's death, I suppose. To whom?"

In her numbed state, his shock tactics were very effective.

"Timmy," she said; and her hand flew to her mouth as her eyes widened in horror.

"Timmy again. Damn it all—you've no idea who's behind him, I suppose. . . . No. The Schmidts. Did you inherit them from Uncle Stephan too?"

"Yes. Damn you, damn you!" She forgot her dignity, and her decision not to struggle, and began twisting frantically. "What are you trying to do? Can't you leave me alone?"

"I wish to God I could. You'd better not do that," he added, his tight mouth relaxing a trifle, as she began pounding him on the chest with her clenched fists. "It's not only undignified, but it has a bad effect on me."

He pulled her roughly into his arms, pinning her hands between his body and hers, and kissing her with an intensity that forced her head back into the curve of his shoulder. After the first second Kate forgot the discomfort of her twisted neck and laboring lungs; she was not even aware of the moment when her body relaxed and her mouth answered the demand of his.

He let her go so suddenly that she staggered, catching blindly at the tangled vines for support, not feeling the bite of them against her palms. Something rustled in the underbrush and Peter whirled, breathing hard. Silence fell; and Peter's clenched hands relaxed.

"I'm tempted," he said, in a voice whose tone belied the mocking words, "to drag you up onto that horse and carry you off. But I wouldn't get far, would I?"

Kate tried to say something, and found that her voice had deserted her. She shook her head violently.

"No," he agreed. "Not with you screaming bloody murder every step of the way."

Kate cleared her throat.

"Anyhow," she pointed out, "you haven't got a horse."

Peter swung around with a vehement remark. Sultan was still in sight, but retreating fast, one eye cocked warily. Peter started out after him.

"I'll be back," he called out. "Try not to do anything stupid between now and six o'clock, will you?"

Kate ran.

She ran faster than she had ever run in her life, ran till her legs ached and the pain in her side finally forced her to slow to a limping walk. The thing she was trying to run away from couldn't be escaped so easily. It rode with her, step for step and yard for yard. She sank to the ground at the edge of the wood, in a tangle of arms and legs and disheveled hair. The wild wind hummed angrily in the trees above.

Her brain felt as if it were boiling like a caldron. A hodgepodge of mixed ideas, emotions, and fancies bubbled and seethed. One thought popped to the surface, and she was just beginning to see it clearly when it broke and sank, and another took its place. She sprawled in a heap of leaves, face hidden in her folded arms. As her frantic breathing slowed, so did the seething thoughts; but the mental terrain that now lay open to her was as unfamiliar as a landscape after an earthquake has tumbled mountains.

For a long time she lay still. How long she did not know, but when she finally sat up and opened her eyes, the sun was sinking westward and the shadows had grown longer. Out of the jumble of wild emotion one predominant feeling stood isolated and unshakable. She marveled that she had not recognized it long before.

Only then did she hear the voice. It must have been calling for some time; it sounded hoarse and frantic. She looked up, and saw Tiphaine standing by the wall.

She must answer; they would be worried about her. Unsteadily she got to her feet and waved. Tiphaine turned, saw her, and ran toward her.

"Kate! I've been so worried. . . . What happened?"

"Nothing happened. I just—went for a walk."

"You look so . . . You saw him, didn't you?"

"Peter? How did you know?"

Her voice was harsh; the younger girl stepped back a pace.

"Why—General Volz called. He said Peter had borrowed Sultan, and wondered if I planned to ride today."

"Oh." Kate started walking toward the house.

"What did he say?"

"Who?"

"Peter, of course. Kate, what's wrong with you? You look sort of drunk."

"It's that stuff Paul gave me, I guess." Kate stopped, turning toward her cousin. She had to look up into Tiphaine's face. "Tiphaine, I've been thinking. We haven't had a vacation for a long time. I think perhaps we ought to get away from here for a few weeks, maybe longer."

"A vacation?" Tiphaine's smooth face was expressionless.

"Yes. Tomorrow we might go to one of the travel agencies, and collect some folders. Maybe even Europe."

"Tomorrow." Tiphaine's face cleared, and Kate felt sick with relief. It was going to be easier than she had thought. "That's a wonderful idea, Kate."

The sound was faint at first, but it rapidly got louder—a wild, rhythmic pounding, like drumbeats. Tiphaine understood its meaning before Kate did; she gasped, turning toward the trees, in time to see Sultan come thundering out into the open. The reins dangled loose on his neck, and the saddle was empty.

Sultan shied violently at the sight of them, and swerved. Tiphaine ran toward him, calling; he came to a crashing stop and stood with his head drooping. Kate followed more slowly. She was a poor horsewoman at best, and Sultan had always terrified her. Nor was she as quick as Tiphaine to catch the implications. Not until she was standing beside her cousin, and caught a glimpse of Tiphaine's face, did she realize what the empty saddle might mean.

"He must have been thrown," she exclaimed.

"I guess so," Tiphaine said slowly.

"Or else he never did catch Sultan." That idea was reassuring; Kate snatched at it. "The brute was running away from him when I left him. That was—oh, a long time ago—"

"How long ago?"

"I don't know. I don't remember very well."

"Kate, you don't know much about horses, do you? Look at Sultan."

She knew that much; she had been trying not to see it. Sultan the vicious was in a state of pitiable terror. Shivering, sweating, nosing at Tiphaine's hand, he did not look like a mount which has triumphantly tossed its rider and run for home. He hadn't gone home. He had bolted, blindly and madly, and by the look of him he had been running for some time.

Kate's knees went weak. She put one hand on the saddle for support, and jerked it away as something warm and sticky smeared her fingers. In silence she held her hand out for inspection. Across the palm there was a wet reddish streak.

Tiphaine said something. Kate didn't hear the words, only a buzzing, like a fly trapped against a window. Inside her head, echoing hollowly, words had begun to form: an insane litany that beat in time with the cold, rushing wind's moan.

"Cold blows the wind . . . cold blows the wind. . . ."

Somehow she got into the saddle. The stirrups were too long, and she couldn't seem to get her feet into them. She slammed her heels into the horse's sides. Tiphaine's hands pulled at her. She shook them off and snatched at the rough mane as Sultan bolted.

Under any other circumstances she could never have controlled Sultan. He was too big and too strong-mouthed. Now he was no longer an animal; he was simply a means of locomotion, and the will that drove her mastered him.

Sultan took the main trail at a dead run. They met no one. The woods were as still as death, shadowy under the tall pines. When they neared the turnoff to the glade, the horse stopped so suddenly that only Kate's taut grip on his mane kept her from flying out over his head. She did not need the animal's signs of panic to tell her the way. A horse had been through the cutoff, though it had not been intended as a bridle trail. The hoof marks were clear on the bare patches of ground off the hard surface of the main trail.

She forced Sultan onto the cutoff, but it took all her will to do it, and that will was fading, with the fear of what she knew she would find. At the edge of the glade he balked, planting all four feet like rocks. He would go no farther. Katharine, perched precariously on his back, felt the shivering muscles under her thighs like an extension of her own shaking body.

The clearing was carpeted with gypsy-colored leaves, but enough foliage still remained on the trees to cut out the sunlight and cast a blue haze over the scene before her. In the shadows the man's body lay face down and utterly still, looking two-dimensional, like a figure cut out of black paper. One shaft of sunlight cut down like a spotlight, gilding the tumbled fair hair. Its oblique path caught the tip of the arrow that stood up from his back like a little banner. The feathers were black and red. In Kate's ears the old song rang with a sick, hollow whine, like a bad recording:

"And he in greenwood now lies slain."

# Chapter

## 10

THE TREES TURNED UPSIDE DOWN, TRUNKS UP AND branches toward her feet. Kate slid off the horse's back, landing on hands and knees.

Standing erect was out of the question. She crawled across the few feet that separated her from Peter. For a long minute she knelt there, hands on her knees, watching gravely as the tip of the arrow bobbed up and down and the trees swayed in a slow, sickening dance. It took her that long—sixty interminable seconds—to realize that the two movements were not the same. The feathers were moving, minutely but perceptibly, with the rhythm of his breathing.

She put out a shaking hand to touch his head, and saw the bizarre barometer of breath jerk more vigorously.

"Don't move," she said, in a voice which sounded too steady to be her own. "You've got an arrow sticking in you."

There was a long moment of silence, while she sat listening to Peter's breathing. It was emphatic and irregular now, punctuated with more peremptory sounds of life. Finally a muffled voice said, "What was that you said?"

"An arrow. In your back."

"Oh." He turned his head carefully, without lifting it, and Kate found herself staring into one half-closed blue eye. The eye narrowed still more as recognition dawned.

"Arrow," he repeated, as if the word were too incredible to believe. "One of yours, by any chance?"

"Yes, it's one of mine." She lifted both hands and let them fall, in a gesture of denial. "But I didn't do it. Probably you won't believe me."

Peter's eye closed.

"How did you find me?"

"Sultan came back alone. There was blood on the saddle."

"Isn't that the title of a song?" The silence went on so long that she bent over him in a new up-surge of terror, and his eye opened again. This time it looked more alert.

"Pull it out."

"Peter, I daren't. I'll go for Paul. He'll know—"

Peter levered himself up on one elbow.

"If you didn't fire the bloody thing, someone

else did. I'd rather not wait around until he comes back to dispose of the remains." His eyes narrowed as he studied her pale face and silently working mouth; then the corners of his mouth curled up in the familiar, detestable smile. "Chicken?" he inquired gently.

Kate took a deep breath.

"Brace yourself," she said, and grasped the shaft, as close to the point as she could.

It had not penetrated as deeply as she feared, but clearly it was deeper than he had thought; he was flat on his face and squirming by the time she had finished. She took advantage of his position to apply a wadded-up handkerchief to the wound, and then held the evidence in front of the face he had turned toward her.

"Hunting arrow," he muttered.

"I never use them."

"I know. Drop it, we shan't learn anything from it. Everyone in town must know your colors. Let's make ourselves scarce."

"Can you walk?"

"I'll crawl if I must," he said grimly, and pushed himself to his knees.

"I have Sultan. If you can mount . . ."

They managed it somehow, though it wasn't easy; by the time Peter was in the saddle, clutching the pommel with both hands and swaying ominously, there was a sizable wet patch on the back of his sweater.

Katharine took the reins and they started off.

Sultan was unhappy, and his gait had never been noted for smoothness; she heard Peter's breath catch every time a hoof came down.

"Hold on," she said, without looking at him. "If you fall off, I'll never get you back up there."

"I'll hold on."

"Peter. What were you doing out there?"

He muttered something that sounded like "later," and swore feebly as a branch struck his bowed head. When they turned onto the bridle path the going was easier, and again Kate found time to wonder at the unnatural stillness of the woods. The shady, sun-streaked leaves seemed frozen, as if waiting. Only the creak of the saddle and the slow rhythmic plop of the horse's hooves broke the stillness. She turned to look at Peter, and saw that he had slumped forward till his head touched Sultan's neck. Her hand loosened its hold, and Sultan stopped. Peter straightened, blinking.

"What's up?"

"I'd better walk beside you, it's safer." She slapped the horse's flank. "Come on, you nasty brute, walk."

"No, wait. Where're we going?"

"To the house, I guess. Then I'd better—"

"Got to talk first," he interrupted. "Can't wait. You know . . . what . . ."

She interrupted in turn, trying to spare him the effort of talking.

"I know someone just tried to kill you. From

the questions you asked me earlier, I gather you've been snooping, as you put it, into the various unpleasant things that have been happening to me. I'm assuming, as a working hypothesis, that the would-be murderer is the person who's been blackmailing me. You think the Schmidts may be involved. It's certainly a possibility. There are a lot of other things I don't understand; I don't know why a blackmailer would want to— try to drive me out of my mind. People who've been judged insane can't sign checks. And I don't know why you . . . why you . . ."

Peter was sitting up straighter and looking more alert. He did not comment on her last, un-voiced question, nor on the faltering of her voice.

"What a pleasure it is to meet someone with a logical mind," he murmured. "That's fine, as far as it goes. But you don't understand the really vital part yet. And I doubt if I could explain it. I'm not even sure I believe it myself. Do you know what today is?"

"Why—October thirty-first. What about it?"

Peter's eyes rolled expressively heavenward.

"Think, Kate, think. It's all there, if you'll just face it. Common garden-variety murderers don't use bow and arrow. In a forest glade, Kate, with a black stone and a babbling brook—in the greenwood, as the poet says. And the date—ah, I see you have thought of it."

The blue eyes met the black in a long, demanding stare; Kate's eyes were the first to fall.

"No," she said. "It isn't possible."

Sultan, sensing her agitation, stamped and snorted; and Peter exclaimed aloud and caught at his shoulder.

"Hurry," he said through clenched teeth. "We mustn't be here after the sun sets."

The sun had set before they reached the house. Behind the skeletal trees to the west the sunset flamed in angry hues of red and orange, scarred by slashes of purple and black clouds. The house swam in the dimness of twilight. There was no light, no sound, and no sign of a living occupant.

Kate, supporting most of Peter's sagging weight, let her held breath out in a sigh of relief. She hadn't wanted to come back here, but there was literally nowhere else to go. Volz's was the only nearby house, and Volz, of all people . . . But the Schmidts seemed to be gone; at least they hadn't heard her come in.

But they might come looking for her at any moment, finding her alone, burdened with an injured man. Peter was conscious, but just barely; she couldn't drag him much farther, certainly not up the stairs. She stood undecided in the dim hall, biting her lip nervously. Would it be better to get him into her car and head straight for town? The car was out in back, and if the Schmidts were in the kitchen, they would hear the engine start up. No, there was a quicker way to get help. She maneuvered her burden into the living room and let him drop onto the sofa. He moved feebly, and fell back; and Kate, rubbing aching shoulders, tiptoed out into the hall to the telephone.

Martin responded instantly, as she had known he would; no surprise, no questions, no delay. Only a few terse instructions and a promise to come at once. Luckily the capsules were in the medicine chest in the downstairs bathroom. Martin had prescribed them for her headaches, but she had never used them—that silly phobia of hers about drugs.

She collected the other supplies she was going to need and fled for the living room, closing the door behind her with an absurd sense that she had reached sanctuary. There was no reason to be afraid now; even if her wildest fears were true, even if they found her, help was on the way.

Peter was trying to sit up when she came in, and he resisted her attempts to get him down again.

"Too dangerous," he muttered. "Kate . . . got to talk. I'm so damned dizzy. . . ."

"Take these." She offered him the pills, three of them, and a glass of water.

"What . . . ?"

"They're for pain. Like aspirin, only stronger."

He was too confused to argue. The pills went down, but Peter refused the water.

"Got any brandy?"

"Maybe you shouldn't."

"I'll risk it. Need something . . . quick."

He swallowed it in one gulp, buried his face in his hands, and then sat up, shaking his head.

"Wow. That's better. I'll need more patching up, I'm afraid, but make it quick. We'll talk while you work."

"Try not to yell," Kate warned as he lay flat, chin supported on his folded arms. "I don't want anyone to know we're here."

"I'm too tired to yell. You think the Schmidts are involved, then?"

"I don't know. That's just the trouble. I feel I can't trust anyone."

"Best possible assumption. That's what we have to talk about. I have an idea that—ouch! What are you putting on that, carbolic acid?"

"Peroxide. Are you all right?"

There was a lengthy pause before Peter replied.

"I'm so sleepy. What was I talking about?"

"I told you not to take that brandy. Hold still."

She applied strips of tape with a hand which was none too steady. It was hard to see, the twilight was so far advanced. But she didn't dare turn on a light. Her ears strained to hear the sound she hoped for, the familiar rattle and clank of the old car. But the windows were closed; maybe she wouldn't hear the car. He could get in. The front door was unlocked.

Peter was so still she feared he had fainted under her awkward hands. The room seemed very dark. And cold. Peter had begun to shiver. She remembered the danger of shock, and squinted into the gloom, trying to find something to put over him. But she knew there was nothing of that sort in the room, not even an afghan.

"Peter. Peter, can you hear me?"

A vague murmur was the only response.

"Peter! I've got to go upstairs and get something, a blanket, or—"

He sat bolt upright, in one convulsive movement.

"You're not going upstairs. We're leaving, both of us. This was crazy, coming here. . . . I've just realized . . . they'll be looking for us, it's dark now, and this is the logical place. After dark . . . before midnight. . . ."

His voice dropped to a mumble, and Kate peered anxiously at the pale oval of his face.

"Peter, lie down. You're sick. You don't know what you're saying."

"Got to get out of here," Peter insisted querulously. "May not know we're here . . . yet . . . but they'll wait. Out there. Go out the window. Around the side to the car . . ."

"It's all right, Peter. Paul will be here any minute. I called him as soon as we arrived, and he said—"

His hands caught her by the shoulders, sinking painfully into the old bruises.

"You did what?"

"Called the doctor, of course. What—"

He let her go, so suddenly that she fell to one side; then he slumped forward, hands buried in his hair.

"God Almighty. I've got to think. . . . What the hell is wrong with me? Maybe it's not too late. The window."

"Oh, no, Peter. Not—"

"You are hard to convince, aren't you? Too damned trusting, that's your trouble. . . . Said it yourself, don't trust anybody." Peter pushed himself upright and stood swaying drunkenly. "Don't wait for me. Run. Maybe . . . not too late. . . ."

"I'm afraid it is," Martin said regretfully.

The overhead chandelier went on, in a blinding burst of light, and somehow Kate found herself in Peter's arms, not quite sure who was supporting whom, but illogically reassured by the feel of him. From under blinking eyelids she saw Martin in the doorway, smiling pleasantly.

"Very touching," he said. "You make such an attractive couple. It really is a pity."

"You don't have to kill her," Peter mumbled. "She'll agree—"

"Too late for that, too. If she'd agreed to marry me . . . But I knew the other day, when I heard her disgusting babbling about you, that I hadn't a chance."

"Then it wasn't you who suggested . . ." Peter shook his head. "I can't think," he said plaintively.

"I see you've taken your medicine," Martin said with a smile. "But you suspected me, earlier; I overheard what you were saying before I came in. Where did I go wrong? I thought I was doing a magnificent job of being the stalwart, loyal family doctor."

"The will."

"Not until then? Well, that is a relief. But I don't think anyone else will find it peculiar. Even the lawyer seemed to think it was reasonable for Kate to leave her money to her sole surviving relative."

"Won't be so reasonable . . . if she dies," Peter muttered.

"Oh, it will seem quite reasonable. You don't know the rest of the plan yet. But you soon will. Come along, both of you."

Now that the first shock of his appearance had worn off, Kate was trying desperately to think. The Schmidts were involved, then; they must be, or Martin wouldn't be so confident of his control of the situation. But he hadn't called them. He didn't even have a weapon. He thought he could easily handle a woman and a man weakened by— drugs, of course. Those pills! Kate's knees buckled under Peter's weight, and as his head dropped onto her shoulder she gasped,

"You've killed him! What was in those capsules?"

"He's not dead, he's just sleeping peacefully. So much kinder that way."

Martin sauntered toward them and Kate sank to her knees, still stubbornly clutching at Peter. He was a dead weight; but as they went down she

felt his elbow dig into her ribs, and she threw herself into her part with abandon, wringing her
hands as she bent over him.

"He's dead, he's dead; you've killed him!"

She slid back out of the way as Martin knelt to
inspect his victim; and Peter's legs came up,
knees bent. But his reflexes were dulled by the
drug; Martin saw the blow coming, and ducked.
Instead of hitting his head, Peter's knees struck
his shoulder and sent him sprawling. Peter got to
his feet, teeth set in his lower lip; and as Kate
sprang toward him he spun her around, put his
hands in the middle of her back, and shoved.

She went staggering toward the window, knowing she couldn't stop herself. . . . Then her outflung hands struck the panel and the door leaves
burst open. Kate went reeling out onto the balcony.

It was not like the sham balconies in the other
rooms, being wider, longer, and railed with stone.
Kate hit the balustrade with a force that knocked
the breath out of her. Clinging to the cold stone
with both hands, she looked back over her shoulder. Framed by the window, under the glaring
lights, the interior of the room looked unreal, like
a set in a play. Peter was down, and decidedly out;
there was no pretense this time about his twisted
limbs and head. He had used the last of his
strength to give her a chance of escape. And not
only her—his only hope of survival lay in her being able to get help. If she was caught, they were
both lost.

The logic was inescapable. The only trouble was, Kate couldn't move.

She couldn't run away and leave him. It was stupid, it was illogical; but for the moment primitive instinct was stronger than reason, and it froze her in her place.

Then Martin rose from beside Peter's body; and, with a queer choking noise, Kate flexed her knees and jumped over the edge of the balcony.

She landed with a thud in a big yew, scratching her arms and face and doing considerable damage to one ankle; but now that the decision had been made, she no longer hesitated. Martin ran out onto the balcony, and she crawled, under the shelter of the yew, toward the corner of the house. Before he could get over the balustrade she broke free, running as fast as she could toward the front of the house.

He reacted as she had hoped. By going through the house and out the front door, he could intercept her on the route she appeared to be taking— from the house to the front gate. As soon as he disappeared into the room, Kate turned.

She was heading for the car, and she was prepared to take some risks in order to acquire a speedy means of transportation; but some rudiments of caution remained, enough to make her stop before venturing into the open lawn behind the house.

It was as well she did so. The car was there, all right; she could see its outlines through the branches of the shrub behind which she cowered. She could also see Will Schmidt. The hood of the car was up, and he was bending over the engine.

Kate gritted her teeth. Damn Martin; he would think of that. When Schmidt straightened and turned, in response to a hail from the front of the house, she knew the car was useless to her. It would take too long to find out what part Will had gimmicked. Perhaps it wasn't even repairable.

Schmidt carefully lowered the hood before setting off at an ungainly lope to join his confederate. Kate grinned savagely. If she hadn't seen him at work, she might have wasted vital moments trying to start the engine.

Instead of backtracking, she slid around the corner of the house in the same direction Schmidt had taken, but at an angle, avoiding the car. As she ran, she fought back a wild desire to go back. They must have left Peter alone. If she could rouse him . . . But the idea was absurd. He was deep in drugged sleep, and too weak to go fast and quietly even if she could waken him. She turned her mind instead to alternate means of transportation. It was miles to town, it would take too long to walk, and they would be searching for her. They . . . She had never realized the terror that could be implicit in a simple pronoun. She didn't know who they were, or how many they were. All she knew was their purpose. But that was enough.

So it would have to be the woods, and Volz's

stables. Sultan had gone home a long time ago, she had been too much preoccupied with more important matters to tie him, and he was not the horse to linger when bed and breakfast beckoned. Volz might be one of *them*; he was a horrible man anyhow, and she didn't dare ask him for help. Timmy, as everyone knew, went to his own room at sunset. . . .

Timmy.

Kate set her teeth and ran faster. Timmy had always made her skin crawl, even before the recent events in which he had been so oddly involved. But in her present mood she was prepared to deal with Timmy, or anyone else near her own size. It might be just as well, though, to take some precautions. She slowed to a walk, forced to do so by the pain in her straining lungs, and put the delay to good use by scanning the shadowy sides of the path. A stout stick and—yes, there was a stone just the right size, small enough to fit comfortably into her fist, big enough to hurt. She would just have to hit Timmy if he tried to get between her and one of Volz's horses.

Or Volz's car? No. The keys wouldn't be in the ignition, they would be in Hilary's pocket, and Hilary would be shut in his own room and disinclined, in any case, to give aid and comfort to anyone. Besides, the car made too much noise.

She stumbled as her weakened ankle gave way, and fell head first against a tree trunk, hitting her forehead so hard that for an instant she saw bright lights whirling inside her eyeballs. With a whimper of pain she ran on. The lights weren't as bad as the other things she kept seeing inside her eyes, the visions of what they might be doing to Peter.

When she reached the edge of the woods she stopped, rubbing her aching head. Her vision was blurred, and she had to blink before it cleared.

What she saw made her stomach sink, sickeningly. The moonlight shone off the polished surfaces of a number of cars parked outside the stable gates, and most of the downstairs lights were blazing. Tonight, of all nights, Volz was entertaining.

Kate slumped against a tree trunk, sick with despair. She couldn't go out there when the house was full of people and the chauffeurs were standing around, smoking and talking. Surely there was someone in the town, someone among the owners of those cars, to whom she could appeal for aid?

She looked again, and gradually she realized that there was something strange about the cars. The weird outlines of Miss Device's old electric runabout were unmistakable. She was one of the sights of the town in that car, sitting bolt upright on the high seat. Miss Device would not be much of an ally. She would twitter and wring her hands.

Miss Device always drove herself. But the others . . . Joan Solomon did too, her white Cadillac was in the lot, parked at Joan's usual, acute angle next to the Senator's Rolls. The Senator had a chauffeur. Where was he?

A cold wind put chilly fingers down her spine, and she knew the answer. In nice weather the chauffeurs hung around outside. On a night like this, with a long party in prospect, they would be in the kitchen, or with Hilary in his room. No, Hilary would probably be helping with the serving. He would be inside.

Kate straightened, her hopes rising. Maybe the situation wasn't so hopeless. She would just have to be careful. But no cars. Joan had probably left her keys. She had lost two cars that way, but she still forgot the keys. But Joan's Cadillac was too hard to get at, through the tangle of surrounding fenders.

The stableyard gates were closed, as they always were at night. Kate sighed. Another wall to climb. At least this was wooden, and slatted, instead of crumbling stone. When she was inside the yard she unbarred the gate to facilitate her retreat. Then she crept toward the stalls.

She had already decided which horse to take. Not Sultan. She would have to ride bareback; saddling up would take too much time. The little mare Starlight was the gentlest of Volz's horses. But with Starlight Kate knew she had to get out of the yard unseen and unsuspected. Sultan could outrun the mare any day of the week, and so could most of the others, especially with skilled horsemen on their backs.

Her skin crawling in spite of her resolve, she inspected all the stalls to make sure Timmy wasn't napping in one of them. Sometimes he did. But he had a catlike regard for his own comfort—or what he considered comfort, which did not include cleanliness. She was relieved, but not surprised, to find no trace of him.

In the silent stableyard, the only sounds came from the horses. Kate jumped as something touched her ankle and then relaxed when she recognized Grimalkin, the stable cat, twining himself around her ankles. He was normally an unsociable animal, but he liked her. Kate stooped to touch his fur, thinking wryly that in this town a cat's approval was not necessarily a compliment.

Her presence acknowledged, the cat stalked off, tail high, and Kate reached in to unlatch Starlight's stall door. The mare turned her head with a little inquiring sound, and Kate grabbed for her mouth. Starlight's melting brown eyes looked calmly at the intruder; she was not alarmed, because nothing alarmed her. Her placid disposition was the reason why Kate had chosen her.

Then the shadows moved.

Kate spun around. Timmy stood in the doorway. His face was a featureless darkness, but she recognized the slight figure outlined against the pale moonlight. She took in a breath which was almost a gasp. The first sight of him had had the effect of a blow in the pit of the stomach. But the stone was in her left-hand pocket. The stick was clenched in her right hand.

"Get out of the way, Timmy," she said softly. "Go back to your own room."

Timmy's shadowy head moved from side to side. His slim body didn't really block the doorway; she could see the cobbles of the courtyard on either side of him. She raised her stick.

"Go back. Or I'll tell Mr. Volz on you."

Timmy's head jerked back, and for a moment she thought her threat had frightened him. Then she heard the soft sounds he was making, and recognized them for what they were; and for a second another fear, the fear of the normal for the stain of madness, gripped her throat. It was then that she saw the others moving slowly in from behind and from both sides. Bizarre, nightmare shapes: a wolf, man-tall, walking on its hind legs; a woman in long black skirts and a stiff white cap that concealed her features as completely as the wolf-snout hid the other face; a crouching dark shape with a ghoul's face that had run like melted lava and shone with a sick green luminescence; a wrinkled harridan with long gray locks streaming under a pointed hat, carrying a broom. . . . A witch, like the witch costume the little girl had worn that night, so long ago . . .

Halloween night. Costume . . .

Kate's reeling brain swayed back from the edge of hysteria. It was Halloween, and Volz was giving a costume party.

She knew the others now, knew the faces—the familiar faces, many of which she had known all her life. Miss Device, dressed like her long-dead ancestress; Mrs. Adams, the witch; Joan Solomon, in a dirty torn shift that showed far too much of her ample figure. There were leaves, dark ugly leaves, twisted in her hair. And foremost among them was General Volz himself, dressed in the tall hat and white ruff and buckled shoes worn by the Salem judges. He was smiling.

"We were pretty sure you'd head for here," he said.

They were all smiling. Familiar faces, looking as she had never seen them look. . . . Her mind made the final, mad connection, and without conscious thought she began to count. Seven, eight, nine. Nine of them. And the others, the four others—that made . . .

"Thirteen," she said aloud; and Volz, following her reasoning with an ease that was the final confirmation, nodded his bullet head.

"Thirteen," he agreed. "That's the proper number. Isn't it, Dr. More?"

## Chapter

## 11

THEY TIED HER HANDS AND FEET, SINCE VOLZ WAS
driving alone, but they didn't bother to gag her.
Kate knew why. The hired chauffeurs had been
left at home tonight; but if they had been here, or
if Hilary heard her cry out, no one would answer.
On Allhallow's Eve the poor ignorant darkies
huddled in their shacks, fearing the powers of
darkness. . . .

Nuts, Kate thought inelegantly, and gasped as
Volz tossed her carelessly into the back seat of the
car. The population of the town, black and white,
knew enough to stay home tonight, but it was not
superstition that kept them in, but a real, tangible
fear. Fear of the superior, sophisticated gentry of
the town, whose combined wealth and power

turned their vicious hobby into an instrument of terror.

Had she been the only blind fool in the whole town? Now that she knew, so many hints and seemingly meaningless incidents fell into place, made horrible sense. But she wouldn't have believed, even if someone had warned her. She hadn't even believed it that afternoon, when Peter had shown her the pattern. The pattern was there, it couldn't be denied, but she had preferred to view it as the result of a suggestion made to a sick mind, carried out with the remorseless, twisted logic of madness. Peter had known the truth. He knew she wouldn't believe him. Peter . . . She turned her head into the slick leather upholstery and stifled a moan. She had failed. And what lay in store for them both was worse even than she had imagined.

Volz's erratic, triumphant driving made even the expensive car ride uncomfortably; she was jolted and jarred, unable to fend herself off from the hard surfaces against which she was flung. Finally she managed to wedge herself into a corner so that she could see out the window. As she had expected, they were heading for her house. The gates stood open, and Volz drove straight in, stopping by the steps with a jolt that threw her forward.

He left her in the car, and Kate tried to pull herself up. Surely there must be something she could do. . . . She wasn't given time even to think. Volz was back almost at once, and Martin was with him. Between them they carried Peter.

When they reached the car, Volz let his share of the burden drop with a thud and opened the back door.

"Couldn't you have waked him up?" he demanded irritably. "We'll have a hell of time dragging him through the brush."

"Feet in first," Martin ordered. "He'll be waking by the time we get there. I timed the injection carefully. But I don't want him too wide awake. I underestimated his resistance once, and it almost ended in disaster."

"We got her back," Volz grunted, jamming Peter's legs into the car. He stood back while Martin efficiently manipulated the rest of the load in. Kate looked hopefully for some sign of awareness, and found none; Peter slid bonelessly down onto the floor, his head and arms on the seat next to her. His breathing sounded odd.

"Yes, you got her back," Martin said contemptuously. He glanced into the car to make sure all was well; his eyes met Kate's and moved away without a flicker of expression. He slammed the door. "Thanks to me."

They moved around to the front of the car and Kate lost Volz's response. It was evidently acrimonious, for as he took his seat Martin said in a conciliatory tone, "There's no point in quarreling. Certainly not tonight. All's well that ends well."

Volz grunted and started the engine.

Neither man, spoke for the rest of the trip, which was incredibly bumpy; they drove straight across the field onto the bridle path. It was wide enough to take the car, but Volz had to spin the wheel like a top to avoid the worst ruts and holes. Kate twisted frantically and vainly as Peter's head slid off the seat and landed on the floor with a thud. Then she leaned forward, electrified, as he muttered something profane.

He was coming around, but it was too late. The car jolted to a stop, its headlights framing the spot she had expected to see: a scarlet trail of poison ivy winding up a tree trunk, and a broken branch sticking out at an odd angle.

The two men got out, and Martin opened the back door. He prodded Peter with his toe and got a half-intelligible epithet in response.

"How's that for accuracy?" he said in a pleased voice. "He can stand now. We'll have to drag him, but that's easier than carrying."

"We? Who's going to carry her?"

"Untie her feet."

"You fool, she'll bolt as soon as we get into the woods."

"With her hands tied she won't get far."

"She'll try it, though," Volz said glumly. "And I'm sick of chasing her around. We're short on time as it is."

Martin pursed his lips and looked at Kate. She stared back at him, wishing looks could kill.

"You would, wouldn't you," he said meditatively. "Well, let's spell out the obvious, shall we? If you should leave us, I will immediately cut Mr. Stewart's throat. It's a quick way to go, they tell me, but not necessarily painless."

He raised his eyebrows inquiringly, waited for a moment, and then smiled.

"I see we understand one another."

They got Peter on his feet, though he kept insisting he wanted to lie down. The final threat had finished Kate; she felt as if her whole body had gone to sleep, the way a foot does when it is twisted the wrong way for too long. At Martin's command she stumbled docilely off down the path. The two followed, supporting Peter; he was grumbling steadily, and Volz added a stream of curses every time they stumbled, which was fairly often.

As soon as they were out of range of the car's headlights, Martin switched on a flashlight which he held in his free hand. He shone it well in front of Kate's feet, but she was unable to protect herself from low branches, and there were stinging cuts all over her face by the time they reached the glade.

There, on another command, she stopped, and stood watching sluggishly while Martin shone the light around. He finally selected a tall pine almost directly across the clearing from the black stone. They stood Peter up against it. As soon as they let go of him, he started sliding slowly down; his eyes were closed and there was a satisfied smile on his face.

Martin, who was holding the flashlight while Volz did the work, said something uncomplimentary, and Volz propped his unresisting prisoner up again.

"He's still too groggy," he said angrily, and proceeded to remedy the situation by a series of sharp blows across the face.

The cure worked a little too well. Peter's eyes opened, and widened in indignation. He grabbed Volz by the ears and brought his knee up. The blow wasn't as hard as he intended it to be, but it was hard enough to flatten Volz. It happened so quickly, Kate didn't have time to react; she had only taken two steps when Martin's fist came down on the back of Peter's neck. By the time she reached him, he was sprawled face down on the ground, and Martin, the flashlight now in his left hand, said calmly.

"I have a gun, but I don't think I'll need it. All right, you incompetent idiot, get up. Must I do everything?"

Volz got up, but not with much enthusiasm. His face was the color of watered split-pea soup. Kate, who had been feeling frantically for what turned out to be, when her unsteady fingers finally located it, a quite healthy pulse, looked up warily as the general staggered toward them.

"You try that," she said, seeing his foot draw back, "and I'll pull your legs out from under you."

"Leave him alone," Martin said wearily. "We've wasted enough time. Besides, we wouldn't want him to miss the little surprise that's in store for him, would we?"

Volz relaxed, diverted by the thought; and Kate, who knew the sort of thought that diverted him, shivered.

"Try it again," Martin said. "Get a rope around his chest to hold him up, then tie his feet. From behind," he added sarcastically. "I thought you were in the army once."

Volz gave him a sour look but obeyed without comment. He handled Peter circumspectly until he had him securely bound; then he stood back and administered a hard backhanded blow across the face. Peter, who had begun to show a faint interest in the proceedings, subsided again, and Martin grabbed at Kate.

"You take the light," he said coldly. "I'll handle her. Can't you control yourself for a few hours, Harry?"

"I don't like him," Volz said simply. "Supercilious bastard . . . So long as I get a chance later . . ."

"That, as you know, will be the Master's decision."

Volz's reaction was surprising and a little chilling. He stiffened, as if standing at attention, and held the position for several seconds before doing as Martin directed.

That was the end of the conversation. Martin went about his business with his usual efficiency. The tree to which Kate was tied was near Peter's, but not quite near enough for her to touch him.

Martin handled her impersonally, as if she were a parcel he was wrapping for the mail. He walked off without so much as a backward glance. Volz followed, carrying the flashlight; for some time Kate could see it, like a giant firefly, bobbing and diminishing along the path. Then it disappeared altogether; and the dark swooped in.

The wind still moaned high in the treetops, but a few stars were visible in the cloudy sky. Something moved furtively in the brush not far away, and Kate wrestled vainly with the ropes. Not that there were dangerous animals in the woods; tales of wolf and bear were still told, but she didn't believe them . . . not really. All the same, it was unnerving to have anything, even a rabbit, approach when you were so helpless. She started when a voice said tentatively, "Kate. Is that you?"

"Yes."

"I was afraid of that. Where are you? I can't see you."

"We're back to back, so to speak. I can't see you either. I wish . . . I wish I could."

"It would help, wouldn't it. I'm sorry; I seem to have missed a good deal this evening. I seem to recall shoving you out the window just before Martin hit me with a mountain or something. I gather you didn't make good your escape?"

"I made it," she said miserably, and in a few sentences recapitulated what had happened.

"Well, don't brood about it," Peter said reasonably. "Thirteen to one is poor odds. . . . Thirteen?"

"Nine of them at the general's. And there are . . . four others."

Silence fell, broken only by the complaint of the wind-driven branches. It didn't seem quite so dark now; Kate's eyes were beginning to adjust. She could see the shapes of the surrounding trees and the menacing bulk of the black stone at the far end of the clearing. She waited for Peter's response with an anxiety which was, under the circumstances, a trifle absurd.

Finally he finished his mental accounting.

"I didn't realize you knew about Tiphaine," he said.

"I didn't think you knew! I was afraid you'd mind, terribly. . . ."

"Why? Oh. It's nice to know my atrocious acting convinced someone. The others must have been laughing up their sleeves the whole time. Tiphaine especially."

The tone in which he spoke the name filled Kate with a reprehensible but very human satisfaction. She said perversely, "I didn't think you could resist her. She's very lovely."

"Fishing for compliments at a time like this? I'll be damned if I'll inflate your ego any further. . . . Oh, there were times when I wondered why I didn't fall in love with her. But I didn't—believe it or not. And when I added up the miscellaneous facts I'd acquired, the conclusion was inescapable."

"It escaped me. Though I've always known there was something wrong about her. Living with her I've seen things—a word, a look, nothing important; but if you'd known Stephan, you'd worry about any child he brought up."

"I did worry. He was obviously serious about his dirty little hobby. Tiphaine had all the earmarks of the convert. Even the change of name, at adolescence, when many of the girls were introduced to the cult. . . ."

"And the name itself."

"Yes, I caught that after I did some reading. And the Folklore Society, the executive committee of the coven. When I think of how they led me by the nose, from the minute I arrived in town, I could kick myself. And I sat there like the sacrificial goat, congratulating myself on my cleverness. . . . I wonder what did go on at those business meetings?"

Kate leaned back against the tree trunk, feeling the rough bark prickle through her shirt and hair. The position wasn't as uncomfortable as it might have been; Martin had tied the ropes tightly enough to prevent escape, but not tightly enough to hurt, unless she moved.

"Peter."

"What?"

"About Mark. I want you to know, before . . . It was an accident, Peter. I didn't mean to."

"I know that."

"How could you know?"

"Because now I know you. MacDonald would have my ears for that remark," he added wryly. "Nailed to his wall. With me still attached."

"Who's MacDonald?"

"My editor."

"Is that what you do?"

"Journalist, yes."

"Journalist? Stewart . . . Is that who you are? I read about you—oh, several years ago. About the trial. They said you were a spy."

"They usually do say that."

"I know you weren't."

"Well, I was, actually. At least I was guilty of conspiracy and aiding a criminal to escape. Unfortunately I was also inept. The escape failed."

"I remember hearing about the execution of the leader."

"I knew Jan at school," Peter said. "That was why MacDonald sent me over there, when we got wind of the revolt being planned. First-hand reports from the rebel camp, that sort of crap. I went—I guess I hoped to talk Jan out of it. We knew it was bound to fail, the Russians have the satellites fast; they can't let any one of them go without losing the rest. Jan knew it, too; but men reach a point of desperation, where nothing matters but the need to act. . . . We almost got out, you know. But Jan had been wounded in the street fighting, he couldn't go fast. I got what I deserved—less, really; they could have shot me. There were times when I wished they had."

The calm, matter-of-fact voice stopped. The tears on Kate's cheeks felt warm in the cold air.

"One of those times must have been when you heard of Mark's death," she said. "Or didn't you find out till after you were released?"

"They told me. They let some letters come through, especially the ones with bad news. The worst of it was that I'd heard from Mark just before I left—one of his hysterical scrawls, full of references to the cold-hearted bitch who'd led him on and broken his heart. The beautiful succubus, La Belle Dame, et cetera. He's my half-brother, that's why our names aren't the same. Younger; I always felt responsible for him, especially after Mother died, even though I knew he was a bloody mess. He was constantly getting into scrapes and having to be bailed out of them, and the scrapes kept getting nastier. That was how he came to the Embassy, in one of those nonessential social jobs; I couldn't think what the hell else to do with him. The letter was typical Mark, full of self-pity and ravings about you. I didn't feel I could take the time to play Miles Standish—or was it the other fellow—not when Jan was in real trouble. So I went east instead of west."

"And you've been blaming yourself ever since."

"I've always blamed myself for everything Mark did. It was Mother, I suppose; isn't Mum the currently popular scapegoat? 'Watch out for Mark, darling, you know he isn't strong. . . . Don't let the big boys hurt Mark, Peter, he's so sensitive. . . . ' She was a very beautiful woman," he added wryly. "It never occurred to me to wonder why two different men had found her impossible to live with."

"No wonder you don't like women."

"You can hardly accuse me of that. . . . Maybe I do. Maybe that's why I was so ready to blame you for what happened to Mark. Transfer of guilt? I hate the superficial psychological jargon we toss around these days."

"You were right to blame me. I'd like to tell you how it happened—"

"I don't want to hear. It's irrelevant."

"Irrelevant? Murder?"

Her voice broke on the word, and when Peter answered, his voice had lost its calm.

"Do you want me to say it, here and now, when we'll probably both be dead before morning? That I'd condone anything you've done, anything you ever will do? If you told me you'd annihilated an entire orphanage, I'd probably just shrug. Oh, God, I've done it again! Always the wrong word . . ."

"I want to tell you about that, too," Kate said softly. "She was so beautiful, Peter. Her eyes were blue—not that dark smoky blue all new babies have, but a lovely clear azure, right from the first day. And bright fair hair, like—like yours. She was beginning to talk; she really was, it wasn't just babbling, she was very precocious. And she was crawling all over the place, puffing—she was so fat—and she—"

The last words were unintelligible even to her. Peter let her cry for a while. Then he said gently, "Can you move, at all? Your hands? Stretch them out?"

Kate found that she could move, though only in one place; by pulling in all her muscles she could slide around the tree trunk inside the ropes. Squinting through the tears she had been holding in for months, she made out the excrescence on the next tree which was Peter. The starlight glinted faintly off his hair. Groping, she felt his fingers meet and close on the tips of hers.

"Feeling better?" he asked.

"Yes." Kate sniffed. "I don't know why I should, but I do."

"Why didn't you marry him? He said he'd asked you."

"After Uncle Stephan died."

"And you inherited how many million dollars. I see."

"It wasn't only that. I guess I was afraid of marrying anybody. I was always a homely girl, and too smart for my own good. But I wasn't smart enough to conceal my brains."

"Why should you?"

Kate sniffed again. She longed desperately for a

handkerchief, and a free hand with which to wield it.

"Because men don't like intelligent women," she said in a muffled voice. "And neither do other women."

"I do," Peter said persuasively.

"Oh, you." Kate laughed; it was a choked, hoarse sound, but it was genuine. "You're different."

"Naturally."

"I mean, you believe in yourself. You're sufficiently competent to accept competence in other people without resenting it."

"There you go again."

"Well, it's true. But Mark—it wasn't self-confidence that he lacked, he thought he was entitled to everything in the world." Kate laughed again, bitterly this time. "The truth is that I caught him with Tiphaine one day. I was already pregnant, and he had sworn lifelong devotion to me. So maybe I was just plain jealous, and to hell with the psychological analysis. I threw him out—out of the house, out of my life. I had—the baby. It was kept a secret, of course; Tiphaine knew, and Martin, but they were the only ones.

"This mother-love business isn't a simple reflex, you know; at first the baby was just a duty, a responsibility. I set up an arrangement, with an apartment and a live-in nurse, in Baltimore, and I went up to see her once a week. Then, after a while, I found I was going oftener, and staying longer. . . . I knew I had to have her with me, all the time. And Mark was being intolerable; he'd gone back to Washington, but he was here every weekend, staying with Volz and harassing me. He knew about the baby, but he didn't know where she was—not even Tiphaine knew that. I got so desperate I even considered marrying Mark, just for long enough to give her a name—so she wouldn't have to grow up with that stigma. Then she . . . she got sick. They go so quickly when they're small."

"And you blamed yourself for that."

"Yes, of course. It was foolish—the woman, the nurse, was the best to be had. She loved her, too. But I couldn't . . . I didn't . . ."

"Did Mark know?"

"Not then. I was a little mad, I think; Tiphaine and Martin knew, they went to . . . the funeral with me. Then Mark insisted on meeting me. It was at night. He asked me to marry him again, and mentioned the baby. . . . I told him then, I think I screamed it at him. And he said—do you know what he said?"

"I think I can guess."

"Yes, you knew him, didn't you? You can imagine how I felt. It was like—offering a child a new puppy to replace the one that died. I wanted to kill him. I did. He had a gun; he'd been waving it around, threatening to shoot himself; but I wasn't impressed because I knew Mark would never deprive the world of anything as wonderful as himself. When he said . . . that . . . I flew at him. Somehow the gun went off. I ran; I knew he must be dead, though they didn't tell me so till next day. It was Martin who found him, and Martin who signed the death certificate. The loyal family friend . . . Your hand's all wet. Sticky . . . Peter . . ."

"The general ties a mean knot," he admitted apologetically. "You sure he wasn't in the navy? Kate, darling, you aren't crying about that . . . ? I appreciate your sympathy, but you'd better save it. For later on."

She turned her head. It was a strain on the muscles of her neck and shoulders, but at least she could see him.

"You have a beautiful nose," she said irrelevantly, and heard Peter snort with amusement.

"Sam was right, as always."

"Who is Sam?"

"Friend of mine. A private detective who once lectured me on the foibles of the female. Whom I hired to investigate you. I don't think I'd feel quite so rotten right now if my conscience were clear."

"Don't think about that. My own conscience is a little smudged."

"I'll be damned if I can see why. If there was ever a born murderee, it was Mark. If he hadn't had the gun, you'd have scratched his face, and he'd have slugged you—he would have, you know—and that would have been the end of it. As for the baby—you surely aren't archaic enough to feel guilty about that? Whereas I—"

"No, I'm worse than you, worse than you," Kate said promptly, and heard him chuckle.

"Okay, this is rather pointless, isn't it? Anyway, I've had my punishment. When I realized I love you—"

"When did you?"

"What?"

"Realize."

"Of all the stupid questions to ask at a time like this . . . I don't like to destroy your romantic illusions, but I think the process began the other afternoon, in this very spot."

"It's . . . a little too much, isn't it?" Kate said after a moment. "I'm sorry; I'm trying not to make this any harder for you, but—"

"I'd encourage you to break loose and scream your head off if I thought it would do any good," Peter said harshly. "But there won't be a living soul in these woods tonight except our friends. Do you realize what a reign of terror this group has imposed on the town? The coven has so many ways of exerting pressure; not only superstitious fear—and there's a lot more of that lingering than we like to admit—but purely physical threats. Good God, these people can literally get away with murder—and produce half a dozen impeccable witnesses who would swear they were some-where else at the time. A doctor has all sorts of chances for skulduggery—drugs, poisons, falsifying postmortem reports ... Then there's blackmail as a weapon of power. It wouldn't do a certain distinguished Senator much good if his associates knew he spent several nights a year trying to raise the Devil."

"And succeeding," Kate said. "The god is incarnate, you know, in the head of the coven, the Master of—Peter!"

"What? Someone coming?"

"No, I just remembered something. Maybe you didn't hear it. Volz was knocking you around, and when Martin made him stop, he said something about getting his chance later."

"Thanks. That makes me feel a lot better."

"That's not the point. Martin answered that any such decision would have to be up to the Master."

"Well, naturally," Peter agreed; she heard leaves rustle as he shifted his feet, and knew he was still trying to free himself. "Can't have the rank and file making such important decisions. Discipline must be maintained, even if ... Wait a minute, I see what you're driving at. I thought Martin was the chief devil."

"So did I. Martin or Volz. Could it be the Senator?"

"Some covens," Peter said, in a different voice, "had a woman leader."

"La Reine du Sabbat," Kate murmured.

"Or the Queen of Elfhame. Scottish custom, if I remember your book correctly."

"Peter, if it's Tiphaine, I don't think I can stand it."

"I know. She's not responsible, Kate. Your esteemed uncle had years to make her what she is."

"Think of her as mad," Kate said bitterly. "That will help. . . . Look, it's getting lighter. The moon must be rising."

They watched in silence as the pale half-orb swam into sight through the tossing boughs. It was on the wane, and gave little light, but to their dark-accustomed eyes the change was considerable. The shape of the glade was clear now, with the black stone standing out like an incarnate threat.

"Running water, and the stone, and the clearing in the woods," Kate muttered. "The classic features of the Sabbath meeting place; and I never saw it. That's why you were here today."

"Yes, I hoped to find concrete evidence of what I suspected; I knew I could never convince you without something definite, I was having a hard enough time believing it myself. But I found nothing. Apparently they don't use this place very often."

"Four times a year. If they go by the book."

"Allhallows, May Eve, Candlemas, and Lammas Eve. I've done my homework, you see. What do you suppose they're going to do tonight?"

"There are all sorts of variants," Kate said. "From a Black Mass, with defilement of the Christian sacraments, to a good old-fashioned orgy, á la fertility cult. The original witch covens tended toward the latter variety, but I expect sophisticates like Martin, who've read the books, have added their own touches."

"Added is about right. The original cult must go back a long way."

"Why?"

"Miss Device's family history is a little bit coincidental, don't you think? And this clearing must have been planned, especially the stone. It's been there for centuries, I could tell that much. I have a feeling, though, that the coven didn't amount to much until the New People arrived and gave it a shot in the arm."

"People like the general. He could contribute such nice—Peter . . ."

"What's wrong?"

"Look. There."

It was dim at first, only a twinkle like that of a fallen star caught among the trees; but the star shone red. A few minutes later she heard the voices.

"They're coming," she said.

"Kate." His voice was rough, no longer pretending. "They'll probably untie us—you, at least—at some point. To arrange the . . . tableau. . . ."

The light was brighter now, and the voices louder. They rose and fell in a strange stiff rhythm that had not yet taken on a tune.

"If they do," Peter went on, "try to make a break for it. Bite, kick—"

"I'm awfully stiff," Kate said, watching the light. Torches?

"I know. But try. Don't head for the path, go into the woods. If they kill you, it will at least be a more dignified way of dying."

"All right." It didn't seem to matter, now.

Torches, yes. The head of the procession came into view; they had to go single file along the narrow path. The torches burned high and fiercely, giving off a dark smoke which writhed and broke in the wind. One by one they came, stepping in rhythm to the odd, jerky tune. It was a dance tune, but the tune had been ancient when the flames of the Inquisition destroyed the reasoning world.

One by one they came, the same eldritch crew she had seen in the stableyard. If they had seemed nightmare creatures there, they were worse now, in the wild wind-tossed clearing, under a flickering moon—visions of a madman's fancy, products of delirium. The weaving line moved out into the center of the glade, before the stone, and each figure flung the torch it carried into a heap of fuel. It blazed up with a roar, sending a column of red flame soaring.

Kate felt Peter's nails boring into her hand. They were circling the fire now, still to the same weird tune; some had produced musical instruments, small drums and pipes and—good heavens, Miss Device's violin. . . .

"And the Hags and Sorcerers do howl and vary their hellish cries high and low counterfeiting a kind of villainous music. They also dance at the sound of Viols and other instruments, which are brought thither by those that were skilled to play upon them."

All by the book—how thoroughly they had done their research. Or was it from minds like these that the material in the books had come? From Miss Device, jerking and stamping, her face rapt under the stiff white cap; from Mrs. Adams, whose coarse gray locks flew as she gyrated wildly? Widdershins around the fire—against the sun, the Devil's direction.

And that tune, that queer jigging tune; she had heard something like it before, in a concert of medieval dances; the melody formless, the rhythm irregular; no ending, no resolution, only an endless repetition. The rhythm lacked the syncopated sensuality of good dance music; it was monotonous, almost prim. Yet after a time the queer beat got into the listener's blood. . . . Kate jerked herself erect, shivering, as she felt her knees and bent arms beginning to twitch.

The circle widened so that the dancers passed within a few feet of the prisoners; but only one paid them any heed—Volz, whose eyes glinted whitely at Peter each time he went by. The faces were terrible in their set absorption; all eyes, except those of the general, seemed to be looking at something invisible to normal sight. Their skins had an odd cast, dusky and greasy, as if they had been streaked with oily soot. . . .

"The fatte of young children, the blood of a flitter mouse, solanum somniferum, and oleum. They stampe all these together and then they rubbe all parts of their bodys exceedinglie . . . by this means in a moonlight night they seem to be carried in the air. . . ."

The witches' flying ointment. It contained other ingredients beside the ghastly mess Scot had mentioned. Belladonna and aconite, hemlock . . . delirium-inducing drugs, when absorbed through a cut or open sore. That was how the medieval witches had "flown" to the Sabbath, in the delirious visions of the drug. By the book; again, by the book. Kate cursed her inconvenient memory. She was remembering other parts of the ceremony.

Tiphaine was not among the dancers. Kate had mentally braced herself for her cousin's appearance—in what *outré* costume, for God's sake, and in what role? A few dancers were so masked and robed as to be unidentifiable, but she would have known Tiphaine by her size, and her grace. The Master, of course, would make his appearance later, on the platform which had been prepared to receive his presence three hundred years before.

The music stopped; not with a resolution, with

a dying failure on a minor chord. The dancers dropped to the ground and lay still.

How long the girl had been there Kate did not know; the slender figure had been masked by the central fire. Now she moved out away from the rock against which she had been leaning. She seemed to walk above the ground, not on it; her slim bare feet—bare, on such a night—scarcely pressed the dry leaves. She wore a costume similar to Joan's, but on her the effect was different; the slender dryad's body shone whitely through the tatters of the scanty tunic. The dark leaves twisted in her hair looked as if they had grown there. She was perfectly at ease, attuned to the fantasy of the coven as she had never been to the real world. The Queen of Elfhame; la Reine du Sabbat; the witch girl, baptized in the Old Religion and raised in its tenets.

Kate heard Peter's voice catch in a gasp that sounded suspiciously like one of terror; her own heart was pounding. This was the closest she had ever come to the reality of black magic. The rest had been stage devices, human perversities, or neuroses; but if Tiphaine had been born in 1610, she would have gone to the stake singing, and cried the praises of her Dark Lord while the flames licked up to meet the flame of her hair.

The girl turned, lifting her arms; and the whole foul crew leaped up, with a wild scream of welcome and adoration. On top of the black stone stood a solitary figure.

It was not his own skin he was wearing, though the garment fit as snugly; no human flesh ever gleamed with that dull scaly luster or gave such a hint of dark coarseness. The hands were like paws; when he raised them in response to the greeting of his worshipers, the sharpened claws glittered in the firelight. The monstrous head was partly in shadow, but the features were not, could not be, human. There was a snout, and a draggle of dark coarse hair, and pointed ears like those of a goat. The head turned, in a lordly survey, and the second face came into view—another set of opposing features on the back of the head. The two-headed god, Janus of the Romans . . .

Peter's hand moved, in a gesture so savage that it twisted Kate's wrist. She cried out; but the pain brought her out of her horrified trance. She saw the poised figure atop the stone for what it was: not a hairy Fiend, but a man wearing a close-fitting garment of leather that covered his entire body, even to the hands. The glitter of those claws suggested a modern improvement on the ancient costume described by so many writers—metal, perhaps. And the head, of course, was masked; the goat-satyr face attributed to the fertility god, the double face found in some of the cults. It was, she told herself with deliberate emphasis, a damned effective outfit, and the young man who wore it suited it well. He must be young; his body was slight, but built like that of an athlete.

The howling circle was in movement again; no

music now, only wild shrieks of adoration. As each worshiper moved to a position directly in front of the stone, he turned and bent back, lifting one foot. Another part of the old ritual; the more perverse form of worship was impractical with the devil up there on his throne. Kate's inconvenient memory was bothering her again—this time with a part of the ritual which she had tried desperately to forget.

"Witches confessing that the devil lies with them, and withal complaining of his tedious and offensive coldness . . ." The fertility rites, and the marriage of the God . . . "There appeared a great Black Goat with a Candle between his Horns. . . . He had carnal knowledge of her which was with great pain. . . . A meikle, black, roch man, werie cold; and I fand his nature als cold within me as spring well water. . . . He is abler for us in that way than any man can be, onlie he was heavie lyk a malt sek; a hudge nature, verie cold, as yce." The hard leather covering of the body; Margaret Murray's reference to the phallic cults of Egypt and Greece . . . She heard someone breathing in harsh, choking gasps, and thought it was she herself. Then she turned to look at Peter. His face was frozen in a spasm of horror and his wide eyes were fixed on the slight, posturing figure on the stone.

As Kate looked back, the leather-clad form flexed its knees and jumped, landing lightly on its feet. He was in splendid physical condition; the movement had looked like flying. But it was a pedestrian stroll that brought the weird figure across the glade toward them. The worshipers fell back before him, with the same archaic, backward bow. Tiphaine followed, two paces in the rear, like a priestess following the sacramental objects. As the figure circled the fire, Kate got a better look at the mask. It was a beautiful piece of work, a clever mingling of goat and human. The straggling beard and muzzled mouth were animal; the eyes, shining out from under heavy coarse brows, were those of a man.

It was the sight of those eyes that gave Kate her first clue, and she felt her face freeze in the same incredulous horror that still held Peter rigid. Pacing slowly, the bizarre shape came toward them and stopped. The clawed hand fumbled at the throat, and the mask slipped up, and off.

The face was Timmy's face. But the thick fair hair, tumbled by the removal of the mask, was not Timmy's. The easy athlete's walk had not been Timmy's shambling stride. The eyes, bright and intelligent . . .

Again the clawed hand lifted; this time, with a very human "Damn!" the man stripped off the awkward glove, and raised his hand to the livid face. The whole fiery birthmark peeled off; and Kate saw before her the face which ought to have been crumbling to dust for almost a year. Mark's face.

# *Chapter*

## 12

HE DIDN'T LOOK A DAY OLDER.

The blue eyes narrowed with amusement as they met hers; the mouth was smiling. He was as handsome as ever, almost too handsome . . . as ever . . .

Kate wasn't aware that she was fainting until she heard Peter's voice, repeating her name. She shook her head, blinking through the gray fog that blanketed her mind, looking, not at the beautiful smiling face in front of her, but at Peter.

Under the ruddy firelight that gave his face a false flush, he was white as paper. The shock had driven the blood from his face, but not from his brain; he knew what she must be thinking.

"He's real, Kate. You didn't kill him. Don't start imagining. . . . Kate!"

"I'm all right," she muttered.

"What," Mark said, "no tender welcome for the dead come back to life?"

That voice—the one that had haunted her for months. No wonder Timmy never spoke.

"I expected more reaction," Mark went on cheerfully. "My fond brother and my—I've always liked the word 'paramour,' haven't you, Kate? So much more refined and Elizabethan than the other terms. . . . But I understand that in this, as in so many of my other specialties, my big brother has surpassed me."

"Blanks," Kate said. "Blanks in the gun."

"Red paint and all the rest," Mark agreed. "Martin was lurking, unseen, in order to bear you away if you overcame your squeamishness and started to investigate the corpse. But you fled, like a nice timid female."

"Why? Why did you do it?"

"Money," Mark said, with an air of pointing out the obvious. "What else? Oh, there were other reasons. Tiphaine has never liked you very much, darling. When Stephan died intestate—and I'm sure he did it deliberately, the old devil—her dislike ripened into something deeper. As for me, it hurts my feelings to be rejected. I've enjoyed watching you squirm."

His gloved hand lifted; the steel claws pricked Kate's cheek. Peter said something unintelligible, and moved his head. Mark turned toward him.

"I've hated you all my life," he said calmly. "It's

quite natural; any psychologist could explain it to you. Gratitude is a fiction; the normal return for favors rendered is resentment. Only imagine, dear brother, how profound my resentment of you! All I ever needed to do was yell for help, and there you were, panting with zeal, ready to bail me out. Only—the last time I yelled for help you didn't come."

"You must have known why."

"Oh, yes, I knew; I read the newspapers." Mark chuckled. "I thought of you often. Prisons in Communist countries aren't awfully comfortable, I'm told. But I thought you'd turn up sooner or later; that uncomfortable conscience of yours. And you were stupid enough to use your own name when you booked your room. Not that I blame you," he added condescendingly. "You thought I was dead, and assumed no one else would recognize the name. Little did you know that we were all ready and waiting for you."

There were beads of perspiration on Peter's forehead; they reflected the firelight like drops of blood.

"I can't get you out of this mess unless you release us," he said.

"I don't need you to get me out of it," Mark snapped. "I didn't really need you when I wrote that letter. This"—his misshapen hand swept out to include the circle of costumed figures—"this is stronger than you ever could be. And I'm its head, Peter. I'm the head devil. The Master."

Tiphaine bowed her head.

Kate looked at her cousin. Tiphaine's eyes were fixed on Mark; they were rapt with a blasphemous devotion. Her fervor was genuine. Couldn't she see that Mark was using her, and the coven, for his own ends?

Kate missed Peter's next comment as her eyes moved from Tiphaine to the other members of the coven. The ceremony was proceeding. Next on the agenda was the ceremonial meal, and if she had been watching the proceedings from some safe, hidden spot, the activity would have moved her to sick amusement. Most of the Sabbath meals, as described by medieval participants, consisted of ordinary food—meat and bread and wine. She herself had expressed doubt, in her book, about the legends of cannibalism and noxious beverages. And this spoiled crowd—perhaps later, when their frenzy had increased, they might be capable of consuming human flesh or urine, or bread made of flour from unspeakable sources. Now they were setting out what appeared to be a conventional picnic supper. Kate's diaphragm contracted as she watched Miss Device fussily weighing down the corners of the white cloth with wine bottles. Red wine. Naturally . . . And what an elegant little supper it was—*foie gras* and caviar and imported cheeses, crusty French bread. . . . Kate suppressed a rising tide of nausea. She hadn't eaten since breakfast, but she wasn't hungry.

Most of the hampers and baskets had been emptied of their contents now; only one large basket still remained, on the ground by the stone. Some special delicacy, perhaps, for dessert. They weren't going to unpack it now, they were waiting for their chief to join them. Mrs. Adams daintily plucked a few dried leaves from the damask picnic cloth; her streaming gray hair fell across her cheeks and chin, leaving the sharp nose in silhouette. Everything was ready. But Mark couldn't tear himself away; he was enjoying this.

"I succeeded old Stephan," he was saying as Kate turned her attention back to the conversation. "He and I hit it off right from the start. It was rather a slap in the face for Martin; he'd been fancying himself as heir apparent. But Stephan knew that for Martin the coven was only a means to an end. For the rest of us, it's an end in itself."

He turned to smile at Tiphaine, and Kate burst out, "For the rest of them, maybe, but not for you. Money, power, control, that's what you want. You asked me to marry you because of the money. When that failed, you staged your own murder so you could blackmail me."

"You have such a simple mind," Mark said fondly. The steel claw touched her cheek again, and pricked a little deeper. "Do you think you were my only problem? I owed a good deal of money, dear, not only locally, but to some threatening gentlemen in New York. Not to mention the irate fathers of certain damsels ... Without Peter to rescue me from myself, my peccadilloes tended to pile up. Since I could disappear, and make money on the deal, as they say here ... Timmy was no loss. And he was so splendidly easy to imitate."

"And we thought someone was using Timmy," Kate muttered.

"But you were perfectly correct."

The fire soared and crackled, sending red flames licking at the lower branches. Kate wondered how they kept the dry leaves from catching. The whole clearing would go up like a torch if the fire got out of hand.

"Being Timmy did limit me, though," Mark went on blithely. "I couldn't get in and out of costume quickly, so I had to rely on my voice to remind you of past events. Peter was more effective; I got a lot of innocent amusement out of watching his performances and recalling our boyhood days, when we sent off for occult literature and tried to conjure up demons in the schoolroom. Yes, he was very useful—until the night when he interfered with me at the séance." Mark lifted a casual hand toward his brother's face, and Peter jerked back, too late. Blood began streaming down his face, and Mark giggled.

"Reflexes a little slow," he said in a voice which was higher than his normal tones. "I don't imagine you're feeling too well, are you? Had a bad day altogether. Well, it won't be long now. I promised the general a few minutes of fun, but don't worry, there isn't too much he can do. We don't want any odd marks which would be hard to explain in a postmortem."

"What are you going to do with us?" Kate hated to give him the satisfaction of asking, but she couldn't help it.

"It ought to interest you. These people have kept the ritual amazingly pure—in the scholarly sense, that is. No Black Mass. So you don't need to worry about being stretched out naked on the altar, or anything crude of that sort."

"Thanks," Kate said.

"Sarcastic as ever." Mark threw his head back, laughing, and caught at the mask as it slipped backward. He readjusted it on top of his head, where it formed a fantastic frame for his young face. "We have to consider the practical problem, you see. When the two of you are found tomorrow, it must appear to be an ordinary murder and suicide. Martin has considerable influence in these matters, but we don't want to take any chances, in case your lawyer gets sticky about the will."

"I see."

"But we can still kill two birds with one stone. Tonight is the night of the Passion—a far older ceremony than the Christian imitation, only two thousand years ago. The god must die, as nature dies, so that life can be reborn in the spring."

"Every seven years," Kate said.

"That's right; you're the authority on fertility cults, aren't you?" His smile was broad and carefree. "But they do it every year, here. A local refinement."

"But you're the—god," Peter said. He was only an amateur at this, Kate remembered; his early religious training had left its imprint, under the layers of adult skepticism, and his disgust showed in face and voice. It annoyed Mark; he made another lunge with his clawed hand, and Peter flinched.

"I'm the god," Mark said.

Then Kate saw what really drove him, under the superficial vices of avarice and cruelty. She looked away, unable to endure the sight of either brother; Peter's sick helplessness was as painful as Mark's madness.

"But naturally," Mark went on in his normal voice, "I don't die. Impractical. And so permanent . . . No, we have the substitute procedure, and a very nice one it is, too. Can you imagine a more appropriate substitute? Tiphaine tried earlier today, but she's not much good with the bow, poor dear. It was a bit premature, actually. All your fault," he added, turning to Kate. "That idiotic song, and your suggestion, gave her the idea."

"But you can't," Kate gasped. "No one will believe . . . Why should I kill Peter? Or is it the other way around?"

"No, no, you had it right the first time. I think,

you know, that they will believe it—once Peter's real identity gets out, which it will. People are already talking about my 'accidental death,' you know. . . . I needn't spell it out, not for a woman of your intellectual attainments."

"And Martin will reluctantly testify that I've been going slowly insane for months," Kate said slowly.

"With Tiphaine and the Schmidts to back him up, I don't see how it can fail," Mark said cheerfully. His eyes moved from Kate's face down to her feet and back again. "There are, of course, certain preliminary ceremonies," he said.

Tiphaine glided forward. Kate thought spitefully that her face had lost some of its unearthly concentration. She was human enough to be jealous.

"They are waiting," she said, touching Mark on the shoulder.

"I'll bet they are," Peter said. "Expecially the old spinsters like Miss Device, and that bored, overweight wench, whatever her name is. . . . How far do your duties extend, Mark? I never did believe those stories of yours."

"Peter," Kate said warningly; but Mark wasn't annoyed.

"I delegate some duties," he said, grinning; and the leering goat's head perched on his brow echoed the expression. "The ritual marriage is consummated with the Queen of the Sabbath." He held out his hand to Tiphaine, and she took it, with a grave inclination of her head. "And," Mark added negligently, "with an occasional carefully selected and honored visitor."

This time Tiphaine's annoyance was plainer, and Mark saw it. Still holding her hand, he pulled the mask down into position.

*"A bientôt!"* he said, and, leading his lady by the hand, started back toward the rock pedestal.

With the incarnate god presiding, the ritual supper got underway. It included a few refinements not ordinarily seen at picnics. The climax of the rite was yet to come, but the participants had already shed several layers of civilized behavior. Volz wallowed like the pig he resembled, cramming food into his mouth and drinking his wine directly from the bottle. As the meal proceeded and the bottles were emptied, Kate was reminded, not so much of the witchcraft reports, as of lurid tales of Roman banquets. Sprawled on the ground, the members were paired, two by two. Perhaps the activities wouldn't have been so obscene if she hadn't known these people so well, especially the older, more respected citizens. . . . Ironic, how she could read and write about practices like these with a cool scholarly detachment, and yet turn sick at the actual sight. The wine was flowing freely, not only into individual mouths, but from mouth to mouth and onto the already stained costumes. But Kate knew it was not the wine which brought the red flush to Miss Device's sallow cheeks, nor the wild glitter into the

Senator's eyes. Volz poured the dregs of his fourth bottle down the front of Joan's inadequate bodice, and bent forward. Kate closed her eyes.

She heard Peter swear, fluently, and without lowering his voice; she heard the leaves in the dark wood rustle as some four-footed creature crept through the night. Remembering her earlier fear of nocturnal animals, she could have smiled. Then lesser sounds were drowned as the music began again.

It was faster and louder now. The dance was different too, though it was just as ancient; the dancers paired off, locking elbows, back to back.

The crackle of dried leaves came again, so close now that it was audible even over the music—if the cacophonous din could be called music. Kate forgot her major preoccupation in momentary wonder. They were at the very edge of the clearing; only darkness lay behind them, darkness and the tangled brush. But surely no forest animal would approach so close.

Then came a sound that almost took her breath away by its very normalcy, in the midst of nightmare. The sounds of a soft, human voice.

"Don't turn, don't talk. Don't look surprised."

For the life of her—and it might have been just that—Kate couldn't repress a start and a gasp. Luckily the others were too concerned with their own activities to notice. Peter was more controlled. His profile, outlined against the dark foliage, remained immobile.

"Jackson," he said, on a long, sighing breath.

"Yes, it's me. Don't let your arms fall when I cut these ropes. Move 'em a little, get circulation back."

Kate kept her eyes fixed on Peter's face, fighting the urge to crane her neck and look back. She knew, by the twist of his mouth, when his arms were freed. Then she felt Hilary's big, warm hands on hers, and the ropes fell away. He held her wrists, taking some of the strain off her numbed arms, rubbing them to get the blood flowing freely. After a few minutes his hands moved to her ankles.

"Kate?" Peter spoke without turning his head.

"Yes, all right. I'm free now."

"Good. Jackson, get the hell out of here."

"I'm staying."

"For God's sake—as soon as we make our break, they'll be buzzing like flies, all over the woods. I'll give you five minutes' start."

Five minutes? Kate wondered whether they had five more minutes—or whether five minutes would be long enough to restore limbs numbed by cold and confinement. Flexing her fingers, trying to stamp her feet without letting the dried leaves rustle, she was still caught by the ghastly fascination of the rite of the Sabbath. Her scholar's instinct, so long dormant, was not dead; if she survived—what a book she could make out of this!

Peter and Hilary were arguing in whispers

which were becoming dangerously shrill. She turned her head to expostulate. Then she heard what Hilary was saying.

"I'm not going anywhere. And neither are you."

Staring straight ahead, hands still behind him, Peter said softly. "We're going, all right. Through you, if we must."

"Why the hell do you think I came? To save you?" Hilary's emotion was so intense that words failed him; he stuttered wildly for a second before he could go on. "Look over there, look—to the right of the stone, on the ground. That's what I came for. And you'll help me, or I'll kill you myself."

It took Kate's incredulous eyes some time to locate the object he indicated. Her mind fought the dawning knowledge as her eyes denied the proof of it. By the stone . . . the basket she had noticed at the beginning of the meal. Only it wasn't a basket. It was made of some plastic material, with metal supports to hold it upright, and attachments by which it could be fastened to the seat of a car. She had bought one like it to take . . . to take the baby . . .

Her stomach rebelled in a surge of nausea so violent it almost bent her over. It was only her imagination, she couldn't have heard it over the screams of the dancers: the high, thin wail that seemed to come from the carrier by the stone.

"Impossible," Peter whispered. "Not even these—how could they? Where did they get it?"

Kate didn't have to wait for Hilary's explanation.

"The Foundling Home. Some of them are on the board. Miss Device does volunteer work in the office. Falsifying records . . . Most of the babies are illegitimate, unwanted. . . . Peter!"

He didn't hear her. He didn't have to; there was no need for discussion of ends, only of means.

"Is it yours?" he asked, and Hilary answered simply,

"I don't know. Does it matter?"

"No." Peter began to shiver, violently and uncontrollably. "Get over there, through the trees, to the nearest cover. When you see me step out and raise my arms, grab the basket and run."

"What are you going to do?" Hilary asked.

"What the hell can I do? Dance, sing, do card tricks. Anything to attract attention. I suppose it would be too much to expect you to have a weapon?"

They were speaking in near normal tones; the frenzied howling had risen to a pitch that made whispering unnecessary. The dancers had abandoned any attempt at rhythm. Miss Device had torn off her cap and was plucking at the collar of her dress.

Kate's hands were clenched so tightly that her nails pierced the skin of her palms, but she didn't feel the pain. That would be the time, when the dancers were locked in the embrace which was the culmination of the rite. They would be blind and deaf to anything else. They were nearing the climax now. But would the sacrifice come first? Each time one of the reeling figures neared the stone, and the pitiful little object beside it, Kate's breath stopped.

She had almost forgotten Peter's question, it took Hilary so long to answer it.

"The general's rifle," he said briefly. "Here."

Peter's right side was the one farthest away; she didn't see his arm move, but she could tell, by his face, when his fingers touched the weapon.

"Maybe you'd better keep it," he said reluctantly. "Can't handle a rifle and the basket."

"Hurry," Kate said. "It can't be long now. Hurry."

Hilary didn't waste breath in answering; she heard the same cautious rustle of leaves which had heralded his approach. Peter said, out of the corner of his mouth, "This doesn't include you. As soon as I move, you run. Straight back, avoid the path."

"If you think I'm going to leave that child . . . and you . . ."

"What are you planning to do, throw stones? If Jackson and I fail, you're our last hope."

He took her silence for agreement. Kate saw no point in arguing; she knew she wasn't going to go. Stones, yes, if that was all she could do. She had left him once before, not knowing whether she would see him alive again; once in a lifetime was once too much, she couldn't do it twice. And the baby . . . Under the impetus of a fear which was not for her own person, her brain began to work more clearly. She would run, but not toward freedom—around the clearing, following Hilary. If any one of the mob defied the threat of the rifle, to pursue the boy and his burden, she might be able to help.

Was Hilary in position yet? She strained her eyes through the smoke and the flames toward a glossy-leaved holly which was the nearest point of concealment. It was a good twenty feet away from the basket, and there was nothing between except flat ground and fallen leaves. There was no sign of Hilary, not even a movement of the jagged green leaves. But there wouldn't be—not until Peter stepped out in full view of the frenzied group and the cold-eyed spectator atop the rock. He had a gun, yes; but what good would that be against a pack of maddened animals?

She looked at Peter. He stood as he had been standing for hours, slightly slumped, his head bowed. It would have taken a close examination to see that he was no longer bound. Hilary had re-knotted the most visible rope, the one that circled his chest, so that a quick movement would release it. What was he waiting for?

Miss Device was the first to go. She collapsed onto the ground, writhing and tearing at her clothing; her face was distorted almost out of recognition, and from her squared mouth came an animal scream. The ghoul-figure at her side— good God, was it Will Schmidt?—dropped down beside her. As if a signal had been given, the others followed; it was a contagious mania, a communicable madness, like the dancing crazes of the Middle Ages or the blood lust that moves a lynch mob. Within moments the glade was littered with moving bodies. The effect was too much, even for someone who had known what to expect; Kate turned her head away. Now, surely, was the time for them to move.

Peter stirred, and she tensed—if further tension was possible. She had been standing poised for flight for what seemed an eternity. But the gesture or word she was waiting for did not come. He didn't even look at her. He was staring straight ahead, his head lifted; the blank pallor of his face and the intensity of his gaze made him look drugged or entranced. Then Kate realized what he saw, and why he had not moved.

High on his black throne, the masked figure surveyed his devotees. Tiphaine was clinging to him shamelessly, but he made no response. The goat's mask held its frozen leer; Kate sensed that, behind it, Mark was also smiling. This was the supreme moment for him, not the sexual release the others sought. There had always been something mechanical about his lovemaking, skilled as it was. Watching other people lose the control he never lost gave him a sense of superiority; and his triumph was intensified by the fact that his brother was a witness to it. One part of his awareness had been, and still was, focused on Peter.

And there it seemed likely to remain. The mating of the god was not part of the communal orgy.

Peter realized this too; Kate looked back at him in time to meet his eyes. They were as empty of expression as was the rest of his face, and his lips barely moved when he spoke.

"Now. Move, damn it; I won't until you do."

She had been ready for so long, her hands braced against the tree trunk to give that one additional burst of speed; now, at the word of command, she couldn't move. The seconds stretched out impossibly as she stood, staring at him with an intensity that made her eyes ache. When she finally forced herself into motion, it was like pulling against something that stretched and held, and hurt when it broke.

She crashed blindly through the undergrowth parallel to the clearing with no clear notion of what she was doing. The crack of a branch across her head stung her into awareness, and she stopped. She was panting as if she had run for miles.

The first thing she noticed was the silence. Now that she was still, the only thing she could hear was the pounding of her heart and the agonized wheeze of her breathing. From the glade, to her left, came no sound at all except the voiceless roar of the fire. She was only a few feet away from the edge of the clearing; the fire glow shone weirdly through the tangled vines and bushes, throwing distorted leaping shadows along the ground. But no sound; no sound at all. Arms up before her face, Kate plunged through a matted curtain of something that was probably poison ivy, and then she saw what had happened.

It had seemed to her that she had been thrashing about in the bushes for long minutes, but no more than seconds could have passed since she darted out of the clearing. It had taken Hilary the same length of time to cover the longer, though not entangled, distance between his hiding place and the rock. He was the first person she noticed, partly because he was the only one in motion; head down, arms extended, he was within a few paces of his goal.

The Witches' Sabbath—an oil, in full color, frozen now into two-dimensional horror. The sprawled, pallid bodies were still; here and there a blank white face lifted blindly. Mark, atop the rock, looked like a statue out of one of the more esoteric museums—an institution specializing in anthropological curiosities. From her new vantage point Kate could see both faces of the monstrous mask; it looked doubly horrifying atop the slender, poised body.

Kate took it all in in a single, panoramic sweep of vision; then she saw Peter, and for one blissfully simple moment she forgot everything else in an upsurge of primitive female admiration.

She couldn't see his face; it was hidden by the stock of the gun and by his raised arm. The marks of the ropes on his wrist were only too visible; in the strange light they looked like ragged black lines, and the flesh around them was swollen and dark. But the finger curled around the trigger of the rifle was as steady as steel, and the muzzle pointed unwaveringly at its target—Mark.

Hilary reached the basket, scooped it up in both arms, and whirled around. One of the panting glassy-eyed figures on the ground heaved itself to its knees with an animal snarl. It was Volz; it would be, Kate thought. Peter's voice echoed emphatically through the empty night:

"Don't move, Volz, or I'll take care of your sacrifice for you."

"Stop," Mark said clearly.

Volz dropped down to his hands and knees.

Hilary had almost reached the edge of the clearing. Kate knew he was running as he had never run before, but he seemed to be moving in slow motion, like a defective film. The clumsy size of the basket hampered him; why didn't he take the child out? He could carry it in one arm and have the other free. . . . Then she realized that the baby might be strapped down. He was almost there; he was going to make it. . . . She had come to think of the glade as danger, the dark woods as safety, but Hilary wouldn't be safe until he reached town; they could still overtake him in the woods with his awkward burden, unless Peter could detain them. How long could he hold them? And how were she and Peter going to get away after Hilary had gone? For the first time in hours she allowed herself the luxury of speculating on the possibility of her own survival.

Hilary was not more than three feet away from the trees when it happened. How long the man had been there, Kate didn't know; he seemed to materialize out of the night, like one of the dark spirits the coven worshiped. She reproached herself bitterly for her fastidiousness; if she had concentrated on the full glories of the final orgy, she would have realized that the paired couples came out evenly. Too evenly. There were thirteen members of the coven. One of them had slipped away earlier.

She might have anticipated his identity even if she hadn't recognized him, tall and lean and confident, wearing a particularly gruesome costume— that of a phosphorescent skeleton, realistically articulated, painted on black cloth. His mask, a cowl-like head covering, was thrown back over his shoulders for better visibility.

He extended one foot and Hilary went sprawling. The basket flew out of his hands and landed, on its side, several feet beyond his outflung, clutching hands. Kate heard the cry clearly this time, and it was the worst moment of a day which had not been precisely pleasant.

Hilary's reflexes were normally superb; tonight they were superhuman. He was up again, staggering but deadly, at once. He turned on Martin, fists clenched, and rocked to a halt. Martin had stepped back. He had a gun. Not a rifle, a hand weapon of some kind. Kate couldn't see it clearly, but Hilary could. His broad shoulders sagged and his face went gray.

"Martin!" Peter's voice rang out. "Drop it or I'll shoot—him."

He couldn't say the name. Kate wondered if he would be able to carry out his threat; and she wondered whether Martin had noticed the almost imperceptible hesitation.

"Go ahead," Martin said.

"I mean it."

Peter's finger contracted. He meant it, all right, but that didn't mean he would enjoy it. Kate wished passionately that she had the gun. She would have cheerfully rid the world of Mark, even without the additional reward of sparing Peter the sin of fratricide.

"Go ahead," Martin repeated. He laughed aloud; the merry, confident sound made the hair of Kate's neck bristle. "I'd planned to kill him myself; I'd be delighted to have you save me the trouble."

Mark had been a silent, interested spectator. Now, knowing that he was immune for at least the length of time it took Peter to figure out his next move, he turned, shoving Tiphaine out of the way with a careless brutality that sent her sprawling. He pushed the mask up off his face.

"What the hell are you doing, Martin?"

"Completing the sacrifice," Martin said coolly.

"You never should have been the head. You cheated me out of my rights. Now I'm taking them back. The others don't give a damn, they'll follow whoever's in control. Go on, Stewart; kill him. When you do, I'll dispose of this interfering young bastard."

Peter stood motionless, his finger still on the trigger. Kate knew he was gripped by the same sick awareness of failure that turned her knees to water. Clearly Peter knew how to handle a gun; but the two vital targets were too widely separated to be covered simultaneously. If he shot Mark, Martin would kill Hilary, and the threat Peter had held over the rest of the coven would be canceled.

She knew she couldn't reach Martin without his hearing her; there were too many dried, fragile objects underfoot, and the glade was too quiet. Once again she heard the thin, wailing cry, like that of some small animal caught in a trap. She turned, in an instinctive response that made her forget her logic.

The crash of the rifle sounded like a bomb in the stillness. Kate's hands flew to her ears; she turned dazed eyes toward the Devil's Pulpit, expecting to see Mark sway and fall. But Mark stood firm on his feet, as surprised as she was.

Martin was down, flat on the ground; Peter had fired at him, not at Mark. His hands were empty, but his arms were moving, groping like separately animated, detached limbs, for the gun he had dropped. Hilary, on hands and knees, was scrabbling wildly among the leaves.

The rifle went off again, and Kate spun around. Peter had fired at Volz, at close range, and missed. The two men stood braced, arms raised, struggling for the weapon. Volz was an obscene, half-naked troglodyte, but the muscles in his squat arms and shoulders were well developed, and Peter had reached the end of his strength. He went over backward, landing with a thud that knocked most of the breath out of him; the rest of it came out in a grunt as Volz's stocky body fell across him. The rifle went flying; and Kate, after an agonized appraisal of the situation, dived for it.

As her fingers closed over the smooth, silkily polished wood of the stock, it occurred to her that she didn't have the faintest idea how to fire it. The thought was fleeting; she bounded to her feet, raising the weapon in the only way that was comprehensible to her then. The butt came crashing down on the back of Volz's round head with a noise that would recur to her, in dreams, for some years to come. At the time it didn't bother her in the slightest. The general slumped to one side, his hands sliding off Peter's throat, and Kate saw Peter staring up at her. His eyes were wide and unblinking; and for a second her overworked heart stopped. Then blood from the reopened cut on his forehead trickled down into one eye, and he blinked. He staggered to his feet and reached for the gun.

In the brief seconds which had elapsed, Hilary's situation had deteriorated. He had the gun, and Martin lay motionless, dead or unconscious, but another danger was creeping up on him from behind as he stood staring down at the doctor.

Mark had vanished from the rock earlier; Kate had noted it subconsciously, thinking it was typical of Mark; he had a well-developed sense of self-preservation. She had underestimated him. To save his position of power he would take a risk, so long as it wasn't too big a risk.

Kate let out a yell of warning, and Peter threw the rifle to his shoulder. Hilary whirled. He handled the pistol awkwardly, as if he had never used one before; but at that range he didn't have to be experienced. Mark was diving at him when he pulled the trigger. The slim, darkly gleaming figure fell like a broken toy, arms and legs sprawling awkwardly.

Peter lowered the rifle; his arm moved stiffly, all in one piece, like a stick of wood. Hilary looked wildly from the huddled body at his feet, to the gun in his hand, to Peter. Then he dropped the gun, and ran. Kate heard his crashing, invisible progress stop momentarily and then go on; he had collected what he had come to get.

Then, and only then, did she remember the others. Miss Device, Senator Blankenhagen of Alabama, Mrs. Adams . . . But when she turned to look for them, they were gone. The fire burned low in the center of a quiet forest glade, empty except for the crumpled dead, and herself, and Peter.

"They've faded away," Peter said, interpreting her look. His voice was flat. "Respectability triumphs after all."

He put the rifle carefully down on the ground, moving like a tired old man, and walked slowly across the glade. Kate followed.

"Looks like the last scene of Hamlet, doesn't it?" There was no amusement in Peter's voice, or face. Going down on one knee, he extended his hand and rolled the still body over onto its back.

Mark had been shot through the center of the forehead—an astonishing shot for an inexperienced marksman. It was a small, neat hole, so neat that it looked unreal, like a painted caste mark, or symbol of the cult. The mask had dropped away in his fall; the tumbled fair hair, so much like Peter's, gleamed golden in the dying firelight. His face looked very young. He was smiling slightly. Lucifer might have appeared in such a form to those who envisioned him as the fallen angel, the morning star; the prince—of darkness, perhaps—but princely nonetheless. "Godlike shapes and forms, excelling human, princely dignities . . ."

She was not moved to mourn for him, though; relief was the strongest emotion she was conscious of feeling. Peter's face was utterly devoid of expression. After a while he stood up. With the tip of his shoe, gently but finally, he turned the body over again so that the beautiful face and staring eyes were hidden. There was some sign of emotion in his face now; but it was an emotion which twisted his mouth into a wry shape, and the bitterness in his voice, when he spoke, transformed the gracious words into a sardonic epitaph.

"'And flocks of angels sing thee to thy rest.' But, do you know—I have my doubts."

Kate reached out for him, but she was too late. He fell like a log, face down among the crackling leaves.

# Chapter

## 13

IN THE DEAD LIGHT OF A GRAY DAWN, THE GLADE looked forlorn and unreal. Kate shivered in the bitter air. The wind had died, leaving swollen gray clouds huddling in the sky. It felt like winter.

The neat brown-and-tan uniforms of the state troopers looked out of place. As they moved about, talking in low voices, she saw one hard young face after another change from cautious incredulity to consternation. They hadn't believed any of the story when they first heard it, even though it came from three separate, hithereto respectable, sources. They believed it now.

Kate wrapped her arms around her body and tried to keep her teeth from chattering. She had warm, clean clothes, but her body ached from lack of sleep and she felt slimy and unclean. A long hot bath . . . She turned the idea over in her mind, luxuriously and longingly. Later, maybe. Later there would be time for other things. But first the explanations had to be made. The dead had to be buried.

And the living had to be tended. She looked anxiously at Peter. He was seemingly quite composed as he stood talking to the lieutenant in charge. Someone's borrowed overcoat, several inches too long, was thrown over his shoulders, and his left arm was in a sling. Now that his face was comparatively clean, its pallor was more evident, and the assorted bruises stood out like the stains of corruption.

Kate wondered when he was going to break down. His collapse earlier that night had been temporary; she had gotten him on his feet without too much trouble, and he had walked unaided down the path to the bridle trail. But he walked like a somnambulist, and she knew that he was only partially aware of what he was doing. He was only responding because it was easier than being nagged.

Mentally she was in much the same condition, too numbed by successive shocks to think of anything except the immediate need. And that need was simple. Escape. Get away. Abandon the whole hideous mess, and find a quiet corner to hide in.

\* \* \*

The night was dark, with only starlight to guide them. Kate turned automatically into the wider expanse of the bridle path and had taken several dragging steps before she saw the faint light glinting off the chrome trim of a dark bulk in the middle of the path. It was Volz's car. How the others had come, and gone, she did not stop to wonder. This vehicle's owner would never claim it.

She got Peter into the car, where he sat slumped and staring, and found, as she ought to have expected, that the keys were not in the ignition. They would be in Volz's pocket. A shudder ran through her at the thought of retracing her steps and searching for them. She would rather walk, impossible as that prospect now seemed. Then it occurred to her that Hilary might have an extra key—some people kept one in one of those little cases under the hood. Wearily she dragged herself out from under the wheel and—found it.

She was back in the car, inserting the key into the ignition, when the long-delayed reaction struck. She fell forward against the wheel, hands clenched around the slippery plastic, and felt the heavy circle shiver with the spasms of her body.

At her side Peter stirred and reached out for her. She transferred her frantic grip from the steering wheel to his shoulders, and went on shivering. It was a much more satisfactory position, and the slow, rhythmic thud of Peter's heart under her right ear was the most satisfactory sound she had ever heard, all the more so because there had been moments when she never expected to hear it again.

As the shivering subsided, she realized that she was clinging like a vine and clutching like a limpet, and making disgusting, feeble noises. It wasn't fair; he had undergone just as great an emotional shock as she, and had taken considerably more physical punishment. No, it wasn't fair . . . but it felt absolutely heavenly. . . . Her mind wandered off into thoughts she would have been ashamed to say aloud; and because Milton had been on her mind ("Better to reign in Hell than serve in Heaven,") she was reminded of the maddening words he had put into the mouth of Eve.

" 'God is thy law; thou mine; to know no more is woman's happiest knowledge and her praise,' " she muttered.

" 'He for God only, she for God in him,' " Peter agreed, in his normal voice. "What brought that on? It's the last sentiment I ever expected to hear from you."

"You might know a man wrote it. Oh, God, I'm so tired."

"Not surprising."

"How are you?"

"Tired."

"Am I hurting you?"

"Your head," said Peter literally, "seems to be right on top of that hole in my back. No, don't move. I guess it's worth it."

"We've got to move. We can't stay here all night."

"Let go of me, then."

"I can't. I'm afraid to. I'm afraid I'm dreaming, and that if I wake up you'll be gone."

"Don't start," Peter said harshly. "If either one of us begins with that sort of thing, we'll be babbling for hours. Do you want me to drive?"

Kate pushed herself upright, and his arms fell away; but they lingered, in passing, long enough to take any possible sting from his last speech.

"No, I'd better drive."

After a few minutes she wished she had let him take the wheel. He might be in poorer physical condition, but he couldn't possibly have done worse, even in his sleep. She felt sure she was hitting every rut and hole in the path; they were both jolted around like ice cubes in a cocktail shaker. The path across the field wasn't much better, but at last she bumped the car onto the highway and pressed down on the gas pedal. Peter roused himself and asked, "Where are we going?"

"I don't know," Kate said blankly, lifting her foot.

"Your friendly local constable won't believe a

word of this. Where's the nearest state-police barracks?"

"Will they believe it?"

"They will when they see what's back there," Peter said grimly, and relapsed into silence.

It was a drive of fifteen or twenty miles, and it took Kate a full forty minutes. She drove like someone who has been drinking, not enough to make him drunk, just enough to be unreliable and yet to be aware of his unreliability. She parked the car, illegally, by the steps of the barracks, and turned to look at Peter. The brief interlude of darkness and silence was over. Now she would have to relive those moments in retelling them. He returned her look of panic with a faint smile and a shrug.

"Take a deep breath," he said, and opened the car door.

As soon as they went through the door, Kate knew that the way had been paved for them. The sound of a baby yelling burst out at them like a siren. At any other time she would have laughed at the look on the face of the young trooper who was holding the squawling bundle over his shoulder.

"A bachelor, obviously," said Kate, holding out her arms.

The young man's professional cool had abandoned him; he didn't ask who she was, or blink at her fantastic appearance. He dropped the bundle into her arms as if it had been red hot, and wiped his brow on his sleeve.

"It won't stop yelling," he explained nervously. "What's the matter with it?"

"Wet, hungry, and sleepy," Kate said. She bounced the bundle experimentally and the yells subsided, though they did not die away completely. "It isn't hurt. It couldn't make that much noise if it were. It isn't hurt. . . ." She sat down abruptly in the chair the trooper had vacated, clutching the baby tightly. It responded with an ungrateful squawl, and Kate started to rock back and forth.

"I can't do anything about any of those things," the trooper said unhappily.

"You must have something I could tear up for a diaper. Don't you men sleep here? An old sheet, pillowcase, something."

"Oh. I guess so." The boy's face brightened at the prospect of handing over his job to a suitable female expert. He turned and caught sight of Peter, who was watching him with amusement; and his face hardened into older lines.

"What happened to you? And the lady—she's been in an accident, or something, too."

"Or something. It's a long story," Peter said. "Take us to your leader, or whatever you call him."

"There's somebody with him now. If you'll tell me—"

"I think we'd better join them," Peter said, gently but inexorably. "It's all part of the same—accident."

"What shall I do with this baby?" Kate turned the unfortunate infant around. "It's a cute baby," she said pensively.

"How can you tell? All I can see is its mouth—wide open. Hell," the trooper said wildly, "bring it along. The lieutenant's going out of his mind now. What's one more baby?"

They found Hilary sitting beside the lieutenant's desk. There were no bright lights; but the air of disbelief was thick. Hilary looked up, startled, at their entrance, and his face broke into a broad white smile of sheer relief that made him look even younger than his eighteen years.

"Man," he said emphatically, "am I ever glad to see you!"

Kate didn't blame the lieutenant for being unhappy. He was a wiry little man, older by some twenty years than many of the men under him, and the remnants of what had been a fine head of sandy hair were standing straight up by the end of the story. He didn't believe it, and he said as much, with amplification.

Peter, who had narrated the tale in a concise, unemphatic manner—with only two small evasions of the truth—made no verbal rebuttal. He simply held out his hands. Some of the swelling had gone down, but the effect was still convincing. Kate couldn't imagine how he had managed to hold onto the rifle, much less get his finger around the trigger.

The lieutenant breathed twice through his nose. "Better put something on those wrists," he said, after a moment. "You, too, miss—er—Doctor. You look as if you could stand a little first aid yourself."

"What I need is a bath," Kate said vigorously, "and I don't think there's time for that now. And Peter doesn't need any first-aid nonsense either, what he needs is a doctor; that wound in his back ought to be looked at, I don't know what was on the point of that arrow, maybe poison, even, and—"

"Poison? Arrow?" The lieutenant's face turned red. "Lady. Please don't say anything else. We'll go out to the woods, where you said, and have a look. I can't be any fairer than that, can I?"

"I'm going to take Dr. More home first," Peter said. "She needs warmer clothing. We'll meet you there."

"And for pity's sake," Kate added, transferring the bundle from one aching shoulder to the other, "Let me do something with this baby!"

The lieutenant knew a woman in town who would take care of the baby temporarily. Kate watched it depart, still howling, over the arm of the trooper who had been designated for this task. She was already forming vague plans for the child; such a dramatic beginning to its life merited consideration, if not atonement. Besides, it had provided the only light touch, and a badly needed one, in the whole horrible affair.

Hilary Jackson, who had listened to Peter's version of the happening with magnificent composure, was not so easy to dispose of. Peter insisted that he be sent home, and the lieutenant was equally determined to keep him. Hilary broke the deadlock himself. He not only had no objection to being detained; he would, he remarked, feel a hell of a lot better with some good thick bars between him and the outside world. Bars, he pointed out, kept people out in addition to keeping them in.

Peter nodded thoughtfully.

"You've got a definite point. For the next few hours, at least. I wish I could emulate you."

"Yeah," Hilary said unemphatically.

The two men contemplated one another in silence for a moment, Hilary looking down from his magnificent height. They shook hands in frowning silence, and Peter turned on his heel and marched out.

Men, Kate thought disgustedly. She held out her hand.

"He might at least have said 'Thanks,'" she said. "Hilary . . . later, when this is finished—"

"Forget it." He grinned, suddenly and charmingly, and the big hand tightened around hers so vigorously that she barely repressed a squeal of pain. "You didn't do so badly yourself," he said.

* * *

Now, as she stood shivering in the cold light of the glade, she tried to concentrate on memories like that, and not on the things that lay, broken and abandoned, on the ground. The lieutenant was converted; one look at Mark's grotesque mask, and the tattered remnants of the other costumes, was enough. Watching his face, which had lost much of its normal ruddy color, Kate wished passionately that she could remain where she was, detached, an observer. But she had to know what was going to happen. And she had to be near Peter when he spoke of his brother.

"I just can't believe it," the lieutenant was saying, as she approached. "The most influential people in the whole damn town . . . Damn it, Stewart, I can't arrest people like the Senator, not on this charge. Witchcraft! I think they repealed the law a few years back."

"I don't give a damn what you do," Peter said wearily. "You'll need legal advice, I suppose. . . . But Dr. More is not without influence herself, you know. At the very least these people must be made to resign from any positions of responsibility they now hold."

"Particularly Miss Device and the Foundling Home," Kate said.

"But people got killed," the lieutenant said helplessly. "I still haven't got that straight. Who the hell killed who?"

"I'm the only available arrestee," Peter said calmly. "I shot Martin. Delightful thought," he added.

"He did it to save the baby," Kate said. "And Hilary."

"Yeah, the Jackson kid." The lieutenant scratched his head. "How does he come into this?"

"He's the hero," Peter said. Only Kate, who had, in some odd way, memorized his every gesture and expression, observed the slight narrowing of his eyes. "He saved us, and the child."

"Yeah," the lieutenant muttered, "and brought the rifle?"

Kate, who had never played poker, barely repressed an exclamation. She still had an intellectual's contempt for nonprofessionals; she had to fight that, it led her into dangerous errors—such as assuming that the lieutenant's bovine face concealed a brain of the same caliber.

"He brought the rifle," Peter agreed. "And gave it to me."

"Then your prints will be on it?"

"They already are on it," Peter said impatiently. "I've admitted killing Martin. What the hell are you trying to prove?"

"The facts. Only the facts. So you killed Martin. That would be after he shot the other guy—your—brother, you say?"

"Can't you leave him alone?" Kate exploded. "He's hurt and sick and he's had a terrible shock. We told you what happened. And if you think he lied about something, you're right." Peter turned on her, his face forbidding, but Kate rushed on. "He didn't kill the general, I did; I bashed his head in with the butt of that gun. You'll find my prints on it too. I did it to keep him from strangling Peter, but I would have done it anyhow, he needed killing as much as Martin did, and if you think I'm ashamed of it you're crazy, I'll stand right up and tell any judge and jury all about it, and furthermore—"

Peter relaxed, his lips twitching, and the lieutenant literally threw up his hands.

"Okay, okay, okay! Take it easy, will you, Doc?"

"And don't call me Doc!"

"Sorry. Look, Doc—I mean, Miss More. I'm not trying to railroad anybody. I just want to find out what happened. I knew there was something fishy; after all these years I've got so I can smell a lie. So now I know. So he was trying to protect you. That's nice. But stupid."

"And superfluous," Peter murmured. "She doesn't need protecting."

"You're so right," the lieutenant agreed.

They exchanged a superior, masculine look, and Kate watched them tolerantly. Under her calm facade her brain was racing.

Peter's comment had been literally true; he wouldn't insult her by such an idiotic lie. He was trying to protect someone, but not out of quixotic gallantry. Even if he was acquitted, Hilary Jackson would be irreparably damaged by being tried on a murder charge. And he wasn't in the clear yet. Neither she nor Peter had been in any condition the night before to remember the one, indisputable piece of evidence which could bring Hilary before a jury.

She forced her eyes from the one tolerable object in the clearing—Peter's face—and glanced around.

One of the troopers had found the rifle immediately; it lay by Volz's body, where Peter had dropped it, and after the lieutenant had examined it, it had been stowed away as part of the evidence. The other gun had not yet been found. They hadn't really gotten around to looking for it yet, being preoccupied with the human remains, and it was probably buried deep in drifted leaves. She knew approximately where it must be—about six feet from the huddled shape of Mark's body. Somehow she must force herself to go over there. And she would have to hurry. One of the troopers was kneeling by Mark, his hands questing through the leaves.

While she was still thinking, Peter acted.

"Lieutenant. Before you take him away . . . may I . . . ?"

"Huh?" The lieutenant looked from Mark's body to Peter's averted face and blinked. "Sure," he said awkwardly. "Al, come over here."

Peter had also mentally marked the spot; probably neither of them would ever forget the details of that night. When his dragging steps had brought him to the site, he stumbled and dropped to one knee. Still kneeling, he covered his eyes with one hand; the other trailed limply at his side, the fingers moving nervously.

Kate saw the young man, Al, turn his head away. He must be new at the job. But Peter's pose and bowed head were genuine enough to bring a quick sting of tears to her own eyes.

When Peter got to his feet, amid a respectful silence, there was something in his right hand. He looked at it dazedly, and held it out toward the lieutenant.

"Here's the gun," he said.

The lieutenant yelped and leaped forward.

"Damn it to hell! Don't you know better than to pick up evidence?"

"Sorry; wasn't I supposed to?" Peter meekly surrendered the weapon.

The lieutenant's reply was heated. When his wrath died down, he gave Peter a look in which annoyance, respect, and a faint amusement were mingled.

"Okay, Stewart, that's all. Get the hell out of here before you mess anything else up. I don't need you any longer. Nor Miss More."

"Thank you," Peter said gravely.

"I'll want to see you, probably later today." The

lieutenant sighed; he looked not like a policeman but like a tired, middle-aged man with too many worries. "God, this is going to be a mess. . . . Where will you be?"

Peter hesitated.

"Baltimore," he said, after a moment. "I'll call you when we've found a hotel."

"Why Baltimore?" Kate asked.

"Do you want to go back to your place?"

"No. No, I don't."

"Nor is the Middleburg Inn a happy choice," Peter pointed out. "We need to get away from Middleburg, Lieutenant. We'll let you know."

They walked side by side toward the path. In deference to Peter's frowning abstraction Kate didn't take his arm, though she wanted desperately to touch him. She knew what was coming, and knew that he hated it as much as she did. Sooner or later the question would have to be asked, but she couldn't bring herself to ask it.

They had taken Volz's car; it was still parked at the end of the path, and Kate got a sadistic, if illogical, satisfaction when she thought of the beating it had taken in the last twenty-four hours.

Peter had taken over the driving as soon as they left the police barracks. She had questioned the wisdom of his driving with one arm and had received a stare of such silent outrage that she hadn't raised the point again. This time, when he was behind the wheel, instead of starting the car, he turned to face her.

"Tiphaine is at the house," he said. "That's why I don't want you to go back there. You can buy a toothbrush in Baltimore."

"Is she—"

"Alive? Not altogether."

"Peter, tell me. I can't stand euphemisms, not now."

"Schizophrenia, I guess that's the technical term. She's completely withdrawn; sits, moves, stands on order, but does nothing by herself. She was well on the way before, Kate; last night she went right on over the edge."

"I see."

"Not much else to say, is there?" His arm over the back of the seat, Peter made no move to touch her. "I've seen cases like hers before. The chance of recovery is not very good."

"I know. . . . What happened to her last night? I forgot about her. Isn't that awful. . . . ?"

"So did I. She must have gone into shock when Mark was killed. The police found her this morning, curled up like a worm, beside him."

"That's why you insisted on stopping at the house before we came out here."

"I spoke to the lieutenant before we left, asked him to get her out of the way before we got here. I didn't know what we'd find, whether she'd be alive, or dead or . . . But I didn't want you to see her. They got her away, through the woods, before we arrived."

He waited for a moment. Kate said nothing, only sat staring down at the hands which lay lax on her knee. Peter started the car. When they were back on the highway, he said, "In a sense she's the most tragic figure of all. I know how you must be feeling. . . . If that foul uncle of yours hadn't gotten his hands on her . . ."

"I don't know," Kate said dully. "I just don't know any longer. What about Mark? You turned out all right. . . . Don't sympathize with me, Peter. It's just as bad for you as it is for me."

"Worse for you," Peter said, his eyes on the road. "It's not my world which has fallen to pieces. Will you want to stay on here, do you think?"

"I don't know . . ."

"It's not all that different from the rest of the world, you know. Human beings are the one thing you can't run away from, and they're pretty much alike." He gave a short laugh. "Full of advice, aren't I? I'm sorry, I don't really mean to sound so smug and omniscient. If you don't want to go to Baltimore . . ."

"You have no idea," Kate said, staring straight ahead, "how wonderful it is to have someone tell me what to do. But it won't last," she added wearily. "I'm not the frail female type. I'm bossy, and arrogant, and conceited; I think I'm smarter than most people, so I don't take advice very well. . . ."

Peter put his foot down on the brake. The car slid to a stop on the shoulder of the road, and he turned to face her.

"I'll risk it," he said.

Acclaimed bestselling author

# ELIZABETH PETERS

brings us

## AMELIA PEABODY'S EGYPT

### A COMPENDIUM

Celebrate mystery's favorite sleuth in
this new collection packed with
fascinating facts and details...
A treasure chest for all Peabody fans!

"Between Amelia Peabody and
Indiana Jones, it's Amelia —
in wit and daring — by a landslide."
—*New York Times Book Review*

0-06-053811-2     $29.95/$45.95 Can.

**Available now wherever books are sold**

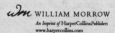